THE DEVIL LAUGHED

A MORIAH DRU / RICHARD LAKE
MYSTERY

THE DEVIL LAUGHED

GERRIE FERRIS FINGER

FIVE STAR
A part of Gale, Cengage Learning

WITHDRAWN

GALE
CENGAGE Learning®

Detroit • New York • San Francisco • New Haven, Conn • Waterville, Maine • London

LIBRARY OF CONGRESS CATALOGING-IN-PUBLICATION DATA

Finger, Gerrie Ferris.
    The devil laughed : a Moriah Dru - Richard Lake mystery / Gerrie Ferris Finger. — First Edition.
        pages cm
        ISBN 978-1-4328-2697-0 (hardcover) — ISBN 1-4328-2697-2 (hardcover)
    1. Murder—Investigation—Fiction. I. Title.
PS3606.I534D48 2013
813'.6—dc23   2013008355

First Edition. First Printing: August 2013
Find us on Facebook– https://www.facebook.com/FiveStarCengage
Visit our website– http://www.gale.cengage.com/fivestar/
Contact Five Star™ Publishing at FiveStar@cengage.com

Printed in Mexico
1 2 3 4 5 6 7 17 16 15 14 13

THE DEVIL LAUGHED

CHAPTER ONE

A local man we encountered on our way to the lake described this summer holiday as, "A stinkin' fart from the devil's arse."

Happy Fourth of July to you, too, sir.

Portia Devon had invited Lake, his daughter Susanna and me to her place on Lake Lanier, a forty-five-minute drive from the heart of Atlanta. Lake Lanier—Georgia's jewel (as asserted by magazine writers)—lies in the foothills of the Blue Ridge Mountains. Upon arriving early this morning and gazing over the lakescape, it didn't look like a jewel. For two years severe drought had plagued the state, adding fuel to the stinkin' fart.

Settled aboard Portia's cabin cruiser, drinks and snacks at hand, Lake piloted us out of the cove into the lake channel. Dodging debris, we drifted past islands where skeletal trees appeared to be standing in mounds of rust—the color of Georgia's soil. "Twenty-five feet below full pool," Lake said. "No wonder we're not seeing many skiers."

Portia said abruptly, "We're wasting gas."

"Say no more, Judge," Lake said and steered us back to the temporary floating marina. On the boardwalk we settled into Adirondack chairs beneath umbrellas to read or play hand-held video games, except for Portia's son, Walker, who continued to grumble about not being able to ride his jet ski.

Portia glared him quiet and lowered her eyes to a red leather volume documenting the latest decisions of the Georgia Supreme Court.

Lake sat back in the cushioned chair, earbud plugged into a news-talk station. Half hour later, he sat up and pulled the plug. "The Department of Natural Resources confirmed that due to atmospheric conditions and fire risk there will be no fireworks on the lake this year."

Susanna and Walker shrieked in protest. Lake held up his hands. "I'll take you both for a slow spin on the jet ski. How's that?"

The glance Portia gave Walker barred dispute so Lake and the kids boarded the old wooden runabout and set out for the marina. Portia turned her attention to her legal tome and I wiped sweat and watched Lake maneuver the jet ski from the cove into the lake's main channel. He was such a lovely man with children, and I was reminded of my biological clock—a reminder I'd rather not be reminded of. Marriage had been discussed, then deferred. We had busy careers—him as a dedicated cop, and me as the owner of Child Trace, a private investigation agency.

Portia raised her head. "Moriah, stop pacing, you're making me long for a soothing cigarette."

I moved to the rail and thought idly about the cove. It was one of the deepest in the lake because the Corps of Engineers had flooded Osprey Waterfall to create the reservoir. I swatted at two June flies playing sex tag. Away they flew into sun beams that sliced into the gloom of trees on the bank. In these sun-washed shadows I glimpsed something in the water. I stretched to tiptoes to make out the wide object. I looked at Porsh. "Something's in the water by the shore."

Portia slid her reading glasses down her nose. "Where by the shore?"

"Where the waterfall was flooded. A long board, maybe the backside of a boat."

"Stern," Portia said, rising and hoisting herself onto a dock rail. She worked her long nose like a high-strung pointer who'd just flushed a covey of quail. A series of speculative noises came from her while she balanced her five-foot, hundred-pound frame on the wooden slat. By this time, Lake had putt-putted the watercraft back to the marina and he and the kids were boarding the runabout.

Portia stretched an arm backward and wiggled her fingers. "Get me the bird glasses."

I got the binoculars from her carry-all. Her fingers tightened over the glasses and her head swiveled over the water. She could be standing in front of a periscope within sight of the enemy. "The stern all right," she said. "Big boat, too." A few minutes went by while she scanned and hummed. Finally, she said, "Ha. Evaporation finally uncovered the *Scuppernong*. Want to bet it's that sailboat?"

Scuppernong. The name floated like warm grease through the labyrinthine folds of my brain.

Lake had beached the runabout. Shading his eyes, he called up, "What's going on with you two?"

"Get ready to push off again," Portia called back. She jabbed an index finger toward the bank. "We're going over there."

Lake looked at me and I said, "She thinks the *Scuppernong* has surfaced."

"Bet you," Portia said, jumping from the rail.

Lake said with whimsical gravity, "The Mysterious Disappearance of the *Scuppernong*."

How many times had I read that oft-printed headline? "It was four years ago, wasn't it?"

"October will be four years," Portia said. She said to Walker, "Hold Susanna's hand and come with me. You can stay with Nanny."

Walker took Susanna's hand and followed his mother. She looked back at us. "I'll call the sheriff. I'll be back, and we'll go see if we're right." *We're?*

Lake pinched the sides of his nose. It hadn't been his case, but the entire U.S. of A. had speculated on the mysterious disappearance of the sailboat. Several counties bordered the lake, and I recalled the squabbles over jurisdictions. We were in Sawchicsee County where the boat lay in the water—if it was indeed the *Scuppernong*. I asked Lake, "Wasn't the main action in Gainesville—Hall County?"

"Hall and Forsyth. Some in Dawson, I believe. Multi task forces across jurisdictions." He puckered his mouth and blew out a soft whistle. "They'll love having their Fourth of July ruined."

"Off-duties will already be sozzled," I said. "Before we go off half-cocked calling authorities, shouldn't we go see if it *is* the *Scuppernong*?" Lake shrugged, and I grinned. "*She* could be wrong."

He put his hands on his hips and looked out toward the boat stern, and then up the hill where Portia hurried with the kids. He said, "She could be."

I nudged his elbow with mine. "You run tell her not to call yet."

His head spun toward me. "I'd rather talk a donkey into getting off its ass."

Even though the bold letters were mostly underwater, I had no trouble reading them: SCUPPERNONG.

"Let's get back to the dock and wait for the sheriff," Lake said. He read the depth finder. "Sixty feet."

Portia said, "*Scuppernong* wasn't that long. It's hung up on something. Rock ledge probably."

Lake cut the outboard's engine, and we climbed onto the dock. Sitting next to Lake on the gray slats, I listened to Portia relate some of what I knew and some of what I didn't know about the *Scuppernong* case.

Almost four years ago, the *Scuppernong,* a thirty-six-foot sloop, had a permanent slip at Swann's Marina in Forsyth County.

One fine October day, two couples set sail from Swann's. After sailing (and drinking) most of the day, at about four-thirty in the afternoon they docked at Trehorne's Marina and Restaurant in Hall County.

One couple, Johnny and Candice Browne, lived in North Carolina, the Cape Fear region. They had come to Atlanta to celebrate the anniversary of their friends, Laurant and Janet Cocineau, who hailed from Wilmington before moving to Atlanta. Laurant and Janet owned the *Scuppernong*.

Witnesses at Trehorne's restaurant say the two couples staggered in on a wave of noise and ordered vodka drinks. Not long afterward, the waitress expressed concern with her manager because the men were harassing her, and the women let their tits hang out of their cover-ups. The manager came to the table. After the Cocineaus apologized and said it was their anniversary, he requested that they "party less hardy." Soon, though, the couples were accusing one another of having affairs with the other. Wife-swapping charges led to hard-core profanity, and the manager told them they had to leave or he would call the sheriff. He had, in fact, already called the sheriff. The couples boarded their boat and went below deck. The sheriff came, took a look at the boat and left. Witnesses said after the sheriff's departure, the men came topside, cranked the motor and churned the sailboat through the no-wake zone.

After whatever happened to the sailboat happened, the sheriff told the Georgia Bureau of Investigation that he hadn't spoken with the four people because the restaurant wasn't going to press charges, and he personally hadn't seen them acting drunk and disorderly. The manager owned up to receiving a hundred percent tip for meals that the four ordered but were never served.

"Truth is, the sheriff was a lazy lout," Portia said. "Didn't want to bother writing a report."

That night, the *Scuppernong* arrived at the Swann Marina, its permanent dock, some time after ten o'clock. Several witnesses confirm that the couples partied on deck, but they weren't any noisier than other boaters, with laughter and music blasting across the marina.

Sometime after midnight, a witness from a neighboring boat heard the *Scuppernong*'s motor start up. She said she saw two men take the boat onto the lake, but later said she couldn't identify them positively as Laurant Cocineau and/or Johnny Browne. The boat never came back to its slip.

That was the last anyone saw the couples alive. Johnny Browne's body was discovered rolling in the no-wake zone of Swann marina. The other three bodies, dead or alive, and the sailboat were never found. Johnny had a nasty crack on one side of his skull that could have happened by various means, so the medical examiner's verdict came out *misadventure*. Authorities searched for weeks and months and came up with zip on the three people. However, they had garnered one unreliable report of the boat.

Portia explained, "It was thought odd that after so many days or weeks, the bodies didn't surface. Bodies, even those hung up on tree branches and in crevices, break up and surface."

"And," Lake said, "the authorities sonared the lake and surveyed it from the sky and couldn't find evidence that the sailboat sunk."

"I saw the planes flying over this area," Portia said, her eyes going to where water lapped at the sailboat's stern. "This deep-water cove is the perfect place to deliberately sink the damn thing."

I remarked that no one could miss the billboard-sized signs

driven into rocks climbing the bank of the cove: *Danger! Deep drop-off. Treacherous rocks below waterline.*

"*If* it was *deliberately* sunk," Lake reminded Portia.

She acted like she hadn't heard him. "It's over a hundred feet out there when the lake's full pool. It was the bottom of a dry waterfall before it was the bottom of this lake." She thought a moment. "The year the couples went missing was the year when two hurricanes deluged Atlanta. The lake was above full pool then to keep from flooding downstream rivers." She put her finger to her lips. "Remember, it was raining that night?"

I didn't remember, but Lake did and nodded.

Portia went on, "A man—can't recall his name—said a couple of campers told him that they saw a sailboat being up-ramped from Landing Creek Park that night. The man is a notorious drunk and not believable."

Landing Creek Park was maybe a mile from Portia's cabin and several miles from the *Scuppernong*'s slip.

Lake said, "I recall the authorities, including the Georgia Bureau of Investigation, couldn't find the two campers. I suspect they didn't look too hard."

Lake's not fond of the GBI.

Portia said, "A drunk and a couple of toke-heads. Weed being involved."

Portia, Lake and I have to be the only three people of our age on the planet who declare they've never done weed. I can't know about Portia and Lake for sure, but I know I haven't. When I was about eight, a twelve-year-old boy in our neighborhood showed some of us younger kids how to huff out of a paper bag. Suddenly, he fell. Passed right out. I ran to get his dad who was in his garage tinkering with his lawn mower. He came running, snatched the kid up, slapped his cheeks until he came around. Then, for the *coup de grace*, unstrapped his belt from his waist. We kids took off.

I got my wandering mind under control and listened to what Lake was saying. "The way the cove hugs the mountain, and being overshadowed by trees, is likely the reason searchers didn't see it from the air."

"It's also murky from silt eroding into the lake," Portia said.

I heard a loud slam—unmistakably a car door—and turned to see Walker running from the cabin, waving his thin arms, shouting, "Mama, sheriff's here. Sheriff's here!"

"Walker," Portia called, pointing back the way he'd come. "You get back up there with Susanna."

Walker about-faced and slow-walked with his shoulders sloped forward. He passed a uniformed man slip-sliding down pine cones and rocks. Portia whispered, "Never met him, but I've seen Sheriff Sonny Kitchens at the local gag-and-vomit porking down biscuits and gravy."

You won't catch Portia porking down biscuits and gravy— more like nibbling oatmeal and dry wheat toast.

The Sheriff of Sawchicsee County stepped onto the planks and held up a hand. "Hey, folks." A pleasing baritone projected from the expanse of his lungs. First impression—exercise freak— biscuits or no biscuits. Broad shoulders tapering to a flat stomach, trim waist, muscular arms. He looked at Portia and said, "Judge Devon, seen you around town." He held out his hand. "Glad to meet you at last. Sorry about the circumstances."

Portia's not much for shaking hands (germs), but she touched his fingers. "And I you, Sheriff Kitchens." She looked out toward the sailboat. "Had to surface sooner or later."

"You positive about what's out there?" His accent didn't have the nasal quality inherent in North Georgia mountain boys.

"*Scuppernong*," Portia said. "We looked."

"You don't say," he said, taking off aviator sunglasses and focusing narrowed blue-gray eyes on the long object. He looked at each of us and sighed deeply.

I looked at Lake. Nothing excited that Atlanta police lieutenant more than getting a lead on a seriously important cold case, but Lake kept his face in neutral. He's not a man who judges, even a sheriff who's blasé when a major piece of evidence comes calling.

"Nothing like a new lead to get you excited, eh, Sheriff?" Portia said. Portia Devon, juvenile judge with the Superior Court, is a woman who judges from behind or in front of the bench.

The sheriff had the grace to grin. Nice teeth, wide mouth. "Didn't happen in Sawchicsee County," he said. "All over in Forsyth and Hall."

Portia countered, "Campers *in this county* said they saw a boat being pulled from the lake."

"They weren't believable. *Scuppernong* couldn't be trailered from that ramp and it was bad out."

"They swore it was a big trailer," Portia said. Judges like swearing, too.

The sheriff shook his head. "Maybe they saw something hauled out that night, but it wasn't the boat that's laying out there now."

"Which *is* in your county," Portia insisted.

"Johnny Browne's body was found in Forsyth," he said. "Those two couples ate supper in Hall County where they had a fight in a restaurant." He rubbed nonexistent stubble on his firm jaw.

"When's your election?" Portia asked, looking up at the sheriff who was a foot taller than she.

He said, "November, and it's coming on quick." His mouth twitched as he stared at the boat site. "Finding the *Scuppernong* here won't make it my case, Judge. It belonged to the Georgia Bureau of Investigation then, and it will now." With much deliberation, he put his sunglasses on.

"Unless the bodies are on it," she said. "Then you have jurisdiction, too."

His upper lip twitched. "I might grant you *one* body."

"That body being?"

His lips came together with tenuous pressure as if conveying to Portia that she well knew which body—that being the body of Janet Cocineau. Many believed that the adulterous Laurant Cocineau and Candice Browne took off for parts of the world unknown.

Behind me I heard men's voices and scuffling feet. We turned to watch five men descending the slope. Two carried diving gear. Two balanced an upside-down inflatable boat on their heads. One man wore a different uniform.

"Forsyth's here," the sheriff said. "We borrowed their fire department's divers." He stepped away to meet the men, saying, "Jawing's over," as if he'd held a committee meeting and it was time to vote. I liked him.

We followed him to the end of the dock. Out on the lake, a boat came on fast, multi-antennae waving, radar rotating.

Velcroing his wet suit vest, one of the divers gestured at the speeding boat with his head. "Here comes Natural Resources."

Lake turned to me. "Told you. Multi task forces."

"Which," I said, "is why Sonny Kitchens isn't too excited about the find."

Lake looked at the sheriff's back. "I don't like the feeling I'm getting."

"Which is?"

"Cool cucumbers have seeds inside, too."

Deputies and divers readied the inflatable boat on the bank at the same time two men in summer suits walked onto the quay. Kitchens turned to Lake. "GBI," he said unnecessarily. "Might as well go home."

Lake said, "Don't be so sure, Sheriff. This ain't a one-dish meal."

Lake must be hungry—cucumbers and a one-dish meal.

Kitchens gave an emphatic nod, jumped off the dock and boarded the inflatable, leaving Portia, Lake and me to answer the GBI's endless, nit-picking questions.

Eight hours later, at sunset, the divers climbed onto the dock, panting heavily.

Portia stepped around the sheriff. With her hands planted on her bony hips, she asked the divers, "Human remains?"

The divers shook their heads no.

The sheriff glanced at Lake then eyed Portia like she was going to be a real smart-ass problem. "I ask the questions."

She jerked her head. "I am not an uninterested bystander, Sheriff."

"No, ma'am, but this isn't judging business."

She turned back to the divers. "What caused her to sink?"

"That I couldn't tell you for certain," one diver answered, looking at the sheriff as if he were informing him and him alone. "The damage is extensive, though."

Portia folded her arms across her chest and looked at Kitchens. "I intend to learn everything about this matter." A "matter" to Porsh is typically something before her court.

Kitchens grinned at her. Why had she taken such a dislike to this agreeable hunk of testosterone?

The divers departed. With Kitchens hovering on the periphery, the GBI, DNR and two forensic experts discussed the best way to lift the boat. Portia was not to be left out, though. She said, "Obviously, you'll float her with inflatables."

No one replied, and she jerkily gathered up her sunscreen, thermos, binocs and leather book. Sheriff Kitchens walked over. "Please, don't be tempted to do more investigating out there.

The GBI will soon have her up and off for a forensic examination."

Letting her sunglasses slide down her nose, Portia gave him her best scathing stare. "You're not being forthright, Sheriff."

With a half-grin, he said, "No ma'am, but I *am* being polite."

He got his campaign hat on, nodded smartly and hurried off before phrases could form in her throat. And that was always fast.

"In other words," Lake said with a grin. "None of your business."

Portia walked around the wooden picnic table ladling baked beans onto plates. Dinner was beans and franks, deviled eggs and store-bought potato salad. The screened porch overlooked the lake and two police guards who had been stationed on the dock to make sure no one got a notion to put on a scuba tank and explore the sailboat.

"Candice Browne had a daughter, Evangeline," Portia said, holding the bean ladle in midair. "Her last name escapes me. It's not Browne; Johnny never adopted her after he married Candice."

Lake looked at Portia, his fork halfway to his mouth. "Evangeline. Not a name you hear every day."

"Candice was originally from Charleston, South Carolina," Portia said, sitting and spooning potato salad onto her plate. "She married a boy in college. Jeez, why can't I remember his name? Something Cajun-sounding."

"So where's Evangeline?" I asked.

"Cape Fear, last I heard, with her aunt. Candice's sister, last name Bonnet. Never married."

"Did you meet any of these people?"

Portia shook her head. "No reason to. I remember the details because of this lake and what happened. I accumulated a file of all the stories written and video interviews."

"What did Johnny Browne do for a living?" Lake said, stabbing at another frank.

"Financial planner, Wall Street stuff, and he owned a vineyard. That's how he met Laurant Cocineau," Portia said. "Johnny's gone bust a couple of times, but he's one of those who manages to recoup and become richer."

"Was he rich when he died?"

"Seems so," she answered. "Candice was wealthy from her first husband who was a banker. I would guess she propped Johnny up in his bad years."

"What about Janet and Laurant? Rich as Croesus, too?"

"Janet was an heiress. Old Wilmington cash."

"And Laurant?"

"He's the poorest of them all. Was some kind of consultant. He's the only one of the foursome who was only married once—to Janet. Damned good-looking man."

He must have been for Portia to comment. She'd been immune to my sheriff's good looks. Maybe it was the biscuits and gravy.

Portia said, "Johnny Browne's first wife was killed in a car wreck and the insurance paid big."

It was all coming back to me, the whole barrel of snakes that surrounded those two couples. I said, "She didn't die right away, and he filed for divorce."

"They were in the process of divorce when the accident happened. Rumor had it he was already hooked up with Candice." She scratched her neck. "Goddamn, wish I had a cigarette."

Lake pushed his plate back. "I'm done."

I said, "Me, too."

Susanna said, "Can I be excused, Daddy?"

"Yes, sweets, you can be excused."

Portia said, "Walker, take Susanna into the kitchen. Tell

Nanny to get you two a bowl of coffee ice cream."

"Oh boy, coffee ice cream," Walker shouted and, running away, almost tripped over his own feet.

Chocolate-loving Susanna turned her head and made a face. Lake said, "Go with Walker, honey."

"Yes, Daddy."

Portia went on to explain that the money accounts of the three missing people had not been touched. She leaned back in her chair, and I anticipated another regret that she'd quit smoking. But she said, "It's funny, too, if any of them are alive. Funny, yet tragic. Johnny Browne, the man who formed the foursome, was the one that died." She raised two fingers to her lips like she was ready to inhale. "You got to like a man named Johnny."

Lake had sat looking thoughtful. "A true mystery," he said. "Three disappear with a sailboat. One dead in the water."

"Reminds me of that nursery rhyme about three men in a boat," I said.

Lake crossed his arms and frowned like a marble had squeezed from my nose. But Portia laughed. *Rub-a-dub-dub. Three men in a tub.*"

Lake asked, "And what, my lady love, brought that into your marvelously arcane brain?"

"Something about it."

Portia said, "She's right. There is something familiar in that nursery rhyme. The original Rub-a-dub-dub was cleaned up for the kiddies. Those ditties are called nursery rhymes today, but back when they originated they were rhyming jokes for adults and, like today's jokes, have a basis in truth."

Lake asked, "Why would three men be taking a bath together? Are we talking gay men, water shortage, or what?"

"Listen carefully," Portia said. *"Rub-a-dub-dub, three* maids *in a tub."*

"Never heard *maids* before," Lake said.

Portia continued, *"Rub-a-dub-dub, three maids in a tub, And who do you think were there? The butcher, the baker, the candlestick-maker, And all of them gone to the fair."*

"Hanky-panky at the fair," I said.

Portia said, "Here's the modern version: *Rub a dub dub, Three men in a tub, And who do you think they be? The butcher, the baker, the candlestick maker. Turn them out, knaves all three.* That's the cleaned-up version for the kiddle-dee-dees. The last line doesn't make sense, does it?"

"No," Lake said.

"That's because important parts of the rhyme are missing and erroneous. The original action takes place at a carnival side show where three *girls* were sitting in a bathtub entertaining men in the audience. When three men climbed in with the girls, the men were promptly thrown out by the fair manager. Now the last line makes sense. *Turn them out, knaves all three.*"

Lake started to sing an old Bobby Darin song: *Splish splash.* He didn't get past the bath part when he asked Porsh, "Can't remember, what's the rest?"

She looked at him like he'd just jumped in the tub with her.

I said, "Unless it's Mozart, Portia doesn't know it. Hum a few bars of Sonata in G sharp."

"There isn't a Sonata in G sharp," Portia said.

"See?" I said to Lake.

Portia, ever serious, said, "The nursery rhyme came into your head, Moriah, because it's about debauchery and what occurred on that sailboat was debauchery."

"Too bad," I said, "there was no fair manager to throw the debauchers out."

Lake stretched and put his hands in his shorts' pockets. "Maybe there was."

"What's on your mind?" I asked.

"A notion."

"That tells me a lot."

Lake hitched his shoulders and said, "Janet's probably dead. Laurant and Candice are somewhere basking with the cash they accumulated before they sank the boat and took off."

"That would make them cold-blooded killers if you believe that theory." I said.

"If I remember, a couple of neighbors suggested that might have happened. If neighbors believe something, it's based on their observations and most likely has merit."

The talk drifted with me wondering what could have happened to the three people. A dead Janet Browne, bones entwined with trash on the bottom of the lake? Laurant and Candice living it up in Canada or South America?

"Who gets the loot?" Lake asked, bringing me back to the moment.

Portia laughed. "That's always the question, *n'est-ce pas?*"

I ventured my thought. "Any crime or corruption attached to any of them?"

"Traffic charges, fines paid," Portia said. "No shit like porn on their computers. Except for Johnny Browne's body, and until the drought exposed the sailboat, they might have been beamed—sailboat and all—up to a spaceship headed for Pluto."

"If they're all dead and their killer or killers sunk their boat, they had some serious enemies," I said.

"No doubt about it," Lake said. "They just haven't been found."

"Could be they met someone up here who took a dislike to them."

"From the many interviews, no one up here knew them."

"A page out of *Deliverance*?" Portia said, cocking a black eyebrow.

I was thinking about the James Dickey book, too. "Maybe the

boat will yield some evidence," I said.

"It will, most certainly," Lake said.

CHAPTER TWO

I picked up the landline handset.

"Moriah," the voice demanded. "Come to my office."

Portia doesn't waste words on greetings and salutations. "What's up?" I asked.

"Remember the sailboat?"

How could I forget? "I saw where they raised it."

"Inflatables floated it free, and then they got a crane to it. Sonny said it looked like somebody took an axe and a reciprocating saw to it. Obviously it was scuttled."

"So you and hunky Sonny are speaking politely."

"After a fashion. I got someone here wants to talk to you."

"Who?"

"Surprise." She rang off, Portia-style. You should see her when she gets impatient with service in a restaurant. No verbal rebukes, just a walk to the door, chin high, high heels clicking.

Sixteen minutes later, standing in the doorway, I was indeed surprised to see the young girl sitting in what is my chair when Portia and I chat over business or have a cocktail at the end of the day.

Portia stood, and the girl looked over her shoulder at me.

Evangeline. You'd think a girl with a beautiful name would be beautiful. But not this Evangeline. She was a lumpy girl with one of the ugliest faces I'd ever seen. Large head, a lot of black hair, black eyes, pug nose, thick lips, high cheekbones, heavy jaws. I'd seen a photograph of her mother Candice in the paper the day after we found the sailboat. Candice was a red-haired beauty. Maybe she inherited her daddy's ugly genes. "Hello," I said, nodding to Evangeline and looking at Portia.

Portia said, "Evangeline, it's courtesy to stand when someone enters a room like I've done."

Evangeline stood. She wasn't more than four feet tall. She bit her lower lip, and her eyes shifted to something she imagined on my shoulder. She held her purse like I might race up and snatch it.

Portia made the introductions: "Miss Evangeline Bonnet Broussard, this is Moriah Dru—and vice versa." With that Portia sat, and I spied her cigarette case and gold holder hiding behind a case file. I also noted that she flipped the switch on her mini-recorder. Like me, she liked to keep a verbal record of interviews.

I extended my hand, and Evangeline took it with two fingers. "Here," I said, grabbing her small hand. "Let's get a good grip on that handshake."

Her face sparked a smile that would light a forest at midnight. In that instant, she was truly beautiful. Not many people are like that. She grasped my hand hard. I ended the shake before my finger bones needed casts. "Let's sit now."

She folded herself into the leather chair, and I fetched its mate from against the wall.

Portia cleared her throat. "Miss Broussard flew from Southport, North Carolina, this morning to meet with me."

Then why am I here?

Having read my puckered brow, Portia said, "You'll know in a second, Miss Impatient. I want Evangeline to tell her story, but first I want to tell you that Miss Broussard read or heard the unfortunate quote I gave to the media." Portia made a face. She rarely talks to the media, but I'd heard and read her inadvertent quote repeated several times. After reporters learned off whose dock the sailboat had been found, they hounded

25

Porsh, crawling up her craw until she snapped, "If you ask me, investigators missed the boat on this one. Literally."

Portia said to me, "Miss Broussard thinks I might investigate better than the authorities. She wants to hire me, but I told her I am not an investigator." Her eyes burned into mine.

"And I am."

"Precisely."

Not so precisely in this instance. After I left the Atlanta Police Department I started Child Trace. I find missing children. Most of my work comes from the juvenile courts, mostly from Judge Portia Devon. I take on private clients, too, but I've never worked for a child. Truth is, I'm never around children much at all until they're found, and then my work is done.

Although Portia waited for me to take up the conversation, I kept my eyes leveled on her mouth. She looked at the girl and then back at me. "You will want particulars from Evangeline."

I held up a hand. "Is Miss Broussard under your jurisdiction?"

Portia said that Evengeline was not, but that as a minor she could not act on her own. Furthermore, she said that Evangeline came to Atlanta with her uncle Baron Bonnet. Her legal guardian was her aunt, Lorraine Bonnet, currently out of the country on business as a trade representative for the state of North Carolina.

I turned to Evangeline. "Why isn't your uncle with you now?"

She opened her mouth but didn't speak, thus resembling a black goldfish. Then she shrugged her shoulders. "He wanted to be here, but I told him I wanted to see the judge alone."

I smiled at Porsh. "She walks into your chamber, just like that?"

Portia flicked her right shoulder and glanced at Evangeline. Something in her faint frown told me she didn't approve—of the action, or the girl, I wasn't sure. I did know that some clerk was in for a verbal whipping.

"Does your legal guardian, your Aunt Lorraine, know you're in Atlanta and why?" I asked.

"I told her by Skype."

"She okayed it?"

"She said it was okay if Uncle Baron came with me."

"What do you want the judge to do?" As if I had to ask.

"Find out what happened to my mother."

"How old are you, Evangeline? Can I call you Evangeline?"

"My friends call me E."

I grinned. "Because it's Easier?"

She rolled her eyes. "I'm twelve; I'll be thirteen September thirteenth. Aunt Lorraine says it's lucky to turn your age on the date of your birth."

"I think so," I said. "It was a good day when I turned twenty-eight on the twenty-eighth of August."

She slanted her eyes away as if she could care less, and I asked her a few questions about her family. Her birth father died when she was three years old, but she said she remembers him. Since I'd already labeled her precocious, she probably did remember him. "What happened to him?" I knew, but wanted her response. You can tell a lot about people who have to answer a difficult question.

She didn't shrink. "He was murdered."

Way too much violence in this story. Sean Tyrone Broussard was a banker, Evangeline said, at the Greater Citizens Financial Bank and Trust in Southport, North Carolina. There was a robbery and he was shot dead.

"Did you like your stepfather, Johnny Browne?"

Wrinkling her pug nose, she hesitated before she spoke. "Well, not at first. But then I did. He got to be nice."

"What was he like before he got to be nice?"

"Mama said he was always nice, it's just that I wasn't, because he wasn't my real daddy."

"It's a normal reaction."

"Yes, ma'am, my doctor said that."

"Is your doctor a psychologist?"

"No, ma'am. He's a psychiatrist, but I don't go to him anymore."

So polite. No teen lingo. "Did you know the Cocineaus?"

"Uh, yes."

The "uh" said a lot. "Did you like them?"

"I did not *not* like them."

"Did you see them a lot?"

"Not a lot." Her brows came together and I saw a storm gathering.

When I asked where she stayed when her mother and Johnny would go away, she said she had a nanny and that her name was Soledad Lopez. "I fired her," Evangeline said. "She was bossy. I can look after myself."

"Who stays with you when your aunt's out of the country, like now?"

"Uncle Baron comes to stay with me. We have a maid, that's still Soledad, and a cook named Benny."

Portia stared at the girl. "Do you have an attorney?"

"Yes, he is Mr. Allister Dames. He's a trustee, too."

Portia wrote that down. "Your mother was a very wealthy woman, I understand."

"She still *is*," Evangeline said.

"Is," Portia said. "I stand corrected."

The girl's aggravation coagulated on her features. "I always have to remind people."

The subject of money continued. Evangeline said she had access to her mother's and father's money through trustees. She leaned forward. "I can pay for you to find my mother, and find out who killed Johnny, if we already didn't know."

"You have someone in mind?" Portia asked.

"Laurant Cocineau."

"Any reason to suspect him?"

"He was in love with my mother."

"You know that for a fact?"

"I have eyes in my head."

I'm not fond of snotty comebacks from twelve-year-olds, but Portia simply asked, "Was your mother in love with him?"

Evangeline hesitated. "He was handsome. She was beautiful."

I said, "That doesn't mean they were in love with each other."

She turned on me. "Johnny was a clown and Janet was ugly. My mother was beautiful but she didn't know what was best for her."

Portia toyed with her pen. "A lot of people don't know what's best for them, but now that the sailboat's been raised, why don't you reserve judgment until we find the people who sailed it that night?"

Evangeline cocked her head. "I can do that. I am fair. Uncle Baron says I have a good head on my shoulders."

"I can see that you do."

"When can you start finding her?" Evangeline said, sharp as a new pencil. "I'd do it myself, but nobody listens to kids—people my age."

Portia breathed in, held the air, then exhaled. "As I have previously said, I am not an investigator." She looked at me.

Vacation was the operational word here. Next week I was headed for the beach, and I'd spoken about it with Porsh, who can forget things when it's convenient. I took a deep breath, too, before I spoke. "I'll have to talk to your uncle, Evangeline. Now, with the sailboat found and being thoroughly examined, the police will pursue the case efficiently. I don't know that I can do better than they can."

Evangeline's body stiffened. This was one determined little

girl. There was a sudden rap on the door, and Portia's clerk cracked it open and stuck his head into the office. "Excuse me, Your Honor, Baron Bonnet has returned from his errand."

Portia rose and looked down. "Miss Dru, I will continue the discussion with Miss Broussard. Talk with Mr. Bonnet in one of the anterooms."

Standing, I gave her a tight-lipped smile. "Sure."

"See me after your interview," she said. She looked at the clerk. "Don't go home until we've talked."

He lowered his eyes. "Yes, Your Honor."

CHAPTER THREE

When Baron Bonnet came through the door of my impromptu office, my mouth dropped enough for him to see the silver fillings in my back teeth if he were close enough. I told myself, *just do not laugh.*

Rhett Butler walked across the floor, or Clark Gable as Rhett Butler. More precisely, Baron Bonnet, playing Clark Gable, playing Rhett Butler. He held a flat-crowned, wide-brimmed hat in his hand.

I breathed from my diaphragm and lifted myself carefully from the chair. "Mr. Bonnet." I came around the desk, extending my hand. "Moriah Dru."

Darned if he didn't have a Clark Gable smile, dimples and all. "Mighty pleased to meet you," he said, touching my fingers gently. Another wispy handshake.

I waved and said, "Have a seat, Mr. Bonnet?"

He adjusted his silk cravat. "Surely, ma'am." Lordamighty, if we weren't going to have a vocal imitation. The gabardine frock coat with velvet collar, cuffs and pocket flaps were enough. But add the silk waist vest, stovepipe pants, and then the voice . . . oh boy . . . I've never liked impersonators.

Sitting, I turned on the recorder and picked up a pen. "I met your niece, Evangeline."

"Corker, ain't she?" He was artful with the slightly crooked smile and eyebrow tilt.

I tapped the pen on a legal pad. "She is that."

"Got her mama's spunk, bless her heart."

Whose heart . . . Evangeline's or her mama's?

He sat sideways in the chair and folded one knee over another. Actually, he had a nice face, a little too much cheek for Rhett Butler, er, Clark Gable. He must have been forty and clearly running to the good life in the hips and chest. He sat back and laid his elbows on the chair arms, gripping the claw ends with his fingers. "She's got this wild hair she wants the judge to investigate what happened to her mama."

"As I told her . . ."

He interrupted. "I can guess what you told her. Just what I told her and her aunt told her. The authorities are all over this case and don't need any PIs messing around, fouling the waters for the real investigators. No offense, ma'am."

My back had arched like a cat's. "None taken."

"I read a lot of true crime novels, and the cops get the goods and the bad guys. Once I read a couple a fiction novels with a private detective, and if the writer didn't twist things around, the cops would of got to the bad boys before he did."

"Fiction novels do twist things," I said. As if novels weren't fiction.

"You want a real cop like a Joseph Wambaugh—boy he writes those crime stories like he really knows what he's doing."

"He really does, doesn't he?" I dead-panned, "Mr. Bonnet, you remind me of a movie star."

He ran his thumbs under his lapels. The big Gable grin lit his face. "I'm a past president of the Rhett Butler Regulars, Southeastern Chapter."

I rolled my lips together. "Let's talk about Evangeline's request."

"You just say no, and we'll be gone out of here."

"Somehow I don't think Evangeline will take no for an answer."

"You got her down pretty good. You turn her down, and I'll take her by the cops and maybe they'll satisfy her."

I couldn't not grin. "Good luck." *On both points—the cops and Evangeline.*

He rose and flicked an imaginary speck from his coat.

I stood and said, "Tell you what, I'll talk to the cops and see how far along they've gotten. It's early days still, but maybe they've made progress. That might satisfy Evangeline. No need for her to shell out any money for a PI." I gave him my best calculated over-eye stare. "We get pretty darned expensive even if we can't compete with the real cops."

He straightened, offended. "Hey, ma'am, money's no object where we're concerned."

"Money's always an object."

"Me and her aunt, my sister Lorraine, we got our own resources to raise E, but she's not short of cash for a little girl."

I nodded.

He pulled at the corners of his waistcoat. "You seriously thinking about taking on E's project?"

I hadn't been until this yahoo came in busting my chops. I came around the desk. "The case has always intrigued me. What happened to the three people on the boat, as well as the boat itself . . ." *Rub-a-dub-dub* popped into my head, unbidden like demons do. "And since I spotted it first in the lake, it kind of makes it personal, you see?"

"Why sure. Like it's personal with E. It's her mama and her step-daddy who she liked all right when he wasn't taking her to task on some pet project or other."

"I can see Evangeline would be prone to pet projects."

"You don't know the half of it. Tries to get folks involved. Save the turtles. Save the cormorants. Pick up trash off the beach. No pesticides on the grapes."

Grapes. That reminded me, and I asked, "What's the name of the Brownes' vineyard?"

He told me that Crescent Moon Winery was prospering due to Johnny's hiring a cracker-jack vintner before he got killed. He also said that he and Lorraine shared responsibility for the operations now, but I detected something dodgy in that statement. He put on the flat hat and said, "You sure you want to get badgered by E again?" He winked, but not subtle enough for Gable.

"Have you met Judge Portia Devon yet?"

"Nope. Hope to."

I let him out, thinking, *When you do, Mr. Baron Bonnet aka bogus Clark Gable, you'll know what badgering is.*

After a second session with Evangeline, I didn't learn anything other than she adored her funny Uncle Baron, but thought he didn't know what was best for her. I agreed to meet her in the morning in Portia's chambers with a decision on representation. I was of two minds. Working with Evangeline could be a pain, but with a bona fide client I could delve into the tragedy to satisfy my curiosity—to say nothing of solving the case, always an overriding goal. There are things a PI can ask and do that cops can't. I just hoped this case wasn't one where I had to put my license on the line for a client I had reservations about. Reservations, I reminded myself, meant reserving judgment. *I would do that. Or try.*

I got up to go. Portia went to her files, then handed me the clips of the *Scuppernong* case. As I was leaving, Baron Bonnet entered. I looked over my shoulder. Portia looked like she'd been plopped into an improv comedy club.

CHAPTER FOUR

Mozart—my cell's ringtone of the moment—woke me at four-in-the-damned-ayem. The cell's LED told me who had summoned the maestro.

Portia. "You at Lake's?"

Oh that I were still at that old cotton warehouse near the railroad tracks in downtown Atlanta, but I wasn't. I was at home in my suburban cottage—left to my mother and me by my father. Now, Mama lived in an expensive place for those who could no longer care for themselves. "No," I said to Porsh. "Lake got a late call last night and I came home." I swung my legs out of the bed because this was a call for action, not reflection. "What's up?" I was already stepping out of my pajama bottoms.

"Get to my place at the lake. They're bringing in a cadaver dog."

I pulled underwear out of the drawers. "For where?"

"The cove." I opened the chifforobe door and pulled a white sleeveless shirt off its hanger. She said, "The pooch got a smell of decomp from the sailboat. I tried Lake's cell. Since when does he work nights?"

"He's lead on a case. He often is."

"Damn. I wanted him there."

Removing a pair of black slacks from the wardrobe, I said, "I'll call him on his personal cell. See if he can be in two places at the same time." Portia didn't remark. "Guess we won't be

35

meeting with Evangeline and her uncle this morning."

"Damn, I forgot. I'll have my clerk call. I'm heading out now. They want the dog there at dawn, in the stillness thereof."

"Makes sense."

"You ready?"

"My eyeliner's going on wrong."

She hung up.

I backed the Bentley out of the garage. If it had been seven o'clock in the morning, I would have trotted up my street to Peachtree where there's a car rental agency on the corner. I love driving the Bentley, but it's old and I want to have her for a long time. She was a gift of sorts from Portia when my beloved Saab got blown up in the service of her majesty, Judge Portia Devon. Long story, but she insisted I buy her mother's car (for five hundred dollars!) now that her mother had, like mine, relinquished the coils of acute intellect and recent memory for the flat-line fuzziness of old times.

I called my office landline wagering that Webdog would be there, asleep on the narrow swayback sofa in my office. Webdog is Dennis Caldwell, the geekiest of geeks and a student at Georgia State University where he's about to graduate. Web has solved more cases from his computer than I have out hoofing it. I tremble at the prospect of his leaving me for some secret government agency where he will design computer architecture meant to save the world. I need him in mine.

"How'd you know I was here?" Web asked around the croaking frog in his throat.

"When I solve this case, I'm buying you an extra-large sofa for your office."

"Just when I'm grooving the one in yours." I couldn't do this job without Webdog. He forgets to eat and stays up all night on his supercomputer inventing platforms and sharpening his hacking skills. "What's moving this time o' day?" he asked.

"I want what you can get on Candice Browne." My agency pays good money to Internet information agencies, but sometimes a deeper probe is called for.

"Candice of the *Scuppernong*?"

"Didn't I say that?"

"I didn't hear it when you yawned."

"Also, Baron Bonnet, Lorraine Bonnet and any other Bonnet related to Candice Bonnet Browne."

"Gotcha."

"I'm on my way to Lake Lanier. A cadaver dog got the smell of decomp from the sailboat now at the GBI yard."

"Rich," he said.

"Get me maps of Wilmington, Southport, the whole Cape Fear area. Find out what you can about the Crescent Moon Vineyard."

"I'm on it."

The Bentley moved with stately grace around curves, up mountain rises and into shallow valleys as the purple veins of dawn lightened the encompassing hills of north Georgia. At Portia's gravel road, the car rocked gently on her new shocks, then purred to a halt next to a pickup truck and two squad cars.

Holding binoculars, Portia flitted down the steps and urged me to follow. A step behind Porsh, I slipped and slid to the dock.

Two men, a woman and a dog were in a boat on the lake. I stared at the dog and shrieked with delight.

Portia shushed me. "She's very sensitive."

"I know that Chessie. Her name's Betsy."

Portia looked at me. "I forgot, you almost went on the K-9 Squad."

That was before Portia talked me into founding Child Trace, which turned out to be the best thing I ever did, except fall in love with Lake.

The red-haired Chesapeake Bay retriever wore a vest, much like a life vest I would wear. I took the binoculars from Portia's hands and brought the two lenses into focus. Betsy's name was on her vest, a law enforcement badge pinned to it, too. She stood in the boat and stared at the water. After several moments, she lifted her head and circled to the other side of the inflatable craft. Maybe fifteen seconds later, she sat and looked at Eleta, her handler. Betsy's body language told Eleta that nothing foul was down there. The pilot cranked the motor, and the boat moved away. A hundred yards or so later, he pulled back on the stick and let the boat meander. Betsy took her stance; front paws on the rail, staring into the water, brush tail a-wagging. These dogs love adventure. It's a game. Betsy pushed back, four paws on the deck again and sat. We watched for an hour as the boat moved further from the spot where the sailboat had gone down, out into the center of the cove. The dog moved restlessly seeking the scent she was trained to find.

Search and Rescue dogs, no matter their specialty, hate to come up empty. I came across Betsy three years ago when one of Portia's runaways decided to take a dive off a bridge to Tybee Island in the middle of the night when no one was looking.

Lowering the binocs, Portia turned away from the search boat with a disappointed slump of her shoulders. Then, quite suddenly, a look of happy surprise grew on her face. Before I glanced up the hill, I knew what caused her glow. Lake.

Sporting a blue straw panama, Lake—of the sure foot— scrambled down the stone-strewn path like it was as smooth as a high school track. We run 10-Ks, but his ankles are thicker than mine.

After he'd kissed Porsh and me on our cheeks, I asked him, "How'd you know where we were?" He hadn't answered his cell when I called several times.

"Let's see," he said. "I had phone messages, a beeper page, and Dispatch told me the judge was waiting for me at the cove."

I studied his face beneath the hat brim. He didn't look frazzled. For someone who hadn't slept in twenty-four hours, now heading into thirty-six, he looked as fresh as the large sunball rising over the water. Me? I was already sweating at the guarantee of another blistering day.

"Betsy's striking out," Portia said.

Lake scrutinized Betsy as she worked both sides of the boat. He said, "Bill, at the Crime Lab, said she alerted, although there were no visible signs of tissue on the boat."

"What part of the boat?" I asked.

"The deck, around a cleat. The galley in a bench locker where they stowed lines. And the head."

"The head? Lots of stinks there." I considered what it meant, which was probably nothing. Betsy had found the scent of dead tissue, but it could be from the killer or Johnny. I said, "Seems a long time in the water for rot to be detected."

"We don't know how large the piece of rot was. Maybe a whole body."

The deck, the galley, the head. Three places, three people. I said, "There would be bones."

"Maybe." Then his stomach growled. He looked sheepish as he put his hand to his belt. "Starved." Missing sleep was a minor issue, a meal was quite another.

Portia looked at him. "I don't know how you can think of food."

He twitched a smile then looked toward the cadaver boat. The rocking intensified, and Betsy's tail wagged like she was about to dig into a pound of steak. Suddenly she leaned over the portside rail, glanced back at her handler and launched herself into the water.

Lake laughed. "I think that means she's found what she's

smelling for."

"That's how she alerts in deep water," I said. "She'll swim to where the odor is strongest."

Betsy circled an area twenty yards from the boat. The pilot edged the craft closer to her, and a DNR man threw a buoy into the water to mark the spot. At the ladder she scampered into the vessel and shook her coat vigorously. Calm and eager now, Betsy waited for her second treat, and Eleta put something between her teeth. Bet it was a liver biscuit. Eleta got the recipe from a doggie bakery.

Lake asked Portia, "How deep is it where Betsy alerted?"

"In full pool, seventy. With the drought, who knows? Forty?"

"Bodies move with the currents and boat traffic," Lake said. "While still fresh, they can tumble a half mile from where they go in."

Portia looked troubled. "Somehow I don't think it's our people."

Lake shook his head and, after a protracted pause, said, "Well, if Betsy's right, somebody went into the lake and is about to come out looking the worse for wear."

Later a cadaver boat drew alongside the other boats. Through the binocs I could see a body bag and men in rubber suits and masks.

Portia folded her arms. "It's almost out of the cove—some killer's plans have gone awry."

"You always think the worst," I said.

"It always *is* the worst."

The body, which I couldn't make out, was pulled up and loaded onto a rubber-covered metal stretcher for its somber ride. The rest of the combined task force including Betsy and Eleta climbed onto our dock.

Eleta extended her hand to me. "I've met the judge, and we've worked together before."

"Tybee," I said, shaking her hand.

She looked at her dog. "Relax." Betsy sat, alert, but with slackened musculature, her tongue hanging out, her pink lips curved into a dog smile.

Portia, not necessarily an animal lover, went over and touched the dog's wet head and scratched her ears. "Beauty," she said.

"We're real proud of her," Eleta said.

"How do you get dogs to do that?"

Eleta leaned against the railing. "First, you've got to have a dog that accepts discipline and obedience; one that likes working with you. But many good SAR dogs are repulsed by human decomp. Only those who accept and are skilled at dead-speak will take on the challenge."

"Do they have to be certified?" Portia asked.

"Sure. Usually takes a year and a half to get cert, but Betsy was ready in eight months."

"What if the corpse has burned?" Portia said, her nose tweaking up.

"K-9s are trained for all kinds of decomp odors, like Nine-Eleven, or bombings, or old burials. Then there's residual odors. Maybe an arm bone carried off by a predator. Water cadavers are a special breed. Betsy, like Labs, loves the water."

"Did you use real dead bodies to train her?" Portia's nose tweaked again in distaste.

"We get cadaver material from the Crime Lab. Others teach from a chemical scent, but I prefer the real thing."

"Grizzly." Portia rubbed her arms like she was cold. The new-morning temperature had to be eighty already.

A call came from the bank. "Yoo-hoo."

I turned around and so did my companions on the dock. "Shit!" I said, hating my outburst. "It's Rhett Butler."

Lake eyed the man and girl climbing the dock steps like he knew things weren't going to work out in their favor. Portia looked like an angry bird of prey. "Why's he here?" She looked at me as if I'd sent Baron an engraved invitation.

"Don't have a clue," I said.

Evangeline skipped forward as Baron watched his step, perhaps to keep his spats pearly white.

"It's not my mama. It's not," Evangeline cried, seeing the cadaver boat pick up speed.

Portia planted her fists on her hips. "Mr. Bonnet, why have you come here?"

"Well, I . . ."

Evangeline had her mouth open to speak when Portia thrust a finger at her. "I asked your uncle." She turned back to him. "How did you know to come to this place, which happens to be my private property?" In court, her black eyes pierced the truth from many a pathological liar.

"Judge," he said, expanding his arms to produce some Rhett Butler charm. "You got your leggings in an uproar."

"*You* have my leggings in an uproar. My lake house is my private affair."

"Why ma'am, your property is the scene of a crime."

"It most certainly is not."

"The news said . . ." He surveyed everyone on the dock to make sure we paid attention. Then he noticed the dog. "My word. Are you the sniffer that found our Candice?"

"No!" Evangeline shouted.

Baron looked at her. "Of course not. Forgive me, E."

He walked to Betsy sitting quietly at Eleta's side. He reached out to pat her head when Eleta said, "She's not a pet, sir."

Betsy's glinting amber eyes dulled and she swayed her wide head toward Eleta's knee in an evasive move. When Baron's hand hovered over a chestnut ear, without looking at him, she showed just the tips of her incisors.

Baron jumped back. "Whoa there boy, it's all right, it's me."

42

He continued to retreat until his backside hit the dock rail.

Lake said, "Mr. Bonnet, answer Judge Devon's questions." He touched the badge fastened to his belt.

Baron took three steps toward Lake, studied the badge and stuck out his hand. "Baron Bonnet, brother of Candice Bonnet Browne."

Lake shook, despite the tightness in his jaw. "Detective Lieutenant Richard Lake, Atlanta Police Department."

Baron called Evangeline. "E, bring yourself on over here."

Evangeline had been eyeing Betsy, who wagged her tail, tongue out, giving Evangeline the merry eyes and upturned back lips as if they shared a funny story. "Cool dog," Evangeline said, and then trotted to her uncle. "Yes, Uncle Baron."

Baron said, "This here's a policeman. Detective Lieutenant Lake." He glanced at me then looked at Evangeline. "We got the police here with us. I don't think we need to . . ."

Evangeline was squinting at Lake. Words burst from her mouth. "That's *not* my mother."

Lake shook his head. "Likely not, Miss Browne . . ."

"Broussard," Evangeline corrected.

"Broussard." His head tilted toward Betsy. "We don't know who Betsy found out there."

"Was the body in the same place where you found the sailboat?" she asked, the dark look of her face enough to scare a predator.

"It went down in a different part of the lake, but . . ."

"What part?"

"I'm not free to say."

"Why not?" Evangeline snapped. "I'm her daughter. I got a right to know."

I had to admire his patience. "It's not my case."

"Whose is it?"

"The Georgia Bureau of Investigation's."

"You still know, don't you? I'm kin. I have a right to know."

Lake looked at Portia. "Judge, you want to tell Miss Browne, er, Broussard, what her rights are?"

Portia didn't hesitate. "Exactly none."

Startled, Baron puffed up. "That's a crock." He sounded very un-Rhett-like.

"Mr. Bonnet," Portia said, "I suggest you shut your mouth before it overloads your brain. The sailboat belonged to Mr. and Mrs. Cocineau."

"My mom was on it," Evangeline said.

"Not when it was pulled from the lake. Now quit being presumptuous."

Lake said, "We know two things for certain. Mr. Browne's body was found almost four years ago in the water and last week the sailboat surfaced. At this time, that's all we know."

"Where's the sailboat now?" Evangeline asked.

"At the GBI Crime Lab, and don't ask me to speculate."

Evangeline crossed her arms and looked down at her shoes.

Portia stared at Baron. "How did you know to come here?"

Baron seemed to understand that the order to explain himself didn't call for movie drama. He spoke naturally when he said they'd heard on the television that dogs were called to Lake Lanier and that the sailboat had provided clues. He said they went to the Sawchicsee sheriff's office, and getting no answer there, traveled on to the post office where they were provided directions to the dock in question.

I thought the bones in Portia's face would come through her pale skin. I didn't hear what she muttered, but I think it started with an F.

Throughout this exchange, Betsy had moved closer to Evangeline. The dog's nose touched her palm. Evangeline looked at Eleta, who nodded. Evangeline dropped to her knees and Betsy tried to lick the pug right off her face. Love at first sight for dog and girl.

I looked at Portia and Lake, a tight, tense twosome, with Baron Bonnet looking very much the odd man out.

Lake went over to him, "Mr. Bonnet, please don't talk to the media until we identify the body."

"And," Portia said stiffly, "don't you tell anyone about this place or come here again without invitation."

"Sure," Baron said, crossing his arms. I figured he'd find the first media mike he could.

Lake signaled me and I walked beside him, off the dock and up the hill. He said, "I'm going to find the son-of-a-bitch who leaked to the press and chew a big piece from his sorry ass."

Some things you just don't want to visualize.

CHAPTER FIVE

I followed Lake to a breakfast place in Yarrow, the county seat of Sawchicsee. Yarrow is your typical north Georgia mountain town. The sturdy red brick courthouse sits in the middle of a park-like acre of land. A favorite son's statue-on-horseback guards a brick path to the granite steps. One-way streets circle the square. On one corner of the square, a newer glass and granite government center housed the tax and tag offices and a lot of other bureaus and commissions. Next to it, a two-story gray limestone jailhouse reminds folks it's not a home-away-from-home B&B.

Lake circled the square then took a side street out to the state road. I followed in the Bentley. Lake lapped the sharp bends like Jimmy Johnson at Daytona, and I'm proud to say the Bentley, stately as she goes, kept pace through the curling and twisting and altogether gorgeous countryside. I was reminded that these mountain towns are known for auto racing. The daring prowess of today's race car drivers, they say, comes from moon-shining ancestors running from revenuers. I don't know about Yarrow, but Dawsonville, not many miles away, hosts a Mountain Moonshine Festival that draws half a million ebullient folks to its tax base. Take that, revenuers.

And was I ready to eat. My stomach reminded me I'd missed two meals. Last night I'd showered, sprawled on the bed, sipped white wine while watching a faux autopsy from a crime scene show. At midnight Lake came in, slipped under the covers and in seconds I found myself in a woozy bodily union. Feeling of velvet and silk, I was back asleep until he woke me to say he'd received a call on his serial case. I couldn't go back to sleep without him there, so I went home to my place in Peachtree Hills, and a few hours later here I was on the outskirts of Yarrow.

I love joints like Trader Joe's General Store and Diner where dried corn cobs swing from porch hooks along with summer sausages and Indian bead necklaces. This used to be the Cherokee Indians stomping ground before they took to the Trail of Tears on Andy Jackson's tragical wagon-train tour. As if to further celebrate that heartrending era, a cigar store Indian stood at the entrance. Lined up in the storefront window were enumerable jars—Cottonwood and clover honeys, jams and jellies, butters of all persuasion—apple, pear, plum—and sauces—Vidalia onion to be sure.

Lake pulled my arm toward the diner. "Shop after we eat."

I glanced over my shoulder at the store. "I'm coming back," I said, giving a thumbs-up to the Indian.

There were two people in the diner. A man's face, half-covered by large eyeglasses, looked out from a window behind the counter where food was passed from the kitchen to the wait staff. Middle-aged though he was, I could still make out the pits left by a cruel case of teen acne. The waitress, standing at the end of the room near a telephone hanging on the wall, looked to be about thirteen. She shuffled toward us, her face showing red patches of brand new blemishes. Dangling from her ears were heart earrings that almost touched her shoulders. Her hair was pulled back in a thin, straggling ponytail, and she wore a faded pink waitress uniform two sizes too large for her.

"Morning," Lake said, his voice resonating in the quiet of the diner.

"Good morning," the girl said. "Sit where you want."

Plucking menus tucked between a napkin holder and condiment tray, I noticed wine and beer on the back of the menu. An all-purpose dunk and dine. The waitress hovered six feet away while we perused the plastic-covered sheets of paper.

I looked at her and she moved closer, her order pad at the ready. I said, "You old enough to serve wine and beer?" I was thinking of the new kind of revenuer. The age-checker.

She jerked back. "Oh no," she said, blinking like windshield wipers flashing. She looked at the man in the window. "Mr. Brunty does the serving."

She tucked hair hanging in her face behind an ear, and her small chest heaved shallowly. I kept looking at her until she felt she had to say something. "I'm here for my mom."

"She under the weather this morning?" I asked.

Lake's eyebrows drew into those curious question marks they can make.

The waitress—Diane—written on her blouse—said, "She's away for a spell."

Lake looked at her. "Away?"

"Eight days now," Diane said, trying to keep her voice from quivering.

"She take off with someone?" Lake asked, and I could have stomped his foot for being so crass.

Diane hunched a thin shoulder. "Could of. I don't believe it, though."

I detected movement in the window behind the counter. The face disappeared, and the man owning it came through the kitchen door. Lake and I picked up menus as he walked around the counter toward us. "Diane?" he asked. "There anything the matter?"

I held the menu like I was studying assiduously.

"No, Mr. Brunty," she said, putting pencil to her order pad. "Nothing."

Lake folded his menu and laid it on the table. His voice was sure and quick. "Big pot of coffee for us two." An index finger went back and forth between him and me. "For me, two eggs, two bacon, two sausage, grits, basket of biscuits, hash browns." He glanced up at Diane. "You got onion and cheese you could put on them potatoes?"

On *them* potatoes? Lake's motto: when in the country, speak the language. If we were in France he'd hack up French, too: *les pommes de terre?*

Diane nodded while scribbling. "Sure do, sir. Anything else?"

"Butter, jelly, blackberry if you have it."

The counter man, Brunty, had stepped back a foot or two. A quick glance and I noticed his glasses emphasized prominent light eyes.

It came my turn to order and suddenly my head was dizzy with indecision. The man standing so near, somewhat hostile, had thrown me off. "Uh, I'll have the same, please. No cheese, no onions."

Brunty walked away, and Diane, with a skilled move, tucked the order pad into her apron pocket. She fetched two glasses of water, set them before us and left to place the order paper on the window ledge. Brunty wasn't standing in the window, but I saw his profile silhouetted on the back wall. He was very alert for something. Diane went to the coffee urns where she poured two cups of hot coffee in so efficient a manner I'd recommend her for a job at a top Atlanta restaurant—if she could serve beer and wine. Yep, she had experience, and I had it figured. Her mom was one of those that disappear for a while. Diane fills in until mom returns from her rendezvous. Things get back to normal until the next rendezvous. People can be so predictable.

An uneasy quietude riffed the air while we waited. I can't answer for Lake, but I didn't feel like talking with the man's ear cupped to hear our every word while he set about fixing our food. Lake's attention was on the road outside. He muttered, "Look at that asphalt shimmer; another hot one."

"Ummm," I agreed.

Diane seemed to float on tiptoes when she brought our plates of steaming food. My typical morning fare consists of a sandwich, usually tomato or cheese. I said, "This platter could feed two hungry truck drivers and their hitchhikers." I punctured an egg and broke apart a biscuit. With a fork, I sopped the yellow with the bread.

Lake looked at my fork, poised above the eggs. "I didn't know you ate eggs."

Tossing my head enough to feel my dark hair fling about, I said, "Nothing wrong with my cholesterol."

He grinned, making my heart sing. "Eat away then. We'll run that fat off you."

"How'd you like to run a 10-K over these hills?"

"Do my flabby legs good," he said, sopping gravy.

Lake's legs are like two iron posts—shapely iron posts.

I looked around. Diane stood at the telephone looking like a kitten in a place that doesn't like kittens, her eyes fixed, her body poised to dash after our every want. She'd refilled coffee cups that didn't need refilling, twice. In my line of work, you learn to figure the age of girls and boys to the month. She might have been an undernourished fourteen, but I'm saying thirteen by the look of her chest and her rear end. True, she was a thin girl with long bones, but even skinny girls get a rounded look once they pass that gawkiness that heralds the onset of puberty. Diane was on the cusp.

"You're staring at her," Lake said.

"Ummm," I said, picking up a piece of bacon.

"You thinking sweatshop?"

"Country ways," I said, chewing bacon. I'm not so fond of salty country bacon and put it down. "Wouldn't be surprised if

Diane got sick, they'd send in her ten-year-old sister."

Lake whispered, "Brunty suspects we're authorities, maybe child legal experts."

"I *am* a child legal expert."

"You going to introduce yourself to him?"

With a casual sweep of my eyes, I saw Brunty looking out the window, his glasses glistening. "I'm going to do worse."

Stymied for a moment because his mouth was full of potato, Lake swallowed and said, "You're going to get Portia after him."

"I'm certainly going to consult Portia. This is her county of residence, and I believe her Superior Court judicial district."

"Good girl. Saving one kid at a time."

I looked at Lake through my rather long, thick eyelashes. He didn't mean to stab with sarcasm, but he had, and he knew it. "Sorry," he said.

Saving one kid at a time was my slogan, when I needed one. Why had he needled me with it now? Probably no reason other than it popped into his mind. But still, the needle pricked. Not that that described my wonderful, but sometimes tactless lover.

"Sorry," he said again. "It's this place." He pushed back his plate.

"You only ate one of each," I said. "One pound of bacon, one pound of sausage, a dozen biscuits."

"I'm not running these hills today," he said, throwing down his napkin.

Diane scooted over, fingers twisting over each other. "Everything okay?" She looked at my full plate.

"Yes," I said, and when she looked about to cry, I said, "Really, I wasn't hungry." I noticed her fingernails, bitten to the quick. "Everything's great. I hope your mama comes home soon. What's your last name?"

She shifted her eyes. "I'll get your check."

★　★　★　★　★

Trader Joe's store was chock full of stuff nobody needs, even as little luxuries. The people in this county were the sort that put up their own jellies and butters and made their own wine. We were Trader Joe's only customers. A tall, thin man stood at the cash register—a real, old-fashioned thing. "Morning, folks. I'm Orell Brunty. Folks shop in my store call me Orell. You need anything, you just ask."

Trader Joe's sounded a lot better than Trader Orell's.

Lake and I said good morning and I pirouetted for the back of the store where shelves were stocked with gallon jugs of Brunty's Suscadine Wine. Lake followed. "I'm going to buy some wine," I told him.

"What?" He calls me a wine snob. "That swill?"

"Sshhhh, Orell will hear. Besides, it can be good."

"Take your word."

"With vineyards in the picture, I have a feeling I need to get to know muscadine and scuppernong wines. You think suscadine wine is a blend of the two?"

"Have you decided to take the sailboat case and rep that pain-in-the-ass *princess*?"

"You just came up with the perfect name for her: Princess Pita. And yes, I am."

"Because a phony Clark Gable put you down?"

"Nope. A dog I know and like, likes a little girl I know but don't particularly like. But I am reserving judgment."

"I get it. I think."

"Dogs are better judges of people than people are of people." I grabbed a jug of Brunty's Suscadine Wine and handed it to Lake.

"I get it. I think."

I led us back to the front of the store. Lake placed the jug on the counter and walked away. I asked the man, "Are you related to Mr. Brunty next door?"

"My cousin," he said and smiled. "You buy some food from him?"

"Just now—big breakfast." I looked to where Lake fingered baseball hats with Sawchicsee County stamped on the bill—$8.99 each or two for $15.00—any color, mix and match.

Orell said, "Hope I don't have to take ol' Scully to task on your eggs. Folks are mighty particular about their eggs."

He had high cheekbones and blue eyes, no glasses, certainly no mirror image of his cousin. And he'd told me Mr. Brunty's first name. I said, "My eggs were perfect. The service was perfect, unusual from such a young girl."

My eyes held his in an unspoken question; then his darted to a stack of cups bearing the Sawchicsee County logo—a waterfall, maybe the flooded Osprey Cove waterfall. He said, "Diane's filling in for her mama that's sick. We're all family around here."

I laid my backpack on the crowded counter, careful of the cups, and ran my hand down to the bottom where my wallet lay. "Are there a lot of wineries around here?" I asked, motioning to the jug.

"Lots of folks make wine from scuplins," he said. "We sell from the Brunty and the Sawchicsee vineyards."

"Scuplins? Is that a kind of grape?"

"Where you from?"

"Atlanta."

"You would call the grapes scuppernongs."

"I see, local name." He nodded. "I was mistaken." I waved toward Lake. "I told my friend your wine was a blend of muscadine and scuppernong."

"No, not a blend of them. They're too much alike, like cousins, you might say."

I grinned. "Like you and Scully?"

He had a funny look on his face. "You might say."

Lake walked up and opened his jacket wide, deliberately showing his badge and the gun in a holster under his arm. Orell frowned and looked at me like he wondered about this *friend* of mine. He addressed Lake, "Do something for you, officer?"

"A few questions."

"You eat next door, too?" He was trying for relaxed, but his bony hand shook when I handed him a twenty for the wine— $15.99, plus tax.

"Food was fine, mighty fine," Lake said. "Service, too. Say, where can I find the Landing Creek Park?"

Orell's shoulder and arm muscles constricted. "That'd be on the county line."

"Thank you, sir."

"Hope you're not fixin' to put a boat in?" Orell said, trying for jolly and being nosy at the same time.

Lake pursed his lips, furrowing his brow. "There a problem?"

"Ramp's closed. The end of it's in two feet of water. Not enough to float a boat. That and trailers gettin' stuck."

"Dang," Lake said, snapping his fingers. He turned to look at me, a sexy smile curving his lips. Then he looked at Orell. "For future then. They got campsites there, right?"

Orell scratched his head with the last two fingers of his right hand. "RV and tent sites. Showers, a grill, fire pits, picnic tables."

"Electricity, water?"

"Surely."

"You have to sign in anywhere?" Lake gave me an adolescent grin. "For future reference."

"Corps of Engineers runs it with the County," Orell explained. "They got entry stations where you got to check in. If you want electric and water, you pay extra."

"I guess I'm living in the past," Lake said. "I thought you just pulled in and pitched a tent or parked your RV."

"Nope." Orell grinned, showing square yellowing teeth.

Lake looked at me and winked this time. "What if, while we're up here, we want a little rowing under the moon?"

I about rolled my eyes.

Orell said, "You got to go to the big marina in the next county."

"Thanks for the info, Mr. Brunty."

"Orell."

Lake nodded, "Orell."

"You want accommodations while you're here, my cousin rents out cabins."

"Your family has quite a presence in Sawchicsee," Lake said.

"Going back six generations—just getting a toehold going by the roots of some around here."

Lake opened his coat to again let his badge show.

Wily Orell hesitated, then said, "I figured you're here because of that sailboat."

"You figured right," Lake confessed. "Sure's a mystery why she turned up in the cove when all the action was in Hall County."

Orell leaned closer, like he'd erected an imaginary picket fence over which to gossip. "Takes someone knowing that Waterfall Cove is the deepest in the lake. Used to be a dry waterfall once." He fingered a cup with the waterfall logo. "Our landmark 'fore the fools came. Ruined everything, building a dam on the river."

"What you're saying is," Lake said, "if someone sunk her, that someone knew about the deep water cove."

"You live here, you know the crooks and crannies of the lake and the rivers feeding it."

Lake said, "If not for the drought, the sailboat would have remained under water."

"The fool sunk it there should have reckoned on drought.

Ever' seven years, just about."

"Have you seen photographs of the people who were on the sailboat?"

I looked at Lake. I had photographs in my car if he wanted to show them, but Orell answered, "On TV, sure."

"Do you recognize them?"

"No, sir. I'd be surprised they set foot in Yarrow. We're off the beaten path, and we only got but one marina, not hardly big enough for their boat." He shook his head. "No, sir, people come to this county from neighboring counties to hunt and fish. You want fancy, you stop off at Cumming."

"Thanks for your information," Lake said, and ambled to the hat table and picked up a powder blue baseball cap. "I'm going to buy my sweetie one of these," he said. I don't like being called sweetie. Lake asked, "How much?"

Orell pointed to the sign. "Like it says—eight dollars and ninety-nine cents. Get you another for fifteen dollars."

Handing me the powder blue, Lake said, "I wear a different kind of hat."

Indeed, he did. As a devoted member of Atlanta's Hat Squad, he'd never go to a crime scene without a fedora—felt in winter, straw in summer. His navy summer straw lay on the backseat of his car.

We left and when we stood by my car, I said, "He was worried about the girl." I opened my car door and climbed under the wheel. "He thought he talked her out of our minds."

"Seems so," Lake said and kissed me through the driver's window. "He's a sly ol' boy."

"You two did an admirable *pas de deux* about the reason we're up here."

"I let him draw me out."

Over his shoulder, I saw Orell at the window, pretending to shuffle the goods stacked there. "He's watching."

"No doubt." He walked to his car, signaled, and said, "Follow me, sweetie."

It isn't lady-like to give a man the one-finger salute.

CHAPTER SIX

Despite the heat, humidity and the lake being at its all-time low, people were making the turn into Landing Creek Park—probably ghoulish gawkers since the sailboat was found not far away. Lake pulled the car into the line, me following, and made a left onto a park road that forked right and left. A sign to the right had an arrow beneath it and a wooden plaque that read: *Ramp and Day Visitors: Use Entrance C. All other visitors: Form an orderly line at the gate.* That gate was straight ahead.

We were ten deep in the straight line. Lake stopped at a sign on the left: *Campsites limited to SIX people and TWO motorized vehicles. One camper trailer or motor home per site. Tents in designated areas.*

Day visitors must depart the campground by 9:30 P.M.

Campsite visitors CHECKOUT TIME 3 P.M. Fee for late departure.

Check-in for reservations guaranteed after 4 P.M.

Length of stay no more than 14 DAYS per 30 consecutive days.

The thought of camping in this heat and humidity with ants and biting bugs had my stomach rumbling, but that was probably more from breakfast fat. If you haven't developed immunity to it, diner grease played hell with gastric juices.

A long wooden cabin with a mailbox in front stood to the left of the gatehouse. A sign said: *Employees Only. No Admittance.* Lake bypassed the visitor line and I followed his car. I parked next to him in front of a rough-hewn cedar building. A Jeep

Cherokee was parked in front and a man in khaki marched out, looking ready to ream us into next month—until Lake got out of his car and flashed his shield. The ranger smiled recognition at a fellow officer and raised his hand. When they met at the steps, the ranger patted Lake's bicep. I hung behind, lest I interrupt official male bonding.

I heard the man say, "You almost missed me. I'm off to Gainesville." He shrugged as if none too happy about that destination.

Lake said, "We won't keep you." He motioned me to step forward, and I checked the man's badge. *Bernard Janeway.* Lake said, "Ranger Janeway, this is Moriah Dru of Child Trace."

Janeway didn't offer his hand and his eyes grew wide. "Are you looking for a child here?"

"Nothing like that," I said and gave him a big smile and extended my hand, which, leaning forward, he took. His hand felt moist and warm, sweaty. The temp had to be ninety-five now.

He said to Lake, "I take it then that you're here in our glorious highlands because of that sailboat."

"Right," Lake said.

I took in Janeway's particulars. About forty, he had gotten a shade soft in the middle—too much beer, perhaps? His light brown eyes tended to shift in their sockets and he constantly finger-combed wilting sandy hair. In his khakis and chest badges, he kept his back straight like he was standing inspection. The red and white castle Corps insignia added a touch of color to his sleeve.

"We can talk inside," he said, turning and leading us up the steps onto the porch, opening the door, then hand-ushering us inside. The cabin was a typical park office—at one end stood an old metal desk with a swivel chair behind it; at the other, a round wooden table with eight chairs arranged for conferences, which, from the dust, didn't happen often. Maps of the park and the cove had been tacked up to my right. Beneath them were shelves with folding maps, periodicals and leaflets. Janeway didn't invite us to sit.

Lake studied a map, then pointed to the boat ramp. "I don't have to tell you why we've held you up?"

Janeway bobbed his head. "The campers."

"I'm assuming you have records of their visit?"

Janeway nodded. "Not here. In the computer. The GBI has the paper originals."

"I'd like to see their signatures—if they signed anything."

Ranger Janeway's mouth spread, showing his whitened teeth. Not exactly a merry smile. "Anna Graham and Gene Poole signed their names in block letters." Janeway crossed his arms and seemed to be waiting for our reaction.

I was the first to laugh. "Quite clever, I thought."

The ranger studied Lake, who is not slower on the uptick than me, just more serious. "Yeah," Lake said, "makes you wonder what they were hiding."

Janeway said, "Kids. We see crazier things here. A volunteer found cigarette papers by the fire pit the next day. Dopers. I took photographs in case we catch up with them." He brushed that likelihood off with a shoulder tug.

Lake looked around. "You have the photographs here?"

"Not here, they're with the other material," Janeway said, shifting from his right to his left foot. "You want to see them?"

"And the sigs."

"The evidence resides with the Chief Ranger. Need his code, and, incidentally, his permission."

"Did the gatekeeper write down the tag number of their vehicle?"

"No, he let it go because it was a dealer tag. He was docked a week's pay."

That'll teach him. I said, "If they took their grass, why leave a pack of cigarette papers in plain sight?"

Janeway twitched his nose. "First off, that's if you believe anything a drunk says."

"Refresh my memory," Lake asked.

"He *says* the kids were smoking dope that night. He *says* they told him about the truck and the boat the next morning before they took off."

"Did you try to find them?"

"Not up to me. The county didn't try. Who knows what the GBI does?"

Lake said, "Speaking of that august agency, I need to get back to Atlanta and talk to the agent-in-charge. We're assisting, not leading the case."

Janeway canted his head and looked like he'd figured Lake out. "You want what my opinion was on a large sailboat being pulled from the lake that night?" Lake nodded. "For what it's worth, pie in the sky. Couple of kids making up names, smoking dope, having fun with a drunk who can't think straight when he's sober."

"The drunk is a local, right?"

"Yeah. Boyd was a good enough fellow when he had his health."

I suddenly recalled his last name, and asked, "What age did Scoggins say the campers were?"

Janeway turned to me, his expression not pleased that once again I'd interrupted male discourse. "He called them teenagers. Do you have a specific interest here? The kids were hardly children."

I opened my mouth to say something clever, but Lake rushed in. "Her interests are *very* specific," he said. Answering for me was something he didn't do. He went on, "Her presence has nothing to do with assisting the *official* investigation, although as a consequence, she usually does." He gave me a that's-my-girl grin. "Miss Dru has been engaged by the Browne family to find out what happened to Candice Browne."

Janeway's eyes shifted like fireflies at dusk. They finally fastened on me. "Let me get this straight . . ."

I said, "My client is twelve-year-old Evangeline Broussard, Candice Browne's daughter."

Lake said, "Miss Dru has excellent qualifications." He grinned. "She was my partner when she was with the Atlanta Police Department."

Uh-oh, I knew where this was going.

The ranger's smile patronized, and I suppose he couldn't help his eye-shift from my face to my chest.

Lake jangled change in his pocket. "Dru always makes me look good; she'd make anybody look good."

Janeway looked at me a twitch too long, then said, "Come by the office in Gainesville in the morning and maybe I can get you a look at those documents." He scratched a cheek with a fingernail. "Since you're not really official, we'll keep the look-see unofficial."

Lake reached out and tapped his arm on the red and white castle emblem. "Good man. You won't be compromised."

The ranger gave a half salute and stepped back.

I said, "I'd like to see that campsite."

"Now?"

"If it's possible."

"Right now I'm . . ."

I looked from him to Lake. "You gentlemen get on your way; I'll mosey over the park."

Janeway went to the desk, opened a drawer and pulled out two cards. He handed one each to Lake and me. "Passes," he said. "Free entry whenever you need to check things out in the future." His eyes didn't quite meet mine. "Miss Dru, follow me in your car. There's a back service gate. You won't have to wait in line." He opened the door for us, then hung back. "I'll be out in a minute."

Outside, we stood at Lake's car. His lips were slits before he spoke. "Goddamn ass-wipes. They never shared that with us."

"Standard procedure for the GBI," I said.

"They had their laugh at the kids' names. What would it hurt to share that detail—in the fucking spirit of cooperation—even if they thought Scoggins' account was a false lead." It's been a while since he's used the F word. He'd weaned himself of that ubiquitous police word because of Susanna, but in anger, he slips.

"Maybe kids of the fake names and Scoggins have nothing to do with the case."

He snapped, "You going to bet your commission on that?"

Before I could lash out, I made an abrupt right and hurried to my car.

"Dru," he called, legging it to catch up. "Dru, I'm sorry."

I whirled on him, suddenly aware that Janeway had come out the door and stopped on the top step. I said softly, "You know what I think. You don't know jack if it's important or not. You hate the GBI keeping things to themselves, as if the APD doesn't do the very same thing when it suits."

"No, I fucking don't like the GBI keeping things to themselves. Or Haskell, if he knew." Haskell commanded APD's Major Crimes squad.

I glanced toward Janeway. "Voice down," I said. "I doubt Commander Haskell knew more than you."

"I'll find out if some douche left me out to dry." He slammed his car door and peeled away.

Janeway came down the steps, his eyes covered by aviator sunglasses. He smiled and said, "The lieutenant doesn't like being kept out of the loop, does he?"

I gave him my best questioning glance. "If these joking kids and a drunken witness are even in the loop."

Smugness edged its way into his expression. "The only way to tell is find the jokers."

"Tell me something," I said.

"More than I already have?" There was a lilt in that last word. Lake had done a good job of pimping me. What we won't do for information.

I spoke with a soft inflection to my voice. "I need to get up to speed."

He crossed his arms and bounced lightly on his heels. "Your lieutenant didn't know about the fake names, did he?"

I shrugged. "You never know with cops. They like to act like they don't know the answers to the questions they ask."

"If you say so," he said and winked.

I had to catch myself from gagging. "Tell me more about Scoggins."

Boyd Scoggins, he said, was a logger who lived off State Road 128, near the dam. He had been fishing that day. As usual, he got too drunk to drive home and, when that happened, Scoggins would bunk down in his truck bed until the gates opened next morning. He always carried food and drink with him.

Janeway crossed his arms and thrust his pelvis. "If you believe a word out of his mouth, he'd have to be sleeping in a cemetery for a rig to pull in like that, which we know didn't happen since the sailboat sunk in the lake."

I think I was supposed to look at his zipper. "It could have sunk days or weeks later."

"Doubtful."

He was right. "Thank you for your . . ."

"See you in the morning?" he asked.

I thought about tomorrow's agenda starting with Evangeline

and Baron in Portia's chamber.

He lowered his voice and said quietly, "I usually have breakfast about eight. There's a diner in the Cross Keys Motel across the street from the office. How about you meet me there?"

My lips involuntarily parted at the overt invitation and his optimistic sideways grin. "I'll need to call you and let you know . . ."

"Write your number down."

I don't like being interrupted in mid-sentence once, but twice is annoying. I scribbled Web's office landline number on my card and underlined his e-mail address. "This is my assistant's e-mail address in case you can't get in touch with me."

His eyelids nearly closed. "He can, and I can't?"

"Web and I are always in touch."

He flipped the card and briefly studied it. "You have a staff; must be a big operation." He paused then read the names. "Dennis 'Webdog' Caldwell. Pearly Sue Ellis."

"A very proficient staff makes my operation what it is."

He grinned and tucked the card in his shirt pocket and looked at his Jeep. Time to hit the road, he was hinting. He said, "Then I'll see you in the morning."

I opened my car door and said, "Right."

"By the way," he said, walking away, "nobody caught the fake names—it wasn't in any report—until we looked up what Scoggins had told us about the campers—and that was *after the sailboat was pulled from the lake.*"

I said, "It was never Atlanta's case."

Turning, he asked, "Why is it now?"

"Has the GBI contacted you?"

He shook his head. "No."

"The sheriff of Sawchicsee County?"

"I get it. We hicks up here got us a cowboy from Atlanta

ready to solve the case before the next episode of *Criminal Minds.*"

"Lake's a good cop," I said. "I wouldn't underestimate him."

"Never underestimate those wearing the big shoes."

Something about you, Ranger Janeway.

"Follow me," he said. He boarded the Jeep and cranked it.

I followed a hundred yards behind until we reached a padlocked, six-foot chain-link gate. The chain link fence surrounded a utility house. Getting out, he unchained the gate, got back in, and I followed the Jeep until we came to another chain-link gate. Once we passed through that gate, he turned and pulled alongside me—driver-side to driver-side. He rolled down his window. So did I. He saluted. "Happy hunting," he called. "Campsite one-thirty-three, a primitive near the shore."

"Which one did Scoggins use?"

"Didn't use one. He parked by a pavilion near the ramp."

"Thanks again," I said.

His sunglassed eyes roamed my face too long before he said, "On leaving, go out the visitor's gate." He paused, and then said, "Call me—anytime." He drove through the gates, rear tires stirring a wake of red silt. I hurriedly rolled up my window.

The first sign read: *Dogs and pets must be kept on leash. No alcohol. Violators will be prosecuted.* The second: *Smoke responsibly. Fires caused by smoking will be prosecuted.* I grinned at the idea of fires being prosecuted. "Sorry, your Honor," the fire flamed.

The innumerable signs at Landing Creek Park—a gorgeous piece of land looking down upon the lake—tried to spoil the view, but couldn't. Waterfall Cove threw sparkles at me as sun rays tried to penetrate my skull and fry my brain. Despite the drought, Portia said that the trees stayed green due to streams that flowed underground. Parking alongside the road, I grabbed my Nikon from the trunk and hoofed it to a wooden sign that pointed me to the *Day Camp Area, Campsites 100–132.* I took three steps and saw another sign: *Grills provided. Visitors to the park may bring tents, camping trailers or recreational vehicles for the day, but may not stay overnight.* Not far away another: *Please do not park boats or vehicles along the road. Park in campsite and boat area. Illegally parked cars will be ticketed.*

Since I parked at the road side, I thought about going back, but what the hell, if Ranger Janeway followed me, he wouldn't be ticketing me. I had the feeling he was somewhere near, watching, and that had vibes creeping along my nerves. Walking the trail, I wondered why he didn't play well on the field of my mind. Nice looking, yeah, flirtatious, yeah, but no more than most men. Professional when he wanted to be. Jealous of Lake, and rightly so.

Just something about you, Ranger Janeway.

I passed immaculate but empty campsites with picnic tables and grills and came to a wash house and playground. The boat ramp lay a hundred yards ahead. To my left, three small trailers were parked, meaning small fishing boats had been hand-shoved into the water. To my right, a pavilion had been constructed with a concrete floor and an oversized grill that was mired in the cement. The structure was big enough for a large family reunion. I shot several photographs. This was where Scoggins settled in for the night.

I came to another sign. *Primitive Overnight Campsites 133– 134.* Getting to them meant climbing higher into the park's interior. Turned out, it wasn't much of a hike until I came to a flattened area numbered 133. I didn't expect there to be inhabitants, and there weren't, not even a whisper of human activity. I looked behind me, down the mountain trail, and saw through a clearing in the pines the lake, brilliant as a blue diamond, a reflection of the cerulean sky. And the boat ramp. I shot the panorama and turned back to inspect the place. The small clearing didn't have the amenities of the day camps, no picnic table or grill. What it had was privacy—pine trees, live oaks with hanging moss, magnolias, slash pine. I clicked away at the tree trunks, like Anna Graham and Gene Poole had carved their initials in a heart with an e-mail address under it, ghost-written like punsters would.

I hiked over to 134, which was a good seven-iron shot through the tree canopy if the golf ball didn't hit a limb. Same layout, same immaculate spot. I shot photographs and walked on, downhill, until I reached a blacktop road where a sign read: *Full-Service Overnight Campsites 135–144.* The terrain here was flat, and a short gravel road through the trees brought me to site 135. A concrete foundation lay ready for an RV. An electric utility pole rose above the foundation and ground faucets stood ready for hook-up. The cement foundation for site 136 was in view, so if I were a camper looking for privacy, I'd go for the isolation of campsites 133 and 134. So, too, would campers wanting to hang out and smoke grass or whatever one smoked or popped or snorted or shot-up. Clearly the lay of the land lent veracity to the campers' story—that a boat, but not our sailboat, had been hauled out of the water on the night they met Scoggins.

I backtracked to the ramp and studied the layout. I don't know boats, or ramps, but whoever sunk the *Scuppernong* could have put his or her boat into the lake from this ramp and then taken it out. Something foul happened here. I like to add caution to my intuition, so with prudence as moderator I told myself it could have happened that way. On the other hand, the drunks on the sailboat could have sunk it, going down with it— their bodies, now bones, stirring the mud that expert sniffer dogs couldn't find. But there were other possibilities, one being that the sailboat had been scuttled some time after the night of Johnny's death, others being too improbable to mention. I looked out over Waterfall Cove, shadowed from mountain and forest, and thought how beautifully sinister it looked. Chills fanned across my ribs, and I hurried down the path, my camera bouncing against my hip.

At my car—hey, no ticket under the windshield wiper . . .

In a literal flash, I knew someone was watching me. The flash had been a shaft of light off glass. Binocs. Apprehension made a run across my shoulders, and I looked up. I hadn't seen the mountain trail twenty yards from where I'd parked because it was partially hidden by drooping magnolias and sweet gum trees. I started the Bentley and drove to the trail, which was wide enough for a truck or Jeep to pass through the trees. I got out and walked to an aluminum gate. As I expected, there was a sign on the gate: *MAINTENANCE. KEEP OUT.*

I took a step and twisted my ankle on a gumball. Damn things littered the ground. I bent to rub the bone and heard a thud behind me. I jumped and landed on my good ankle. On top of the gumballs and pine needles lay a rock. Not just a rock, an aggregate of concrete and cement about ten inches in ragged diameter. Backing away to the shelter of a young magnolia, I glanced up, past the fence. The trail curved around a bluff. I didn't see anyone—nothing other than trees and limestone cliff, but someone had tossed a man-made rock down. I picked up the rock and about-faced. Folding the rock between my arm and right side, I hurried to the Bentley, my ankle yelping. Highway 128 took me out of Sawchicsee County in the direction of Atlanta and home. I needed time to think, a bath and eight hours of sleep.

CHAPTER SEVEN

"Could have been a wild hog," Lake said from his cell phone.

Sure glad I told Lake about the rock. "Why not a snake? Country snakes get big enough to move a twenty-pound piece of concrete."

"I'm just sayin'," Lake said. "Or a deer running from the hog."

"I didn't hear a ruckus."

"Deer are very quiet animals."

My lover, the woodsman. "So are humans who want to scare the crap out of me."

"Consider this, my love. Nobody up here knows anything, or they're keeping their collective mouths shut, so why would *they* want to scare you?"

"*Someone*, not *they*. Considering people up here carry guns and bows and arrows, I'd say it was meant to scare me. What's the percentage of the rock hitting me smack on the head and braining me?"

"I don't want to contemplate that," Lake said.

"Contemplate this. Janeway didn't leave the campground, but got up on that bluff . . ."

"Oh, but he did leave."

"You were already gone."

"I was watching him from some jerk's driveway. Janeway pulled out of the campground and drove toward Gainesville."

"How thoughtful, pimping me out then hanging around to

rescue the damsel if she got into distress."

"I'm the one that got into distress."

"Does this distress have something to do with the aforementioned jerk?"

"This local yokel knocked on my window and told me I was trespassin' and to get my tail off his land. He carried a shotgun. Nice folks up here."

"I rest my case about people carrying guns around for just such transgressions. Did you follow Janeway?"

"All the way to the state highway."

"So it wasn't Janeway, but since we haven't kept a low profile up here, it makes me very curious. What's going on in Atlanta?"

"Meeting with the GBI, sheriffs, us, pooling information, results of investigation, of which there are none."

"You chewed butt when you got back."

"Bet your own sweet butt. I'm convinced no one at APD knew about those kids' names."

"That's because the yokels up here didn't get the punny names, nor did they believe their story."

"Ask your hacker if he can run them down."

"My hacker's working overtime."

"He loves it."

"Can't deny it. My love to the GBI."

"Speaking of which, that's why we can't have dinner together. The meeting will probably go into the evening with dinner after."

"Booze and broads?"

"Booze for sure. I probably won't get back to my place until late. You coming there?"

I might be sorry later, but I was flat beat. "No, love, I'm heading for home and a soaking bath. Call me Ineta Drink."

"Well, I'm no Bud Wiser," he said. "Make sure you lock your doors."

★ ★ ★ ★ ★

Ah, the healing powers of a good night's sleep and a healthy breakfast of dry cereal, skim milk, coffee and toast. After which I started for north Georgia. I hadn't talked to Lake, and I told Portia I'd meet with *our* clients—Princess Pita and The Baron— this afternoon.

"*Your* clients," she said.

Webdog had given me Boyd Scoggins's mailing address yesterday. Route 128, Box 44, No More, GA. No kidding—No More, Georgia. Web also provided directions to Scoggins's No More cabin, located in the piney woods just north of Yarrow. For a mountain homestead, it wasn't hard to find.

At ten o'clock the Bentley soldiered up the red rutted trail until we reached a wide spot in the pines. A log cabin had been built at the top of the trail. Beyond it, I made out ramshackle outbuildings and a couple of chickens scratching in the dirt. And darned if there wasn't a satellite dish on the cabin's roof. Welcome to the modern world, oh pioneer.

Eight hunting dogs rushed to my car. A cabin door opened and a woman came out. She looked to be about ninety, a hard-living specimen. Cigarette dangling from thin lips, she had a shotgun pointing at the ground. I don't blame her, living on the mountain, no neighbors, no one to hear a call for help; I'd have two shotguns, one for each hand, and a few more dogs.

Warily, she moved closer to the car as I rolled the window glass into the door. The closer she got, the younger she looked.

"Who you?" she said, spitting out the cigarette and stomping it.

"My name is Moriah Dru," I said. Final countdown, she was in her rode-hard fifties.

"What you want?"

"To talk to Boyd Scoggins," I said.

She let out a keening sound only a wolf would understand. It went on and on. I waited until she stopped. Half the dogs got bored and wandered off into the woods. One fat guy, reminding me of a hot dog, looked up at her with the saddest eyes.

She shifted the shotgun, now holding it across her standing lap, and leaned toward the car. "He ain't talkin' to no one no more, lessen you dig 'im up and put some strings on his mouth." She cackled like one of Macbeth's demented witches.

"I'm so sorry," I said and opened the door half way. "Are you Mrs. Scoggins?"

"Stay right there," she said, and angled the shotgun more toward me.

"I'm staying," I said, pulling the door to.

"What you want with Scoggins? I'm the missus."

"Talk about the sailboat they found in Waterfall Cove."

"Tch. Didn't believe ol' Scoggins then. Now's no different."

"Can I have a word with you then?"

"A word, heeee-heeee." She approached the window, scooched down, peered in and up at me. I'm six feet tall and my head nearly touches the liner. "You a smart-looking thing. Where you from?"

"Atlanta." I knew that would bring a yowl.

But it didn't. She withdrew her head and stood. "Been there some," she said, looking for a moment like she would recount some jovial incident. "Liked it when I was a girl." She moved back. "You can get yourself out." I did and towered over her. She broke the shotgun and slung it over her shoulder. "Who sent you here?"

"No one sent me, exactly."

She glared through a gathering of wrinkles around each eye. "Who sent you, *unexactly*?"

She had some smarts with words. "I asked around."

"He don't live here or anywhere else no more."

Janeway held back telling me Scoggins was dead. Why? "I'm

sorry for your loss," I told her.

She made a sound like a whoosh from the back of her throat. "Death bein' what it is." She turned her back and walked ahead. "C'mon up to the porch. Tell me what you wanted with Scoggins, s'if I didn't know."

The house looked solidly constructed on a foundation of heavy stones with the heart pine of the cabin pitched rock-hard. Mrs. Scoggins sat in one of a pair of newish rocking chairs and I sat in the twin. I like rocking and gazing at a view. Here, pine woods climbed higher on a neighboring mountain and appeared to float in a light purple haze. A cool sadness spread through me. Uncomplicated beauty does that. As the woman said: death being what it is.

"You can talk now," she said, rocking a little, a twinkle starting somewhere in the back of her retina.

I talked. "When the sailboat and the folks on her went missing, campers at Landing Creek Park told Mr. Scoggins they saw a tractor and boat trailer back down the ramp and pull a sailboat from the water."

When I paused, she said, "Ummm, Scoggins said that, more or less. Who told you?"

I would keep our word with Janeway. "I believe it was reported in the Atlanta newspapers."

"Used to take the papers 'fore Scoggins got bad in the knees. Foresters don't need bad knees and a bad back. Didn't see Scoggins name in the papers for sayin' what he said."

Back-track time. "I'm probably mistaken, but the official reports said Mr. Scoggins spoke with young campers that night."

"I got it from the horse's mouth hisself," she said, rocking forward, stopping. "Scoggins was drunk, but that don't matter. He can—could—see and hear and smell just as good as you and me, drunk or not. He did a bit of cannabis in his time. Used to grow it back up the hills. Got a fine and six months, so we

74

don't do that no more. Made some money, we did."

"What did Mr. Scoggins say about the teenagers at the park."

"Why'd you call them teenagers?"

"The reports . . ."

She waved away the reports. "Fergit them. Papers lied, the law lied. Those folks was full grown."

"What did Mr. Scoggins tell you specifically?"

"*Specificly*, Scoggins said he shared his food and bottle with them and they lit him a toke. He says he went sound asleep in the back of the pickup after that. Out like a light, he said. That was Scoggins, head to the pillow, and out like a light."

"Did Mr. Scoggins see a sailboat raised from the water?"

"What did I tell you? He passed out in that sleeping bag he carries around. When you pass out, you don't see nothin', no matter how good your eyes see."

I grinned, then looked solemn. "Can I ask what happened to Mr. Scoggins?"

"He had the cancer," she said and rocked back.

So much for suspicion. A rock thrown down at me; Scoggins killed for his knowledge.

Then she said, "Sonna-bitch that shot him waited six months, he won't be getting hisself killed by the state."

Welcome back suspicion. "They caught the shooter?"

"Not yet, but we will."

"When did this happen?"

"Three weeks now."

"Where?"

"Out back a here, by the shed where Scoggins kept himself. Hunter, they said. Bah, Scoggins knew a few things people didn't want known."

"Like what?"

"You sure are nosy." She crossed her arms and set her mouth.

"It's not personal," I assured her. "I'm not broadcasting your business."

"I know what you're about," she said, staring into my eyes, making me blink. "I ain't talkin' 'bout folks around here."

"Mrs. Scoggins, I want to know all there is to know about those people at the campsite. They likely weren't your neighbors."

It was as if she didn't hear me. "See here, 'round here, we're all related one way or other. But that don't mean we like each other, and that don't mean we don't do no harm to each other. The Lord made people to hate each other so as to keep the numbers down. I seen on TV, rats go crazy when they get to be too many." She yanked her hands apart. "Tear each other up. Same way with people, kin or not."

She rose and held out a strong hand. "Be on your way, miss. I told you all I know to tell."

I walked to my car feeling her philosophical eyes heating the back of my blouse.

Chapter Eight

"Go see Sonny Kitchens," Portia said. "Tell him about the girl. Ask him what happened to her mother and her father. Her whole fam-dam-ily."

"He has no reason to give me that information," I said. "I'm not the law."

"He gives you grief, tell him I'll be up there jumping on his ass before he can . . ."

"Is Sawchicsee County in your district?"

"The very edge of my district. One of those counties where people deal their own justice and fly under the judicial radar. But when I need to act up there, I don't care about folk justice."

"I'll tell him you deputized me."

"You tell him you're working for the State of Georgia, the Juvenile Courts. He can call me."

"I like the part about you coming up and jumping on his ass. At least he's got a nice one."

Portia disconnected, and ten minutes later I climbed the four steps to the Sawchicsee County Sheriff's Department—the two-story gray limestone building next to the new government center's architectural mediocrity.

A scrawny guard, wearing a hat that threatened to slip over his ears, consulted his list. "He ain't in," he said.

I looked at the clipboard in his hand. "It say when he'll be back?"

"Nope. He got bidness in the county."

I was tempted to ask if it had anything to do with sailboats, but better judgment intervened. I reached into my backpack— which I had brought around to my chest—to get a calling card. The guard called, "Freeze right there, miss."

Hand in mid search, I looked at him. "What? I'm getting a card."

"You want to hand me a card, you go though the checkpoint machine, otherwise you keep your hands in plain sight."

I took my hands out of the bag and held them up. "What is it you don't like? My height? The color of my hair? My Atlanta accent?"

He rested his hand on a beeper. He didn't sport a gun that I could see. "We got our procedures, ma'am, just like y'all."

I'd gone from *miss* to *ma'am* in thirty seconds.

I turned for the outside door and waved. "Thanks."

Halfway down the steps, I saw an unmarked Crown Vic coming down the one-way street off 128. The driver stopped the car next to mine. Sheriff Kitchens got out and looked up the steps at me. He grinned and I grinned back. How could I help it? He said, "Well, well, someone I want to talk to comes to me."

I put my hand on my chest. "Me?"

"You."

"What about?"

"Your visit to Connie Scoggins."

I think of a Connie as a lithe blonde cavorting on a beach blanket. I asked, "She call you?"

"Let's say I know you were there."

"You following me?" Could he have been at the park, on the cliff? The man with the nice rear end?

He leaned his head toward the building across the street. "Let's go into the courthouse. They serve a good cup of coffee."

"I could use one. By the way, your jailhouse guard could use a lesson in civility."

He twisted his lip. "We like him like he is. Overzealous."

We walked diagonally, disregarding the traffic light, side-by-side, me almost as tall as he. Cars slowed for the sheriff, people inside waving. People must be used to him walking like he owned the street. A young female driver, dark hair, wearing sunglasses, yelled to him, "Hey, Sonny, you're lookin' fine today."

When we reached the path to the courthouse, he asked, "Your visit to the jail got anything to do with your visit to Connie Scoggins?"

"I have a few questions Mrs. Scoggins raised."

"Are you going to lay some cock-eyed theory on me about that boat and the campers?"

"Cock-eyed, not yet. Were you in the park yesterday?" *When concrete aggregate was tossed down at me.*

He said he wasn't but that he knew Detective Lake and I went there and talked to Bernard Janeway. "What'd you find out?"

"Things that make me curious, one being Ranger Janeway."

He let a small ticking silence slip in before he said, "Government official. Important *federal* government official."

Inside the courthouse, the foyer floors were exquisite green marble, and eye-high frescoes told the story of the founding of the county. The walls above rounded together to form a dome. "Lovely," I said.

A screening machine met us, this time with armed deputies at each side. The man and woman were friendly. Maybe it takes a sheriff at your side. Sheriff Kitchens said, "Too bad we have to spoil the insides of this place with these ugly machines, but we have to be prepared when someone goes nuts."

I went through the machine, my backpack on a runner coming out the other side. "Ever happen?" I asked.

"Not on my watch. It's nearly fifteen years now that we had a nutcase in the court room. His mama, who was nuttier, came in with a shotgun. Held up the judge, sprung her boy, and disappeared from the county."

"Never to be found?"

"Nope. We got their particulars in the system if they ever show up. Won't, though. They have kin in Canada. Heck, it was only a breaking and entering into a vacant house."

We trod the worn wooden steps into the basement. The smell of coffee and cinnamon mingled with the mustiness of old—old wallpaper, old moldy plaster, and old polished furniture. We passed several rooms piled with old file boxes. He waved his fine hands at the doors. "Soon all that's going to be input into the computer, with originals stored in the new building."

I got a tray and slid it along the chrome rungs of the cafeteria line. Not much selection, but the sweets beckoned after this morning's Spartan repast. Further along were three coffee urns: *Columbian. Decaf. We proudly serve French Mill Coffee.*

"French Mill, strong stuff," I said.

"Strong stuff for a strong lady."

"That's better than being called nosy."

"That must have been Connie," he said, a smile lighting his earnest gray eyes.

The sheriff got two sugar donuts with his French Mill. Cops and donuts. I quit counting the number of sugar packets at five that he opened and poured into his coffee. Then he dumped half the cream jar in. He had the kind of physique that would always be solid, even if he put on weight, which seemed likely.

I stirred my coffee like he did even though mine was straight. I think it's an advantage to go first, so I said, "My story or yours?"

"Let's start with why you went to Connie Scoggins."

"Talk to Boyd. I didn't know he was dead."

He kept stirring and bobbing his head to the rhythm of his hand.

"Was he usually reliable?" I asked, tearing apart the cinnamon roll.

He smiled and I smiled back. Talk about woolly. "Scoggins was a good forester until he got bad knees and a bad back, then when he got the shoulder thing he couldn't get work and took to drinking more."

"And fishing," I said, chewing.

"Yeah, the man fished." He took a bite of donut and talked around it, politely keeping his mouth as tight as possible. "He told the truth about going to Landing Creek Park and putting in and fishing until dusk. I know he was there because I saw him out on the lake. He doesn't admit to being drunk that night." He swallowed a gulp of coffee. "He always carried this sleeping bag. Had a few too many DUIs. I've seen him sleeping all over this county with a tall tale to tell next morning."

"And you believe that on the morning in question the tall tale included the people at the campsite." I blew on the coffee before putting my lips on the rim of the cup.

Fret wrinkles creased his forehead. "That mess happened over in Hall and Forsyth. Not our problem. All we had was a drunk who said he shared his sandwiches and liquor with kids smoking dope and telling him about a boat. Yes, I believed it was a tall tale told by a drunk."

He seemed peeved when I said that Janeway told us about the campers' word-play names, although he didn't think they were of any importance, just young people thinking they were cute.

"Janeway's not from around here, is he?" I asked, then bit into a cinnamon strip.

"Back east. Wants to go back there. Good riddance." He sat

his cup on the table. "You know what OCD is?"

"Obsessive–compulsive. I got that from all the signs in the park."

"He's a stickler about order. And don't go breaking the rules." He seemed to be warning me about something other than obsessive signage.

"Tell me about Boyd Scoggins's death."

Sonny related what Connie told him, and that was that Scoggins was drunk the day he went up the hill to a shed in back of his house. He was shot in the head and that it could have been a hunting accident. No hunter came forward, not that anyone expected one would. The medical examiner ruled it death by misadventure with a firearm.

I said, "I saw eight or ten dogs roaming the property. They bark like hounds from hell."

"Which would naturally lead you to believe whoever shot him knew the hounds, wouldn't it?" he asked, a cynical smile bunching the muscles of his mouth.

"Who found him?"

"Connie, once she figured he'd sobered up."

With a last gulp, I finished my coffee. "Connie said everyone in the county was related."

His gaze was cool, assessing. "She's not far off. She's my cousin by marriage to Boyd." He scooted his chair back and rose. "I'm going for more coffee. You want some?" He took my cup, brought it back full, placed it before me, sat, and said, "Is that all that brought you to my little fiefdom?"

"Where'd you go to college?" I asked.

He gaped, and then smiled. "North Georgia Tech. You came here to ask me that?"

I shook my head. "Curious is all."

He said that he studied electrical engineering and could wire a mean lamp. He'd never lived anywhere but north Georgia and when his term was up as sheriff he was going to run for the county commission. He had been married once, but his wife ran off with a tobacco farmer from West Virginia. He sipped coffee, and then looked at me, meaning, *Now let's get on with it.*

"Lieutenant Lake and I had breakfast at Trader Joe's Diner. You know my work, don't you?"

"Private detective. Your clients include Juvy Justice and Social Services. You were APD."

"My concern is Diane, the waitress."

"Diane Parker?"

"How old is she?"

He sat back, his eyes shifting upward, then to the side. "Fourteen thereabouts."

"I think twelve," I said.

"What's the problem?"

"Child labor laws."

He exhaled like something in his chest just let go. "Diane's filling in for her mama."

"She told me her mama had been gone for eight days. Has she returned yet?"

He leaned back and shook his head. "But no need to get the state into this, Miss Dru." He blew out his cheeks like I was the evil east wind.

I said, "The state allows for exigencies like sickness when help is needed, but I can tell Diane's a seasoned waitress. Fourteen is the age at which kids can apply for a job, but they can't work twelve-hour shifts."

He turned his butt sideways and drummed the fingers of his right hand on the table. "Any man pays attention to Linette and off she goes with him, particularly if he likes to gamble, too."

"Where's Diane's father?"

"I don't think anyone knows. Linette raised the kid by herself.

Had a couple of abortions. All in all, Diane's not turned out half bad."

"Who stays with her when her mama's gone? Relatives?"

"None around here. I keep an eye out for her."

"Look, the laws aren't onerous, but I can tell you this. If Judge Devon gets the employment department handling this, they'll turn it over to Social Services because of her mother's activities. If you don't want that, if the community doesn't, you'll have to find a solution."

"Judge Devon will come down on Linette, won't she?"

I explained Portia's attitude. As long as Linette didn't do drugs and wasn't a habitual drunk or a child beater, she could go wanderlust all she wanted. "But there has to be a responsible adult in the house when she's gone. Do you know how to get in touch with Linette?"

"No, but I'll take care of Diane, don't you worry."

He rose and so did I. He placed the campaign hat on his head.

As we walked up the steps to the rotunda, I asked, "Has the body in the lake been identified?"

He came to an abrupt stop. "Linette always turns up."

"Male or female?"

"Female, but that's a big lake so don't go connecting any dots."

"Not until they appear," I said. We walked past the guards and outside. He shoved his hands in his trouser pockets and said, "I'll put out the word—the blue-eyed righter of wrongs has come to Sawchicsee County."

I reached in my backpack and drew out my card case. "Here's my card. Call me when Linette shows up, or call Judge Devon. If you don't, she'll be calling you."

Without a word, he tucked the white card in his shirt pocket.

I followed him across the street to my car. "You leaving us now?"

"One last question."

He looked as if his endurance had come to an end. "I can't stand here all day answering questions I don't know answers to. First thing I got to do is get over to the diner and tell Scull Brunty he's going to have to find himself a new waitress for this afternoon and evening. That's going to make him real unhappy."

"Don't you think it's odd that Scoggins was killed three weeks before the sailboat surfaced? Someone might have been nervous about evaporation."

"Hunting accidents happen all the time."

"What's in season to hunt?"

"On one's own land, everything."

"Who lives behind the Scogginses?"

"National forest land." He grinned, but without much mirth. "So much for one more question."

He raised two fingers to his hat brim. "Now, have you a safe trip back to Atlanta. I'll get things straightened out."

In the car and rolling, I called Webdog. "Get me all you can on Boyd Scoggins, who was shot three weeks ago in a supposed hunting accident. Wife's Connie. You may find something on her. Also Linette Parker."

"I'm on it."

"Now here's where your real talent rises to the fore. Two campers were at Landing Creek Park the night Johnny Browne died and the sailboat presumably sunk. They signed in as Anna Graham and Gene Poole."

Web's laughter floated through the ether. "Pretty good, I've heard better."

"Maybe this isn't the first time they've used those names and maybe they've left a cyber trail."

"If they use social networks, they might use those names with avatars."

"Also check out Ranger Bernard Janeway. Army Corps of Engineers."

"Got it."

"That ought to keep you off the streets for a while."

"You know what I say. Bring it on, Boss, bring it on."

"I'll have more, bet on it."

"Thickens my gravy."

That Web, always up on the latest jargon.

CHAPTER NINE

We gathered in an antechamber. Baron Bonnet rested the heel of his palm on an arm of the brown leather sofa. Evangeline sat at the other end, jiggling around, getting under Portia's skin. Portia sat in a Chippendale chair at the escritoire and I sat at her side. The elegant room served many functions behind the austere courtroom. It was a place where witnesses could regain their composure, where alternate jurors camped out waiting to be called, where lawyers consulted with clients.

Baron shot the cuff-linked sleeves of his fancy white shirt and fretted with the crease in his trousers before folding his hands on his lap. He drawled, "I have all day, Judge, but I presume you don't."

Tight-lipped, Portia peered over half-glasses. "Nice of you to get the ball rolling, Mr. Bonnet." She looked at me. "You have the completed contracts, haven't you, Miss Dru?"

"I have, Your Honor. All that's needed is Mr. Bonnet's signature, witnessed by the Court."

Evangeline stiffened so quickly I thought she might throw her back out. "What about me?"

"You are too young to enter into a contract in this state," Portia said.

"But it's my plan."

"What is your plan?"

She glanced at Bonnet, then back at Portia. "To find my mother."

"A plan is one thing," Portia said. "It can change at any time. A contract is binding until a given period of time expires or all signers declare it null and void, which means . . ."

"I know what it means," Evangeline said. "It means over with."

Portia stood. "Near enough."

"I want to sign the contract, too," Evangeline said.

Portia stepped away from the escritoire where three copies of the contract lay. She faced Evangeline. "Very well. It's meaningless, I want you to understand, but you can add your name beneath your uncle's. He is acting as your guardian ad litem."

"That's because you appointed him."

"Yes, in the absence of your parents." Murderers could warm Portia's heart before this child. Portia addressed Baron, Evangeline and me. "A guardian ad litem in this case has been created by a court order only for the duration of this contract for monies paid for investigative services, with no guarantee of success on the part of this court or Miss Moriah Dru. It, in effect, protects Evangeline Broussard's rights in court if the contract is contested."

"Who would contest it?" Evangeline asked.

"Your aunt. Your trustees."

Evangeline giggled, and Baron said, "We've discussed the details of the money with my sister, Lorraine, and Evangeline's trustee, Allister Dames. He has presented you with a written affidavit that he will provide the funds necessary to honor the contract."

Portia extended her hand, "Mr. Bonnet, if you will step over here."

Two Cross pens lay next to the contract copies. Baron rose and pulled at his vest. "Pleased to, Your Honor." Evangeline followed him.

"We'll execute three copies, one for the court, one for you,

Mr. Bonnet and one for Miss Dru." She looked at Evangeline. "Yours is also your uncle's."

Evangeline wisely kept quiet. I signed my name three times then Portia beckoned Baron. Sitting and lifting a pen, he flourished his name on all three. Evangeline signed two copies with her name, and on the third, she wrote what appeared to be a novel.

Portia signed on her lines, picked up the metal press with the court seal and punched the appropriate spaces. Evangeline said, "Aren't you going to seal my name?"

Giving the girl a look a hawk gives a rabbit, Portia gave the contracts a tight-fisted second punch and handed out the signed, sealed contracts.

Evangeline had written on mine: "This is for my mother, Candice Bonnet Browne, who I will find if it takes me to the day I die."

Which I found touching and could mitigate the pain-in-the-ass part of her personality—could, but probably not. When I looked up, Portia was heading for the door.

Speaking over her shoulder, she said, "Miss Dru, can I have a minute?"

I looked from Baron to Evangeline. "Excuse me."

"We shouldn't have secrets," Evangeline said.

I resisted slamming the door, but put a little extra wrist into closing it. Portia sat at her desk eyeing her cigarette holder.

"Why us?" she said, not looking at me.

"Because you bad-mouthed the authorities and your highly quotable quote landed in the newspapers."

"Keep reminding me. I need to put on the hair shirt, atone for my immoderation."

"Absolution will come."

"You, too, my long-time friend, should put on the hair shirt for agreeing to work for that precocious little horror."

"Aw, she's not so bad, really. Besides, I'll get absolution when Baron hands over the certified check."

"Money has a way of mitigating culpability." She ruffled her shoulders. "Go back now and deal with the little horror, although I must say the addendum to her signature drew a sigh."

"She is a sincere child."

"Save me from sincere people. They're only artful."

"I gladly grant you that, Your Honor."

Portia picked up her short, gold cigarette holder. Not since she left law school have I seen her smoke a cigarette without it. She tossed it aside. "Moriah, find out what her plan is. The child is not without guile." She huffed and sat back. "Give me a late bloomer over a cerebellum wunderkind any time."

Her Walker was just such a child. Maybe that explains why he'll have a nanny until he leaves home.

I held the certified check, made out to me for a hundred thousand dollars. I thought in reverential tones, *a hundred thousand dollars*—plus expenses. A hundred thousand dollars to find Candice Bonnet Browne or the facts of her whereabouts, if deceased. Evangeline didn't seem concerned about the Cocineaus. I'll give her the benefit of the doubt and believe she thought finding her mother would find them.

I left the antechamber with Baron and Evangeline. Outside, treading down the steps with them, Baron said, "Did you read the paper this morning, Miss Dru?"

"I did," I answered.

Evangeline said loudly, "That article's a lie. My mother most certainly would not run off with Laurant Cocineau. She could barely stand his braggadocio."

I said, "Yet your mother and your stepfather were great friends with the Cocineaus."

90

"It was mostly Johnny who was friends with them because of Crescent Moon Winery."

Baron raised a hand as if asking permission to enter into the conversation. "Laurant Cocineau wanted to buy a vineyard."

"He wanted to buy Crescent Moon Winery," Evangeline said in precise tones.

"He hadn't a chance." Baron said.

"Then why did he buy land and a house down the road?" Evangeline said, a direct challenge to her uncle.

"To turn it into a new winery," Baron said.

We were at the bottom of the steps. Baron looked at me. I think his thick black lashes were mascaraed. He explained that Laurant Cocineau got the vineyard bug and that he'd traveled to some remote places in the Carolinas and Georgia, places that grew a lot of grapes and made wine. Cocineau, according to Baron, became inspired and after careful consideration decided the best place to set up shop was Cape Fear.

"Did Laurant hang out at Crescent Moon, learning the craft?" I asked.

"Bah," Baron scoffed. "He thought himself a connoisseur. Too high and mighty for learning. The kind that thinks he's an instant genius about everything that takes his fancy."

Near the parking garage, Evangeline said, "Laurant came to our house a lot."

I asked, "Did Janet come with him?"

"She didn't like the country."

"What's happened to the Cocineau's Cape Fear house since they disappeared?"

"It's still in the family," Baron answered. "His nephew Emile comes and goes. A wastrel, by my reckoning. The boy paints."

Evangeline said, "Right now he's too old for me, but I'll probably marry Emile some day. Have you heard from him?"

Since this was the first time I'd heard *of* him, I hadn't

expected to. "No, I haven't."

"Lives in England," Baron said. "Don't worry, he's on his way here to stake out his claim, you watch."

Webdog said, "Got info on the Bonnets. You won't believe."

"Let me make a wild guess," I said. "They're related to Rhett Butler."

"Not bad, not bad. First clue?"

"He dresses antebellum, speaks Charlestonian and . . ."

Web interrupted, "Whatever else, his Charlestonian speech is genuine."

"I'm listening," I said.

"Ever hear of Stede Bonnet?"

"Uh, off the top, no. But just a minute. Some hinge in my mind wants to open and spill memory . . ."

"The gentleman pirate, he was known as. Born in sixteen-eighty-eight into a wealthy English family on Barbados. He inherited land and money after his father's death along about sixteen-ninety-five. He married and was a major in the King's Guards, but, according to the story, his wife's nagging drove him to piracy in seventeen-seventeen."

"You're making that up, Web."

"I'm not married, so why would I?"

"Point taken."

"Anyway, this dude in the fancy pants and periwig, who owns a plantation, who has no sailing experience, names his sloop *Revenge* and attacks ships along Virginia and the Carolinas. Somewhere along the line he met Blackbeard, aka Edward Teach. Blackbeard knew an idiot when he met one and managed to trick Bonnet into coming in with him. In actuality, Bonnet was a prisoner of Blackbeard's, but to make a long story short—my concession to your dinner plans—Bonnet somehow got himself a pardon by the North Carolina governor so he could privateer against the Spanish fleet. A true nutcase of narcissism, Bonnet decides to pirate again, so he carried on under the name Captain Thomas."

"Our present-day Bonnets are related to this vain pirate?"

"Indeed, they are."

"Most interesting, Web, but I've got to meet Lake for dins at four."

"Four? That's lunch."

"You need to get out and do some fieldwork," I said. "Cops eat when they can."

"Okay, so I'm hurrying. Bonnet, despite being a gentleman, was especially vicious. Whenever he would visit Charles Town to whore and drink, he'd leave with a citizen who did not go with him willingly. He would demand a ransom and if it wasn't paid, he keelhauled the citizen. You know what keelhauling is?"

"When one is roped and dragged under a ship. C'mon, Web, I got to do my nails."

"The citizens of those seaside towns had it to the gills with our gentleman pirate, so the leader of Charles Town sent Colonel William Rhett to capture or kill him. Bonnet was captured on Sullivan's Island, tried in a court of law, denied clemency and hanged in seventeen-eighteen. He was thrown into the marshes where the crabs had a free dinner."

"I'm on my way out to *eat* dinner, Web."

"Pass on the crab cakes."

"That it?"

"William Rhett, ring a bell."

"Rhett Butler? William Rhett? Is this an Anna Graham gone wrong?"

Web snickered. "Rhett is a surname, an Anglicization of de Raedt, brought to South Carolina by William Rhett. Margaret Mitchell chose the name for her black sheep charmer from Charleston."

"Am I to believe the Bonnets think Mitchell modeled her charmer after Bonnet the pirate, but named him after the man who sealed his fate?"

"Despite his cultured charm, Rhett Butler was a gunrunner, an outlaw, a kind of pirate. He landed in jail and got a pardon. He, like Stede Bonnet, partook of the lovely ladies above the saloon. Today's Bonnets glory in the connection to Mitchell's hero."

"Dandy, but that tells me nothing about Lorraine and Baron."

"Get to that after you've wined and dined."

CHAPTER TEN

Lake wanted Hastings Seafood and I wanted Il Vesuvio. I won. No seafood for me.

I turned off Peachtree onto Marietta—a hodge-podge street with short skyscrapers, banks, shops and cafes. Going west, I passed the newspaper building, Centennial Park, CNN and the Omni Hotel. Then into the mix were hundred-year-old warehouses and chi-chi inner-city restaurants, bumping brick facades with auto and motorcycle repair shops. I parked beside Lake's unmarked car in the lot of one of the established neighborhood eating places.

Il Vesuvio's bricks were painted to look like a postcard from Italy—boats bobbed at a wharf, a towering mountain in the background. Burglar bars covered the stained glass of the entry door. One of the leaded panes had a neat round hole in it. I slipped inside the small vestibule, then walked into the bar.

Ah, the smell of Italian—not too much garlic, nor fennel—floating on air-conditioning. Lake sat on his usual barstool gabbing with the bartender. When he saw me, he grinned and said, "Dru." The way he said my name melted my sinews nearly to the point of collapse. Which I did, against him.

Joey the Barkeep pulled at a tap and said with a smile, "Officer Dru."

I put my arm through the crook at Lake's elbow and pecked his cheek.

"You can do better than that," Lake said, threading his fingers in mine.

Winking at Joey, I rubbed my nose on Lake's cheek and made my alto voice very husky. "Later."

"Tonight sounds like your lucky night, Ricky," Joey said.

If that sounds like a regular routine, it is.

A year after my fiancé was killed, Richard Lake and I were assigned to patrol Zone Two. It was a good thing and a bad thing. The good thing was we liked each other and became lovers too fast for our own good. The bad thing (for me) was he got a promotion to homicide, and I didn't like my new partners. They thought they were taking Lake's place in my bed. I bitched to Portia, who is a sucker when it comes to old, unhappy friends. I didn't have a law degree so she couldn't help me there, but she told me she had a great idea. "You always liked working with children." From the time I was eleven, I was the neighborhood babysitter. I adored every one of those kids. Anyway, Portia's call instigated my *raison d'être,* as the French call it. My reason for being.

Lake's voice brought me back to Il Vesuvio's. "How's the new client?"

"I am now wearing a hair shirt," I said, catching the Amstel Light Joey skated down the bar.

Lake signaled for another Sam Adams, then said, "I ran into Portia when I went to get a warrant. She said you needed to cut loose of the little horror and her handler." He grinned and pushed back wisps of black hair hanging on his forehead. His face is all angles and irregularities that blend into one delectable whole. "Ricky," as the lady cops coo at him, has a groupie following and Portia is not immune to his charms, either.

"How's your homicide?"

" 'Cides," he said. "The cases are confounding. Three murders—all elderly women with little or no money. One knifed, one strangled with a rope and one shot. One raped in the usual place, one in the anus and one in the . . ."

I held up a hand, meaning *stop right there*. "I can guess." I liked this pre-prandial conversation about as much as crabs feasting on a Bonnet in the marsh.

"The killer's running out of weapons, to say nothing of . . ." He paused, narrowing his eyes to observe me. "You're turning green. Not like you. Not like when we were partners. Remember that time we found the body in Otto's men's room? There wasn't a two-inch square of flesh that hadn't been knifed."

"How could I forget that lovely scene?"

"I bring it up because you were so unwavering in dealing with gore. I was proud of my new partner."

"I puked for days afterward. Can we change the subject?"

"Sure, my lovely," he said, clutching me around the waist. "Mia will be calling us soon for dinner. What would you like to talk about?"

"The body in the lake."

Lake laughed and so did I. "Didn't I say unwavering? Let's see, prelims say she'd been in the water about a week. Strangled, can't tell yet about rape. Blond hair, unknown color eyes, you know how that is, not much left after . . ."

"Here's a riddle for the great detective. Any woman in the state missing that fits the description?"

"Not yet—unless . . ."

He'd stopped for me to fill in that blank. "Diane Parker's mother, Linette."

"It occurred."

Then I told him about Stede Bonnet, winding up with the crab thing.

"Oh, so that's why you opted out of your favorite seafood restaurant."

I heard a noise like static behind me and turned the barstool.

Mia, the restaurant owner, stood waiting for us to notice her. She asked, "You ready to eat?"

Turning to her, Lake asked, "What's for dessert?"

The man and his sweet tooth.

Mia said, "Spumoni and a nice almond vanilla crème brûlée."

"One of each," Lake said.

"None for me. I had dessert this morning."

"I'll take hers," Lake said.

"Make that spumoni then," I said, slipping off the barstool, grabbing my beer and following Lake into the narrow, low-lit dining room, heels clicking across the black-lacquered concrete floor. The murals on the walls had been painted by a starving artist for free meals twenty years ago. As usual when we eat this early, we were the only diners in the place.

We ordered. Me, veal Parmigianino; Lake, pizza. I asked Lake, "Did you know that Laurant Cocineau had a nephew, Emile?"

He swallowed the last of his beer. "I recall a nephew. GBI was happy to see him go back to England."

"Baron says Emile stays at the Cocineaus' Cape Fear house when he comes over to the colony."

Mia uncorked our favorite Chianti Classico Reserve and poured a little into Lake's glass. "Fill 'er up, Mia," he said, waving away a taste test. "It's always excellent."

"For the price, it should be," she said. Mia must think we're on the dole. The first bottle is on her. When we're not working, we pay for the next.

When she left, I said, "Want to talk about my visit with Connie Scoggins and Sheriff Kitchens?"

"As long as it doesn't involve seafood," he said. "I'm still suffering from rejection."

While scarfing down antipasto—olives, salami, provolone, pepperoncini—I told him about Connie Scoggins. He finished his first stem of Chianti and said, "But does it have anything to do with us finding the sailboat three weeks later?"

"I don't like coincidences."

When I recounted my visit with Sheriff Kitchens, he said, "You sure seem to get along with the yokels—er—locals. Kitchens doesn't give a damn about the boat found in his yard. He's thinking about his election."

"You think about your promotions," I said.

Lake sized me up with that sideways look he bestows when about to correct my mistaken idea. Fortunately for me, the food came and Lake tucked into his pizza, folding over a large slice, while I cut my veal.

"For your edification," he said, chewing and not looking at me, "my promotions come directly from my performance as an investigator. I set out to be the best cop I can be, and therefore promotions come my way." He finished that piece and folded another slice, studied it like it was not quite right, then let it unfold itself on his plate. He stared at me with piercing dark eyes. "Your sheriff gets elected because he's related to half the county, and the other half is in his debt for taking care of them by circumventing the law, a la Diane and Linette Parker. God knows what and who else he protects and from what."

Before steam started coming out his ears, I said, "Darling, Lake, you are exactly right." He frowned. I reached over and put my hand on his forearm. "I can't imagine why I say some of the things I do. My sheriff is nothing but a fixer for the county."

He patted my hand. "You don't mean a thing you're saying."

"I do, love, I do."

"You admire that sheriff." He bit off a chunk of pizza and winced. I think he got his tongue.

My eyes flicked with delight. "You're jealous."

"Hell I am."

I put up a finger and air-struck a 1. "One for my side. I'm

usually the green-eyed monster."

"Admit it, you think he's—whatever you think."

Boy oh boy, hallelujah. We'd had it out not long ago over a woman who'd been calling me saying Ricky was going to leave me for her. I'd leapt to conclusions and was wrong.

He ate the last bite. "Guess who I saw today?"

"That blonde bimbo reporter . . ."

"Don't go there, Moriah Dru, or you'll get no dessert."

I held up both hands. "I give up."

"Billie Nikkel."

"Billie?" I automatically smile at the image of the short impish photographer. "I haven't seen her in ages."

"She came to see me."

"Billie? She shooting the Hat Squad's photographs these days?"

Lake explained that Billie wanted to extend her photographic career into darker areas like working for lawyers, shooting people doing what they weren't supposed to be doing—for love or money. Billie wanted to know the legalities and Lake had explained the laws to her.

I said, "Billie's so gifted she doesn't need that kind of work."

My cell played the concerto, and I looked at the display. "Portia."

"Answer the summons from the judge of judges."

No chit-chat-Portia said, "Your clients are about to drive me crazy."

"They should be home by now."

"They are. Baron called me. Really, Moriah, you need to give them your cell phone number. This is your case."

"What's the matter?"

"Emile Cocineau is raising hell."

"The nephew? He's in the states now?"

"Somebody stole his uncle's will."

Emile had, according to Portia, taken legal papers from his lawyer's office and his bank safety deposit box and hid them in a hidey-hole safe in his floor. When he'd gone to fetch something, he'd found the floor safe gone.

"What's that got to do . . ."

"He's blaming the Bonnets. Says they're trying to cheat him out of his half of the Crescent Moon Winery."

"His half? Baron said . . ."

"Don't put faith in a word out of their mouths. I called Webdog. You have a reservation on the six-twenty-five to Wilmington. Good luck with the precocious horror and her idiot uncle." She hung up.

I glanced at Lake. "Into the jaws of the opposition."

Mia sat three desserts in front of Lake. Lake looked at me and said, "They're your clients and they have a lot of money." I held my stomach like I was trying not to throw up. Lake pushed a dish of spumoni toward me. "Something sweet to take the sour out of your mouth?"

"*Mal appétit!*" I said. "Emile Cocineau is claiming Crescent Moon Winery is half his. He also claims his uncle's will was stolen from a safe that was stolen, too."

Lake picked up a spoon and, poised to attack the first spumoni, said, "Curiouser and curiouser."

I said, "I might be able to give Billie some work."

"Follow the dodgy sheriff?"

"No, Gainesville tomorrow. Unless you'd like to meet with Janeway."

"Out of my jurisdiction. What about Pearly Sue? She can handle a camera and she'd be a helluva lot cheaper than Billie."

"Pearly Sue is bullying the state department again. An Arab father refused to return his kid to his custodial mother in Atlanta. You'd think these women would learn. Marrying outside your culture and bearing children is asking for grief."

"Love and the drive to procreate trumps good sense."

"Ah, so."

"You're not leaving today, are you?" he asked.

"I must, I'm afraid."

"No tonight for you and me?"

I reached over and pinched his cheek. "Love in the time of pitas. Now get me to the plane on time."

In the trunk of my car, I keep a travelling bag packed, good to go for three days, everything I'll need unless I'm going to the White House for dinner. Which isn't likely on a moment's notice, which reminded me I was invited to the White House this coming September to receive high praise for solving a cruel kidnap case.

Before I'd finished that thought, Lake had eaten the last forkful of crème brûlée.

Chapter Eleven

The commuter got me into the Wilmington airport at eight-forty, right on time. I can't sleep on the widest, roomiest planes, but these little commuters drive me insane. I mentioned I'm tall. The space for my legs is getting shorter with each trip. On landing, I congratulated myself that I could unfold my body and limp down the aisle without screaming. I wove through the passengers in search of car agencies. Web had booked a mid-size Buick, which I parked beside the Happy Haddock Inn, near Long Beach on the Atlantic Ocean.

With my cell to my ear while hurrying through Atlanta's mess of an airport, Web acquainted me with the fish for which the inn was named. I can't believe I actually listened to his erudite prattle when he said that the haddock has a black lateral line running along white skin, not to be confused with the Pollock, which has a white lateral line running on black skin. He went on to say that haddock have a distinctive dark blotch above the pectoral fin known as the devil's thumbprint.

I'm not sure why that made me pause and shiver. Would the devil be with me all the way to Cape Fear, his thumb ready to grind on me for being greedy and a traitor to my cause? I had sold my soul for a hundred grand. *No you didn't, you're working on a high-profile case worth every thousand-dollar bill.* The devil, riding high on my shoulder, thumb poised, reminded me that I wasn't looking for vulnerable kids in trouble, but that I'd used an obnoxious rich kid to hunt adults who were damn well able to take care of themselves. But had these adults been able to take care of themselves and where were they? Checkmate. *I am not a candidate for the devil's thumbprint. So thumbprint that on your own forehead, oh pitch-forked one.*

I shook myself and brushed off my shoulder. *Go to hell and stay there.*

I like old-fashioned inns near the sea with their wide porches so you can look out and see the boats come in or go down to the beach to collect shells or sink a line. As the sun settled on the western horizon, dads and kids were coming in from the shore. I like inns that are no more than three stories high and four suites to a floor. Webdog seeks out places like this, ones with natural clapboards and white deck rails. Sitting on stilts covered with latticework, I figured the inn was a par four from the water's edge—for me, a driver and a four iron. It has been so long since I played golf, I'm probably being optimistic about the four iron.

Despite my favorable opinion of the inn and my need for sleep, I didn't get any. The mattress was too soft. Sleeping with Lake had turned me into a torture board aficionado. The suite's small refrigerator ran loud, the sheer curtains let in too much moonlight—not that I don't like gibbous moons and starry nights by the sea—but all this contributed to my agitation. I worry when I don't have a clear idea where an investigation is going and when I have the devil . . . *don't go there* . . . when I had a client I'd signed up out of pique and a shadowy case that promised to become inexplicable. Lake would always help me out when he could, but the *Scuppernong* case wasn't remotely connected to his series killer. At least I hoped it wasn't. At some point I dozed off and woke to a watery sunrise coming through the gauze curtains. Trust me, heavy drapes promote sleep.

I ordered room service—a big plus for the Happy Haddock. Most inns require you to go down in your jams, robe and slips to get a cup of coffee and be of good cheer with the innkeeper. I sat at the desk, wi-fied my computer, flicked the snaps on my briefcase and clicked the remote until I found local news on television. Rain today for the beaches, dry inland. A warning about riptides after a tropical storm at sea came close to the shore. A fatal crash in the middle of the night on Plantation Road. Three inebriated teens meet Mr. Telephone Pole. A walk for Breast Cancer starting at The Grove. Family Pyrate Night, seven to nine, admission free at the Southport Community Building. That must be the seventeenth-century spelling of pirate. I switched to CNN and opened the files on the *Scuppernong* mystery. While I was reviewing my handwritten and computer notes, a reporter from Atlanta came on the screen, reporting from some dock on Lake Lanier. It wasn't Portia's, I could tell that. With sadness, I listened. The Georgia Department of Natural Resources divers found a body near where the *Scuppernong* sailboat had sunk in a deep cove. The body was identified as Linette Parker of Sawchicsee County, Georgia. She was not one of three people on the sailboat, now missing for almost four years. The reporter ended by saying that the Georgia Bureau of Investigation scheduled a press conference for five p.m.

I looked at the file, at Evangeline Bonnet Broussard's telephone number. I'm sure the only reason she hasn't been calling since midnight is because, one, she doesn't have my cell number and, two, she doesn't know where I'm staying. Portia and Web swore secrecy.

Sigh. I had to call her. I did so on the inn's phone. I did not want her capturing my cell number—ever.

"I am your client, Miss Dru," she said by way of hello—no missing Portia with Evangeline around.

"I know, Evangeline," I said, "but I got in late and in need of rest. What's up this morning?"

"You have to go see the sheriff."

"Not the police?"

"None of us lives in a town. We're unincorporated."

Evangeline appeared in my mind as a thirty-year-old ugly, bossy woman. "Then I shall go see the sheriff. Where is Emile Cocineau?"

"In jail."

"What for?"

"He hit Uncle Baron on the chin."

I thought I was going to be the first in this drama to take a crack at him. "Where are you?"

She said she and Baron were on the way to see Sheriff Ben Avlon and that the sheriff's department was in Pardo Town. "It's on a map." She hung up. Portia in training.

What, I wondered, had prompted Emile Cocineau, of the sophisticated name, to punch Baron Bonnet on the chin? I would soon know and turned my thoughts to Sheriff Ben Avlon. Like Sonny Kitchens, he owed his office to the Anglo-Saxons and their shires and reeves. My brain cells are loaded with things no one needs to know. The shire-reeve was the keeper of the county and acted as judge and law enforcement officer. In the American colonies, of which North Carolina was one, he served the courts' orders and writs and inflicted punishments—stocks, lashings, brandings, cropping of ears and the hanging of pirates and slaves.

Which would mugger Emile Cocineau get? Lashes? Branding?

With little trouble, I found the right building and parked. Two deputies raised the American flag as I got out, entered the building and passed through security. At the same time I saw Baron and Evangeline coming toward me. Evangeline's feet and arms performed some kind of South American dance that propelled her forward at remarkable speed while Baron smoothed his way with a pronounced sway. I don't remember that Gable or Rhett walked like that.

"Emile's gone," Evangeline said with all the drama she could conjure.

I took a step back. "He broke out?"

Baron twitched his upper lip, most likely at Evangeline's histrionics and my gullibility, and spoke like an orator. "As an officer and a gentleman, I refused to testify to the incident and the sheriff dropped the charges. Emile was released and left minutes ago."

Evangeline wrinkled her face. "That's not it. The sheriff said there would be no charges since I kicked Emile first."

Princess Pita strikes again. I said, "I was hoping to . . ."

Baron held up a hand. "We had a conference with Emile and his lawyer. One of the conditions of me keeping my silence was that Emile talks to you and lets you see the crime scene."

So much for the officer and gentleman speech. "The floor safe? He agreed?"

"As soon as the sheriff gets down here, we'll get on over to the Cocineau place."

A door opened. The man who stepped through it was undoubtedly the sheriff. Ben Avlon was a mature, pretty-boy blond. His hair was graying at the temples, but silky and abundant on top. The wind would have its way with his pompadour. The tiny muscles around his eyes were aligned to give them a hard coldness. His forehead was etched three lines down, like a writing tablet. His expression spoke of the gravity of his position.

He stuck out his hand. "You must be Miss Dru."

My hand met his. "I am."

"Pleased to meet you."

"Pleasure's mine," I said, taking back my hand.

"Well, if you folks are ready, we'll head out to Beggar's Grind."

Taking out my keys, I told Baron I'd follow him.

"You ride with us," Evangeline said.

Reluctant as I was, I needed to get up to speed with these two, so I put away my keys. I moved toward the passenger door, but Evangeline opened the back door and waited—for me to get in. It was awkward, but I slid inside and she closed the door with a smirk. Children are not tactful, and I reminded the devil beside me that not all children are vulnerable and need my services, so go to hell. Had I been in a helluva mood the last few days, or what?

With the sheriff in the lead car and me settled into the leather seat, I asked, "What happened yesterday?"

Baron turned his profile and spoke out of the side of his mouth. He said that the Crescent Moon vintner, Domingo Cardona, telephoned to say Emile Cocineau was at the gates raising hell, claiming that by a documented agreement between his Uncle Laurant and Johnny half the winery was now his. Emile told Domingo that the raised sailboat proved that Laurant was dead. As the heir, he had a right to tour his business.

If that were true, it made sense, but I didn't say that to Baron and Evangeline. We'd left the outskirts of Pardo Town and were traveling a winding ribbon of a road south through scratchy pine land. Baron said, "We'll come to the winery shortly. For your edification, I'll give you the lay of the land."

Evangeline said, "I will. The winery is on the east side of Hardee Road outside Varnamtown. My house is on the west side. Aunt Lorraine has a place two miles from us, but she moved into our house."

Baron said, "My permanent home is in Charleston, but currently I am caretaker at Lorraine's place but I lend a hand at Browne House."

My head reeled. "How did you and Emile get into a brawl?"

"Emile departed the property, but when I pulled the car into the driveway, he comes rip-roaring up. Almost hit my backside, damn him."

"All this because of what?"

"He accused me—*me*—of stealing his floor safe."

"Me, too," Evangeline said. "I'm a Bonnet. He said Bonnets were liars and thieves because of our pirate ancestors."

"Is that when you struck him?" I asked Baron.

"I did not. I asked to see proof of his accusation. He offered none; instead, he called me a thieving moron. By God, I'm a man of peace, but I won't be called a thief or a moron."

"Me, either," Evangeline said. She turned in her seat to face me. "So I kicked him in the leg."

"The bastard grabbed her," Baron said. "A little girl, for the love of God, and started shaking her. I said, 'Mr. Cocineau, you are rattling the girl's brain. Please discontinue immediately.' "

Sure, that's what he said.

Evangeline said, "When he stopped shaking me, I kicked him again, and then—"

Baron broke in. "I told him to leave. He charged me. I put up my hands. He drew back his fist and landed a punch on my jaw." He rubbed it where I hadn't seen a bruise.

"I kicked him for trying to steal my birthright," Evangeline said. "Even harder."

"So he called the sheriff?" I suggested.

Evangeline said, "He ran like a coward and called when he got home."

"It wasn't I who called the sheriff about the fisticuffs," Baron said. "I am a man of honor and this dispute is between two gentlemen."

"Emile is no gentleman," Evangeline said.

Since I was to meet the man, I reserved judgment on that.

Evangeline said, "We are coming to Crescent Moon Winery." She pointed left. "Look."

Baron pulled off the road while the sheriff kept going.

The buildings of Crescent Moon Winery stood behind an iron gate hung on two stone posts. On top of one post was a statue of the Greek god Dionysus—also known in the Roman pantheon as Bacchus—holding a grape vine. A small satyr looked up at the great god. I said, "Dionysus, god of wine, theatre, grapes, madness and ecstasy." On the other post, Artemis stood, one arm raising a crescent moon.

Baron pulled back onto the road. About a mile up, he said, "To your right is Browne House." I couldn't see the entire house for the forest, but I saw the gates and a roofline. Up the road, black angus cattle grazed. Baron said, "We sharecrop the fields, and the University of North Carolina uses our pastures for its herds."

"I'm going to the University of North Carolina," Evangeline said.

God save the dean. "What are you studying?" I asked.

"Agriculture. Wine-growing in particular." She spread both arms. "All this will be mine, once we find Mama. She inherits from Johnny, and I will inherit from her."

Inheritance seemed to be the byword this morning. Johnny Browne died having fathered no children, but who else might show up to claim inheritance—nephews, cousins? Already, Emile Cocineau, no blood kin to Johnny as far as I knew, presented himself to claim a share, which made me wonder what the state of North Carolina had to say about the presumption of death in the case of Candice, Laurant and Janet.

The law regarding the presumption of death after an unexplained absence of seven years began around 1800. Before the end of seven years, anyone wanting you declared legally dead had to offer evidence that you weren't alive. After seven years, anyone wanting you declared alive had to furnish proof you were not dead.

Georgia's presumption of death begins after four years, and for the missing three sail-boaters that would be coming up in October. Many states, I knew, waived arbitrary presumption. Given the trail of electronic records that living people leave, it might seem arbitrary, especially if someone faced danger. Probate judges use the preponderance of evidence rule. If it points toward death, the missing person is declared dead; otherwise, the greedy must wait sometimes beyond seven years.

I asked, "What is the period of waiting in North Carolina for a person to be declared . . ."

"Five years," Evangeline said. "But Death in Absentia in Georgia is four."

Birthright? Death in Absentia? What does Princess Pita read at bedtime?

Baron said, "If Georgia declares those three people legally dead, then it is presumed a judge in North Carolina would go along with that court."

Question: did the two in the front seat want Laurant, Candice and Janet declared legally dead or, as Evangeline believed—or as she *said* she believed—that Candice was alive? Anyway, they had the presumption laws nailed to the last subsection.

We turned into a narrow country lane, rocked across the gravel for a hundred yards or so and came to a signpost. The white-on-red sign said, "Beggar's Grind. 1888."

Farther up the road, a two-story stone building with a tin roof had me smiling. Set in a landscape of hardwoods, dogwood and magnolia, the scene could have been hanging in the Louvre. The bright red wheel next to a wall and the dry waterfall identified the stone building as a grist mill. Most old mills are dilapidated, but this one was in pristine condition. I asked, "Is the mill in use?"

"As an artiste's studio," Baron said, his scorn clear. "Cocineau imagines himself a painter."

To say nothing of what Baron Bonnet imagined *himself*.

Past the mill, Baron drove over a wooden bridge to a house that, although set in the same idyllic woods, would not light up the architectural world. Brick and stone, it was long, low and built probably in the fifties, an asymmetrical rectangle with a cross-gabled roof and large overhanging eaves. The gardens were nice, flourishing with rhododendrons and ferns.

"You stay in the car, E," Baron said and braked the car next to a split rail fence.

"I will not," Evangeline said.

"Stay quiet then," he acquiesced.

A man stood on the front porch that was gained by a series of three concrete paths, each having two step-ups. Emile Cocineau, I presumed.

The sheriff had parked up the lane, near a red barn. Emile met us at the bottom of the paths. He nodded to the sheriff; then his eyes met and kept mine until he blinked. He grinned that I'd outlasted him. "You are the private investigator from Atlanta?" he asked, his baritone voice implying reservation.

"Yes." He made no move to shake hands, nor did I. "Moriah Dru."

"Emile." He looked at the sheriff. "Shall we go inside?"

Except for the van dyke beard, he looked the image of his uncle in photographs. Dark full hair, dark eyes, full lips, even teeth. A tall slender man, he reminded me of the late Yves Montand—sans beard.

Inside the rambling ranch, it appeared the previous owners had left half their furniture for the new owners—the half they didn't like—a stew of early American, French provincial and

Mediterranean.

Emile said, "E, go into the kitchen. Drinks in the frig."

"I'll come with you," Evangeline said.

"No," Emile insisted. "You remain in the kitchen or in this lounge." He pointed toward an entertainment center. "You know how to work the satellite dish."

She folded her arms across her chest. "I am a participant in this."

"You are not an adult, and this is an adult matter."

Evangeline recognized hard-shell opposition when she heard it because she sulked to the entertainment center, opened the double doors to reveal a big, old television, picked up the remote and started pressing buttons. The television screen took a while to come to life.

Avlon addressed Emile. "You folks go ahead. I'll check things in the house unless you have an objection."

"None," Emile said and led the way down the hall. I noticed a billiard table in one room; in others, stacks of boxes, bedsteads, rickety furniture. The hall ended at a door leading into a large circular room. I remember from an architecture class I once took when I considered becoming an architect—in my dreams—that this was the hallmark of fifties ranch houses. This was Emile's bedroom. A king bed sat in the middle of the room, no head or foot boards, flanked by a couple of nice dressers and a cheval mirror. Such was the extent of the furnishings. Except for a braided rug between the bed and a window. *Don't tell me this is where his floor safe was?* I can't think of a place more obvious. Why would anyone choose a floor safe? They're complicated and expensive to install. You have to cut a slab out of the floor, dig a hole, put the safe in and pour concrete around it. This keeps the water out—but doesn't always in my experience—and is supposed to be burglar-proof.

Emile raised the rug to expose a cut-out square in the wooden floor. He grabbed the recessed handle and raised the square, then motioned us forward. I looked into a wreck of a hole. The safe had not been surrounded by concrete, but a wooden structure that was ripped apart.

"Lock, stock and combination," Emile said, glaring at Baron.

"Who installed the safe?" I asked.

"It was here when Uncle Laurant bought the place," Emile explained. "The lock is electronic so you could change the combination any time."

"But if it's not in concrete . . ."

"It was bolted in and it weighed more than a hundred pounds."

"What was in it?" I asked.

"My uncle's will, his financial papers like his stock portfolio, and a signed codicil that said if anything happened to Johnny and Candice Browne, Laurant Cocineau was to take possession and control of the assets of the Crescent Moon Winery." He looked at me. "Not the land, just the business."

"Poppycock," Baron said. "Lorraine and I . . ."

Emile glared at Baron, then spoke to me. "He was to put in trust half the profits for Evangeline and once she reached twenty-one, Uncle Laurant was to become a fifty percent partner with her. If either didn't want to stay in the business, it would be for one to buy the other out. As it appears now—that Uncle Laurant might not be alive—then I—"

Baron's mouth popped open. "That's the most ridiculous—"

I interjected, "Sounds to me like a prescription for a feud. But you are all assuming something that is not a fact. We only found the sailboat, not the people on it."

"It stands to reason—" Emile began.

Baron broke in, "They drowned in the lake."

"I understand Evangeline has trustees," I said.

"What does a trustee know about wine-making?" Emile

asked. "Besides, she's a long way from claiming inheritance."

"What did your uncle know about wine-making?" I asked.

He leveled smoldering eyes at me as if I impugned his uncle. "Uncle was a quick study. Ask around, you'll find out."

I certainly would. "Why do you think the Bonnets had anything to do with the robbery, if there was a robbery?"

Avlon came into the room.

Emile pressed his lips, and then spoke. "There was a robbery, Miss Dru. Are you starting a fight with me?"

The sheriff stepped closer as if to block a punch. "No use getting cantankerous, Emile."

"Anyone implies I'm lying . . ." His mouth twisted.

"What evidence do you have that the Bonnets stole the safe?" I asked.

"They're the only ones who benefitted."

I glanced at Baron. "Did you know about the codicil and will?"

"Of course not, it's preposterous. Johnny wouldn't do such a thing. Candice would be outraged if he passed over Evangeline for a stranger."

"My uncle and Johnny were hardly strangers," Emile countered. "And he hardly passed over his *step*-daughter."

"Who knew about the safe?" I asked.

He explained that only the Brownes and Bonnets knew of its existence, that he kept diamond jewelry and a valuable coin collection there. He said the last time he opened the safe was in April. "I come here in the spring. The light's good in the mill for my work."

"I hear you paint," I said.

He lifted a sneering lip at Baron. "That is correct."

Sheriff Avlon said there was no evidence of a break-in and that the safe would have had to be hoisted by at least two very strong thieves. The rope burns on the side of the boards told the story of the leverage used. Emile looked at Baron and said leverage could allow someone small and older to lift the safe.

Baron snorted. "Contact my neurosurgeon about my *older* back."

The sheriff crossed his arms, his patience at an end. "We'll continue to investigate the theft of your safe, Emile. Meantime, don't go accusing people of stealing when you have no proof."

Emile flashed his hands through his hair. "Motive, Sheriff. The Bonnets had motive and all the time in the world to raise that safe."

"Hard evidence," Avlon said. "Take my meaning, Emile?"

Emile nodded and turned on his heel to lead us out of the room, down the hallway into the lounge where Evangeline sat sipping a cola and thumbing a magazine she held upside down. With the television off. Easier to eavesdrop.

We walked outside, the sheriff leading the way down the paths, Baron and Evangeline following. I'd hung back to get elbow to elbow with Emile. "I'd like to talk to you alone."

His mouth slid sideways. "What about?"

"Your relationships to those missing and deceased from the sailboat."

"You want my side of the story?"

"Yes."

He paused a step. "You work for Baron and Lorraine."

"More accurately, Evangeline," I said, "but I'm past client loyalty. I also work for myself and it was I who spotted the sailboat's stern in the lake."

His shrug was classic Gallic. "I have nothing better to do."

"Thanks."

"Where you staying?"

"Long Beach at Happy Haddock. East Beach Drive."

"Dinner?"

"All right."

"I know a good place. Quiet. Private."

"Sounds good."

"Be back here at seven-thirty."

"Back here? I was thinking . . ."

Evangeline had paused and looked back, then hurried to where we stood talking, her face warped by suspicion.

"Thank you for your time, Mr. Cocineau," I said. "Please be patient. Let the sheriff do his work."

"Patience is not its own reward, Miss Dru. It's for the thieves among us." He turned and walked up the path, up the steps, across the porch and into his house without looking back.

"Dweeb," Evangeline said. "I wish I could kick him again."

"I thought you wanted to marry him."

"I will when I change his attitude."

"That might be a good thing, if he's correct about that codicil. Married people can get along when working together."

"He's not correct."

"Right now it's his word against yours."

She gave me a nasty glare and said that Johnny and her mother would never give Laurant any part of Crescent Moon Winery. She claimed she overheard them talking after Johnny hired Domingo from California."

I said, "Interesting."

"You can learn a lot from me," she said. "You don't need to talk to that cheater and liar."

I walked away, she followed and we joined Baron at the car. "Where to now?" he asked.

"I'm going back to the inn and get in touch with my associates," I said. "See what progress they've made."

"You have to report to me," Princess Pita said.

I said, "I give an oral report once a day. I write up reports weekly. Interactions with clients do not require an oral report. Right now you know everything."

She looked like a doubting monkey. "Where are we going when you finish talking to your associates?"

"*We* are not going anywhere. I'll spend the rest of the day talking to people who knew the Brownes and the Cocineaus."

"I can help you with that," she said.

"Evangeline, I don't want to say you will only get in the way, but you will only get in the way."

Her face scrunched up. "I . . ."

"Don't say anything you might regret. Listen to me, you will inhibit conversation. I want the truth about the missing people. People I interview are not going to say anything disparaging about Johnny, or especially—"

"There's nothing disparaging to say about my mother."

"I'm sure I'll find that out."

"You have to tell me what they say."

Dratted brat. I opened the car door and got inside. Evangeline slammed her door. Baron pulled away. I looked back. Emile was standing in the plate glass window, most probably laughing.

CHAPTER TWELVE

Riding back to the sheriff's office with Baron and Princess Pita was enough to give a woodpecker a headache, what with listening to Evangeline and Baron run down Emile and his uncle, Laurant. I had no appetite for lunch with them. Baron got huffy when I turned down his charming proposal of a nibble at the Lemon Sole, seaside, under a large umbrella, a few pre-prandial bloodies while we waited for noon. That would be two hours of drinking before eating.

Evangeline reminded me that she expected a full report by dinner, which Uncle Baron would be preparing for us. I said I was sorry, I had a conference call with Lieutenant Lake and my staff. Certainly I wasn't going to tell them I was having dinner with Emile. I hope they didn't tail me, and I'd certainly be on the lookout. I can lose tails. I can even let the tailer know I know and that he's lost me. So tedious, though.

"Is this conference call about my case?" Evangeline asked.

"Among others," I said.

"I thought you were going to drop everything . . ."

"No," I said, with finality. She huffed but didn't say another word.

As clients go, Princess Pita wasn't the worst, but close.

Baron dropped me off at the sheriff's building. Uncle and niece bid me a curt good day with a promise to be at the Happy Haddock first thing in the morning. I said I hoped to finish up today.

Driving away, I speed-dialed Webdog. "Web, give me something good before I rip off my clothes and backstroke the Cape Fear River."

"That sounds like a client problem."

"Speak up. I'm recording."

"No luck yet with the Anna Graham and Gene Poole," he said, a grouch in his voice. I recalled how certain he'd been that they'd be a cinch to track by leaving a trail of fairy dust up and down the information highway.

"What about Lorraine and the Crescent Moon Winery?" I asked. "I'm going to pay a visit."

"I gave you the story of the Bonnets and their relationship to Stede the pirate. His later-day descendants were born in Charleston. They are Lorraine Darlene Bonnet, aged 40; siblings Roland Creed (who is deceased), 51; Baron Lionel, 47; and Candice Bonnet, 38."

After a deep breath, he went on, "Lorraine Darlene never married, rumored to be a lesbian. I'm e-mailing you a photograph. Not a lovely woman. A little on the gnomy side."

Now I knew. "So's her niece."

"There's a fly in Lorraine's face cream. The Internal Revenue Service."

"Web, you didn't hack into the IRS?"

"Didn't have to. Court records courtesy of Dirk's." Dirk's Detective Agency was the all-around outfit we used most because his information was always reliable. His excellence warranted his high price. Web said. "Anyway, ten years ago Lorraine was investigated and charged with fraud. She had two Social Security numbers and kept two sets of books on her consulting agency. She settled the case and paid for forgetting to declare a couple of hundred thousand.

"Baron never married," Web continued. "Graduated in arts from some arcane school—uh—here it is, Banifit Theatre for the Performing Arts. He tried it all, improv, stage work, etc., he never got past the yokel level."

Most of what he told me about Candice Bonnet Broussard Browne I already knew. "Any record of her having met Browne before the bank robber killed her first husband?"

"My mind sinks with yours. Nothing with Dirk's."

"How much did Princess Pita inherit?"

"A triple stack left in trust." Web's way of saying three million. "Broussard bequeathed a buck to Candice, which tells you something about the marriage, but he never changed the benny on the life insurance policy taken out by the bank on its key directors."

"Interesting what money does and doesn't do."

"Now, we merge Johnny into the Candice resume."

I already knew that Johnny had gone bust more times than balloons at a kids' birthday party. "He was on the bricks when his first wife, Della, was run off the road by a hit-and-run driver—who was never found. Della died six weeks later never having recovered from a coma. With the insurance cash, Johnny sank a ton into Crescent Moon Winery."

"So bereaved Johnny Browne, bon vivant, a-hole, meets bereaved Candice Broussard," I said.

"I've been working for you too long. I've come to not like co-incidences like Broussard's murder and Della Browne's car accident. Both bringing riches to their spouses, who meet up and vow to live happily ever after. Dirk said that the insurance company investigated but eventually paid."

"I'll get Lake to call and talk cop-to-cop on the case. Do me a favor and work up a sketchy report, make it suitable for Princess Pita. Now tell me about the winery."

"The land used to be a tobacco farm and orchard. Two families owned it before Johnny. Both went broke. Sad to say, Americans are becoming wine snobs and scuppernongs and pears don't cut it except for communions and bar mitzvahs. The first few years were a disaster, but then poor Della met up with an irate driver on the interstate and voila, Johnny's got the cash to hire a wine-maker from California. Name's Domingo Cardona. Apparently he's worth the big bucks. The business was growing when Johnny was killed. Now the winery wins awards. Bring me back a fruity merlot, will you?"

"Sure will. I'll call later. Work on Emile Cocineau, Laurant's nephew."

"Right-o."

I drove into the parking lot of my temporary home, the Happy Haddock, grabbed a towel and strode to the seashore. Having foot-raked several cigarette butts off the sand, I spread the towel, sat and rocked my rear-end until I was comfortable, and then called Lake.

"Getting ready to leg it out of here," he said. "What's going on?"

I told him to record what I learned from Web. He turned on his phone recorder and listened while I recounted the info. Concluding, I said, "I'm particularly interested in the deaths of Della Browne and Sean Broussard and if Johnny knew Candice before Sean bought the farm."

"Sure, sweets, I don't have anything else going," he said. "Dead people stacking up in the streets. Atlanta's practically on fire. The drought is killing more people than the drug dealers."

I whined, "Oh my poor darling, I know."

"But you come first."

"And," I continued, "I also know you'll hand this off to the GBI, which will piss them off because I bet dollars to a police car full of donuts, they don't have the connection."

I heard the sigh. "I need a vacation."

"Come to Cape Fear."

"What are you doing now?"

"Going to a winery."

"Nice. I'm off to an autopsy."

"You don't do autopsies."

"Got to. Nobody else I can send."

"Hope the body's fresh."

"It's not."

Domingo Cardona was a slender Latino with a mop of black curls circling his head like Caesar's. In his forties, he had fine brown skin and black eyes. He'd acquired a permanent sun squint, and his constant smile-flashing disconcerted me after two minutes. I find lean, dark-haired, dark-eyed men sexy, but unlike Lake, Domingo Cardona tried too hard.

With two dogs following and my elbow in his palm, we sauntered up a concrete path, past a long natural oak building that had once been a tobacco barn. Lush rhubarb plants grew alongside the barn and crape myrtle trees brushed my cheek with their purple blossoms. While we walked, he transferred his hand to my shoulder, letting it linger there before slipping it down my arm. The other hand was in constant motion as he spoke. "I love to exhibit the Crescent Moon Winery," he said. "It is pure pleasure for me."

"It's a pleasure for me to be here," I said.

He pointed over my shoulder. "Our aging takes place in the barn you see here, while our café and gift shop used to be an outdoor fruit and vegetable stand. The tobacco farmer built it to bolster his income when he planted his orchard. He sold berry and muscadine wines there right on the road with peaches and pears." For no apparent reason he flashed yet another beatific smile.

I scanned the landscape. "This is truly a beautiful place."

We segued onto a walkway between the barn and a white limestone building. He threw his arms wide to take in the barn

123

and the pristine structure. "This is my passion. The boutique winery." He looked up. "See the azure sky, not a cloud; the grapes, they are very happy as they soak up the sunshine and nutrients from the first flowering."

"When did they flower?"

"In June." Broadly winking, he added, "So, too, do I flower in June."

What could I say? I pressed my lips into a half-grin.

His hip settled into a slanted slouch, one arm swaying gracefully toward the building. "We shall go inside the wine tasting room and have a wafer and a little Pinot Gris Chardonnay."

This was shaping up to be a drinking morning. "Little early for me to be . . ."

"Ah, nah, nah. Just wait. But first, we go into the store and meet Bobette."

Bobette Ritter was a plump, rosy-cheeked woman. Domingo explained that as manager she arranged the making of wonderful jellies, preserves, sauces and salsas. He loved to spread his arms. He performed a three-sixty around the room. "She fills our shop with books, wine art, center pieces. If it's wine-related, we have it. You must pick something out before you leave."

"My goodness, can I have one of each?"

"If it will make you happy," he said, sailing on through the room, me on his heels, out the door, down the walkway, through double doors into the converted barn. Silver containers taller than I took up most of the space. "Fermenting tanks," he said, rushing past them into the next room.

Barrel rooms are a delight. Weighty wooden casks lined the walls. "All our wines are blended," Domingo said. Talking about wines makes me glow, but at some point we were going to have to talk about the reason I came. He was saying, "We blend our wines prior to aging. This year we do a very fine merlot with equal parts cabernet sauvignon and cabernet franc. Such a lovely structure, I cannot wait to show it off. I predict it will take a national ribbon next year."

Side-by-side, his roving hand sliding between my shoulder and arm, we went into the tasting room. The aroma in a tasting room is indescribable. I'll try, though: fruity, lightly leather, masculine. An S-curved oak bar had been built and twelve oak barstools gathered around it. Domingo directed me to a stool and went behind the bar. Racks upon racks of wine lined the wall. He expertly removed a cork while he talked. "Pinot Gris is French. It means 'gray pinecone'." Staring at me, he batted his long black eyelashes like a flamenco dancer might. "Pinecone, eh?" He grinned. "Those French, huh?" He'd executed a perfect Gallic shrug.

He sat two white wine stems on the rich planking and poured two inches. It wasn't as cold as I expected. "Pear," I said and pushed my glass toward him for more. Definitely my morning for drinking.

"You think?" he said with a roguish leer. "Pear?" He spread his arms, bottle in one hand, and laughed. "We do not reveal our secrets."

"I bet you added pears."

"You would lose. It is a Pinot Gris and Chardonnay blend, each grape adding its own fruitiness and texture. It has a marvelous nose."

He reached under the bar and brought out a plate of wafers and thinly sliced cheese. "Do I give you too much information?"

"No." *Yes; although I like learning things, I yearned to get to the point of why I had come.* "How long were you with Johnny before he died?"

"Ah, I have bored you and now you want to talk about sad things. Well, I was here almost two seasons before he passed on. Not very long, but we were making good progress."

"Did you buy grapes?"

"No, Mr. Browne did that, but I put him in touch with some excellent vineyards in this region. For many varieties you need elevation to grow good grapes. Now I am the buyer."

"Do you buy from Georgia vineyards?"

He laughed. "Georgia? We have enough scuppernongs here, but those mountains are the gift from the wine gods, so beautiful and perfect for growing certain varieties, the Mourvedre, a must to blend Chateauneuf-du-Pape or the Grenache, to give structure. Mourvedre, the name of the wine made from the grape, rolls off the tongue, but we here have a nickname for it. We call it Big Red. Very robust, like the mountains."

I thought about Orell's wine.

Domingo was saying, "You must taste our Chianti from the Sangiovese grape. The grape, known as 'the blood of Jove,' is grown exclusively for us. It is a grape that takes its time to mature."

"Not scuppernongs or muscadines then?"

"Ho no," he laughed. "Now we tour the vineyard."

In the café and gift shop, Bobette handed Domingo a basket and a blanket. *Blanket. Oh my.*

We left by the side door and Domingo set us a quick pace through the pleasant rolling countryside. There was a fresh sea breeze, and who would have thought so close to the sea that there would be these hills with lines and lines of grape vines marching across them like soldiers determined to take the fort.

"The sea," Domingo said, kissing his grouped fingers, "she kisses the grapes good morning and good night with breezes from around the world. But only certain varieties can grow here. That is why we import."

We reached the grapes, their vines hanging on wooden slats.

"*Vitus Rotundafolia,*" he said. "Pampered by the gods right here in North Carolina." He grasped a handful of the round green grapes. "They love their native land, warm and humid.

They do not need a longer winter like European varieties. We blend the varieties to make a wonderful wine that people on the eastern seaboard adore, and we are finding a market abroad."

At the end of the row, he paused to fondle a grape. "We also use these grapes with European varietals for fruitiness and texture. They are the wine gods' gift to us, too."

He was into wine gods.

We walked through a meadow, and I glimpsed sideways at Domingo because he was quiet for a change. Then he said, "We will sit and sip some wine and eat *foie gras,* then we will talk about what is necessary to discuss." He looked through his lashes, something he probably practiced in the mirror when he was an adolescent trying out his wiles. He wouldn't be one to say something self-deprecating like, *I know it is not for me that you are here . . .*

We skirted an orchard and arrived at a small stream where water lilies floated on slender stems. Two logs had been lodged in the gravel bank with strips of four-by-fours, creating a bridge. Domingo held my hand and led me onto the first plank. The bridge was sturdy and in five steps I was across. Six yards ahead, we came to a small patch of grass. He laid the hamper on the grass and spread the blanket. "It is my favorite place to come and have a repast of wine and *foie gras.* It is one of the pleasures of living. Beautiful nature, a fabulous wine, a beautiful woman to sit by your side . . ." I sat at the edge of the blanket and he stretched next to me, propped on his elbows. He aimed his deep brown eyes at me and said, "It was Plato who said wine is a gift from the gods. I say it all the time, as you have noticed." When I didn't reply, he sat up and opened the hamper lid. Strapped into the lid were three bottles of wine. Removing one, he raised it and said, "A simple beverage, a marvelous dinner partner, a work of art, wine is a treasure. Do you agree?" He reached into the hamper for the stems.

I nodded. If only it were Lake sitting next to me in this idyllic place.

"Cabernet Franc," he said, showing me the label. "Mostly blended with Cabernet Sauvignon and Merlot." He had decanted the wine and poured a finger for me. I ran the pretty red liquid around the inside of the glass bowl and then sniffed. "Tobacco, violets," I said.

"It is the soil. It comes from the West Virginia mountains."

He laid out toast points and pate. I'm not all that fond of goose liver, but how could I object? I tasted the wine. "Feels good in my mouth and doesn't taste too green."

"I marvel at your discrimination. We try to emphasize the fruit by delaying harvesting to minimize the green leafy notes." He cocked his head and smiled without showing his teeth. "Now, the time has come. I can tell you are anxious to ask me questions, and I have decided to be frank with you."

"Johnny Browne."

He held up his glass. "To the late Mr. Browne."

I raised my glass. "To Mr. Browne."

I asked and he told me that he was the manager of operations and answered to no one. "I don't get involved in politics. It would ruin me as an artist."

Was I going to have to pull teeth? "Who's the money-man?" He shook his head. "Who writes your checks?"

"That, Miss Dru, is my business. Please—don't—I won't talk about present-day business. Maybe others involved will. I am not alone in all financial matters." He launched into programs that he and Johnny dreamed up before Johnny died, the wine tours, wine art, civic involvement, anything to avoid talking about the man, which annoyed me because he had promised to be frank. "Sounds busy and exciting."

"It is that, Miss Dru."

"Dru."

"Domingo. We've been talking and eating for quite a while and we are just getting around to first names."

"What did you think of Johnny Browne?"

"I did say I would be frank, didn't I?"

"He's been dead almost four years. Perhaps it is time."

"So we can speak ill of him?"

"If it helps me find his murderer."

"There would most certainly be a murderer when it comes to Mr. Browne, but why are *you* trying to find his murderer?"

"I thought Baron would have told you. Evangeline hired me."

"That one. She *must* have her own investigator."

"You know Evangeline."

"After it happened, she begged me to go to Atlanta and find out why her mother was missing. Me? I am a wine-maker, not a policia."

"I also happened to have a personal interest. I found the sailboat in the lake."

"And you are an investigator?"

I smiled. "I'm a child finder, but in this case I'm finding *for* a child."

"I hope you do so. I will help all I can." He swallowed a sip and pressed his lips. "Mr. Browne spent money freely if it was for something for himself and for his fun." He held up a finger. "However, he had a temper and often shorted his suppliers, finding little things wrong and wanting to knock off the price. One supplier came here and called Johnny a grape thief to his face and threatened to settle the debt himself. I have to tell you that to stay in business after he passed on, I had to make many amends all up and down the region. My suppliers now know that I will not steal their grapes. All wine-makers reserve the right to refuse inferior fruit. Sometimes a crop stays on the vine too long or the weather affects the grapes. The supplier says they are fine, I demur. There's always a tussle. That's the unpleasant part of the business."

"So you made up with this name-calling supplier?"

"I might have for all I know because I did not see him, and Johnny never confided in me. I paid every debt of Johnny's whether it was warranted or not."

"What was your personal relationship with Johnny Browne?"

He hunched his shoulders. "He left me alone and only once threatened me. I was at fault. I would have been bereft to leave here. It was exciting to me, the prospect of turning a poor winery and vineyard into a rich one."

"Johnny let you be an artist."

"He left me alone to develop the wines I wanted to. I love blends, and . . ." he raised his empty glass, ". . . making the most of a fine variety." He divided the remaining wine between us.

"Why did he threaten you?"

"I anticipated that you would ask, and I will tell you." He sipped, then reached into the lid and brought out a second bottle. It was blue glass with a crescent moon on a white label. He opened it and said, "He shall breathe."

"I have to drive to Southport," I said.

"You will not become inebriated on these wines."

"What's that one?" I said, pointing to the blue bottle.

"Blueberry wine."

"Sweet?"

"For dessert. We will have a biscotti and a glass of the blueberry wine. It is something you will want to take home with you."

"You saved the best until last?"

"All my wines are the best—in their place."

I pressed my lips. "Please go on."

"It was about Candice."

Why wasn't I surprised?

He went on, "She came on to me, I swear to God." He looked at the cloudless sky. "I am not shy with women. I love women, beautiful women especially." His eyes narrowed to become doe-like. "I could love you."

I leaned back and twisted my lip, *dream on.*

He understood. "I see that you are not interested in me. I love women who are interested in me. You love another man, true?"

"True."

"Mrs. Browne pursued me. She came to the winery. I tried to avoid her. You can ask Bobette."

"I might."

"Please do. Bobette told me she was dangerous the day I came here and met Mrs. Browne. 'Stay away from that one,' she said, and I could see my career going into the toilet if I found myself in the same room with her, alone."

"And you did."

"I was setting up for a wine tasting for the Rotary Club. She is a member. This day she came in unexpectedly and put her arms around my waist. I was bending forward counting the whites in the refrigerated case. I turned around and found myself in her arms and then she was in mine. She wore no bra, nor panties. She had a powerful aroma. She kissed me. I kissed her back." He ran his fingers through his hair. "We continued to kiss with our tongues. She reached for my zipper. I pulled the straps of her sundress down to her waist. She had me . . . my . . . well it doesn't matter, the particulars. I heard quick footsteps. Mrs. Browne ran into the locker." He pointed at a door in the corner. "And I knelt on the floor and pushed my shirt back into my pants but I could not zip my trousers. When he walked in, Mrs. Browne came out of the locker with two wine bottles and said, 'Sweetheart, we're counting the Pinot Gris for tonight. Do you know how many are coming?' Mr.

Browne was coming around the bar and I had to get up, although I couldn't zip. I turned to retrieve two bottles of Pinot Gris out of the cooler. I held them in front of me and stood. Mr. Browne was red in the face. He wasn't fooled. Mrs. Browne wriggled her fingers and left."

"Then what?"

"Mr. Browne always carried a gun on his ankle. He reached down to his shoe and pulled it out of the holster. He didn't point it at me, but he said, 'Candice is mine. Nobody touches her. Not even you, Domingo. I don't share. Not even with you, Domingo.' I started to say something, but he raised the gun toward the wines in the racks on the wall. 'See the crescent moon on the top of that liter of champagne, Domingo?' He shot it square in the middle. The bottle exploded. He left." Domingo paused to huff air. "It still lingers, the fear I felt that day."

"Did you have a girlfriend?"

"You are very perceptive. I went right out and got me one. I have had several since. I am not a man to settle down."

"You and Candice didn't end there, did you?"

"Mrs. Browne would catch up with me in the vineyard when she knew Mr. Browne would be away, buying."

I looked around the lovely glade. "Did you bring her here?"

"Many times after that occasion."

"Other women, too?"

"Many, yes." He sighed. "It is my nature."

"Did you kill Johnny Browne?"

He didn't look surprised that I'd asked. "I never even wanted to," he said. "I never wanted Mrs. Browne for myself alone. I liked to make love with her because she liked to make love with me. We did not love each other, but we enjoyed each other."

"Johnny never knew?"

"I believe that he did, but I also believe that he had *other interests,* too."

"You live dangerously."

"By then, he could see that I would make his winery a success beyond his dreams. He gave me more pay. I came from California. My old winery wanted me back at twice the price. But I fell in love with Crescent Moon. Mr. Browne looked the other way."

"Did you know Laurant?"

"I did."

"What did you think . . . ?"

"I thought him the most dangerous man I'd ever met."

"How so?"

"He had a cold soul. He had to have money to make him happy, which was never enough. He took what he wanted. He did not give a damn about anyone else. I warned Mrs. Browne to keep away from him."

"Candice doesn't seem the type to listen."

"No." He blew out his breath. "Whatever happened on that boat, it was brought about by Mr. Cocineau and Mrs. Browne."

"Do you think they are alive?"

He said he believed that they were alive and living in Rio because they'd taken two trips when Johnny went out of town for wine conventions. "Mrs. Browne confided this to me and that she told her husband she was going to Paris to shop. She had a friend who covered for her."

"What do you know about Laurant's nephew, Emile Cocineau?"

He laughed and poured two small glasses of blueberry wine. He laid biscotti on a china plate and handed it to me. "Sip and tell me?"

I sipped. "It's dry. It's sweet but not too."

"Because the blueberries are picked at just the right time."

"We had blueberries in our back yard. The birds ate them before they were ripe."

133

"We're one step ahead of the birds."

"It's delicious," I said and meant it. "It could go with meat."

"Yes, but you wine snobs would laugh us vintners out of the blueberry patch."

"Emile Cocineau," I said, wriggling my shoulders. "Then I must go."

"I hardly know him."

Something in his expression—evasive—made me doubt that. "He claims to have ownership, or will have ownership in this vineyard, if Laurant is declared legally dead."

Domingo shook his head.

"Do you believe him?"

"I concern myself with grapes and wine. I do not listen to rumors that do not concern me."

He gathered the detritus of our repast and stowed it in the basket. He held out his hand and I took it. We'd sorted out the man–woman sex thing, so I didn't feel threatened. His hand was scaly and warm. At the stream, at the log bridge, he let go of my hand and I stepped onto the four-by-four span, except my sole didn't land solidly and my right ankle turned. The same damn ankle I injured in the woods. He caught my elbow as the logs started to roll. "Be still," he cautioned and I straightened. The logs sank back into their bed and we walked on across. "Are you hurt? Can I help you?" he asked.

"No, I'm fine. It's nothing."

Damn thing hurt like hell, but I walked through the orchard and the vineyard like it didn't.

CHAPTER THIRTEEN

Domingo was quite correct. I felt no ill effects from his wines; nevertheless, I drove the speed limit, stayed between the lines and even took the precaution of pulling over to a stop before I called Webdog. "What else you got for me?"

He rattled off a bunch of boring stuff about Janet Foster Blair, the old plantation money heiress who divorced a diplomat quadrillionaire for Laurant from Quebec, owner of Talisman Corporation, a consulting company of obscure enterprise. Laurant's father had a top security clearance from the United States government. Long dead now, Web speculated that Laurant's father may have been a spy."

"How did you find that out? No, don't answer that. But I like the way you speculate."

"To speculate, per chance to be right."

Laurant inherited little from his father, then he married Janet and suddenly he's on easy street and looking to buy anything he can get his hands on—with her money. They bought boats, gold, a restaurant franchise in Florida that went under—on and on until I told Web I got the picture. "I'm almost to my destination, is that it?"

Web's voice got very confidential sounding. "He looked to buy a vineyard."

"I know that. Rumor is he wanted to buy Crescent Moon."

"Here's the really good part. A fight broke out between Laurant and Johnny. The sheriff got involved because a gun was

135

involved. The scandal got out. Laurant and Janet handed over the family plantation to lessees and moved to Atlanta. A year later, again Laurant got the yen for a vineyard in Cape Fear. The Brownes and Cocineaus reconciled, and Laurant bought a place called Beggar's Grind up the road from Crescent Moon. Four years ago, he applied for a license to turn a grist mill on the property into a winery and retail store. Nothing came of it."

Probably because their plans were foiled by the Scuppernong tragedy.

"Their Paces Ferry house was on the market when they disappeared," Web said. "Two point three mil."

"That all come from Dirk's—or hacking?"

"My superb skills at *detecting* a hacker."

"Someone's trying to hack you?"

"The nerve! But yes, I detected a cyber stalker. No trouble finding who was on my tail. A reporter for the Atlanta newspapers snooping into the lives of the *Scuppernong* people. I know who he is. He's not a bad hacker. He told me what he had when I gave him a little info, nothing he didn't already know. So we developed this back and forth. Candice was pretty chatty about the past and her affairs. According to the reporter, Candice and Laurant were having an affair. She told her best friends that they got it on in the swimming pool. Johnny didn't much care, it seems, but Janet would get on a tirade. She threatened to divorce Laurant if she found out, and she was the snoopy type. So the lovers did lap dancing."

"So clever, Webby."

Webdog, the ultimate geek, is in love with his supercomputer. If he ever had sex with a human—man or woman—it would be a complete, utter shock to me. If I walked in on him diddling an orifice in his computer, that would not be a surprise.

"When is the reporter going public with this info?"

"Bits of it are public, but he's doing a full-page take-out on the couples, the vineyard, anything he can dig up. He's traveling to Wilmington in a day or two, soon's he wraps up another piece."

"Stay in touch, pick his brain, but don't share the good stuff."

"Got it."

I was told the sheriff had gone to Sunset Harbor and was directed to follow Highway 211 South to where it feeds into Sunset Harbor Road. That road met up with Lockwood Folly Road. I followed Lockwood Folly for a short stretch until I saw two squad cars parked at a pier. Ben Avlon was on the lookout for me and waved. Apparently his office had radioed that I was on the way. He directed me to park in a sandy spot near him. "Sorry if I'm interrupting you, Sheriff Avlon," I said.

He shook his head, a signal to be quiet. He stepped toward his deputies and whispered. A discordant wail startled me. I looked over and saw a van backing away from the pier, a medical examiner's van. When it turned and drove up the road, Avlon came to my side. "Drowning. Old story. Two boys fishing, one falls in, the other dives in to save him, the savior goes under, the first boy surfaces and crawls up the piles."

I looked over the murky water. "Is this the Cape Fear River?"

"Nope, the Lockwood Folly River. It goes out to the Intercoastal. Cape Fear dumps at Wilmington."

"I saw the movie and always wondered why it's called Cape Fear."

"Wasn't always," he said, motioning me toward his car. "Let's get a cup of coffee, do a little talking before I got to get back. I'm not hungry; I ate a late breakfast–early lunch. You can ride with me."

"I'm not hungry, either," I said, hoping I didn't reek of alcohol.

As he drove, he told me about the cape with the chilling

name and the river with a laughable name. "The cape's name appears on early maps as 'C. of F-a-i-r-e.' The spelling of 'Faire' got mangled into 'Feare.' There was certainly nothing to fear of the river because it's mainly inland, going north of Fayetteville." As he spoke, Avlon drove through the charming fishing and tourist village. "The Lockwood Folly is a different story. Depending on the tale you believe, a group of settlers led by a man named Lockwood colonized the banks, but the good Mr. Lockwood didn't bring enough supplies and got into a dispute with the natives, so the colony disbanded. What remained was called Lockwood's Folly and the name stuck to the river and inlet. Both rivers show up on a map in the mid-sixteen-hundreds, making the Folly and the Cape Fear two of the oldest named rivers in the state."

I love a man who loves history.

He pulled up to a beach eatery with a lighthouse and starfish painted on the glass. Inside, we sat at a booth with red leather-ette benches and a white Formica top. I was admiring how spic-and-span the place looked when the waitress came forward, looking me over with an unpleasant wrinkling of her nose. I looked at her left hand. No ring. I'd already noticed the sheriff didn't wear one. The waitress's eyes would never come in contact with mine again unless I got up and did a jig in front of her. She put a hand on her hip and said to Avlon, "I see you're getting your substation."

"If we can find the place for it," he said.

She canted her head to one side. "Glad y'all didn't pick us taxpayers' pockets." She laughed at herself.

"We're good so long as the druggies keep smokin' and snor-tin' and shootin'."

"Try and stop 'em," she said. She waved her hand as if it didn't matter anyway and asked, "What can I get you this time of day?"

"Cup of coffee." He looked at me.

"Same," I said, looking at the waitress who had turned to fetch his order.

When she left, Avlon shook his head in a *can't do nothing about her* kind of way. The waitress brought little bowls of sugar, the pink substitute and a chrome jug of cream. She put a hand on her hip—why do they do that?—and asked him, "You want water, sugar?"

He shook his head no and she left.

He picked up a pink sugar substitute and ripped it open. "We got a pretty big county and we can't be in all the unincorporated outposts at the same time. We need the substations, but the commissioners want us to fund them without taxpayer money. If the drug money runs out, we won't be able to keep them going."

"Drug money running out? Not unless you stop doing your job."

"Thing is if it did run out, we wouldn't need the damn substations. Damn drugs doing a helluva number on our kids."

"You got yourself a catch-22."

The waitress brought our coffees. When she set mine on the table, some slopped out.

Avlon's was lovingly placed, the handle turned to fit his right hand. "Sugar, you just signal when you want more, yours is a bottomless cup, like always." Turning, she slanted her hips away.

Avlon hadn't so much as tensed a tendon so I couldn't tell if he had the hots for her or not. He said, "Now, you came all the way down here." He raised his cup and blew on the hot coffee. "Tell me why."

"Information."

He sipped and nodded. I drank and set the cup down. Worst coffee I've ever tasted.

I told him that my staff was researching the Brownes and Cocineaus and their connections here. I said I knew about the fight between Johnny and Laurant and that it involved him.

His eyebrows rose at the unexpected statement, then he shook his head. "Not me, my predecessor."

He said that before he was elected sheriff he was a lawyer in Southport and that he had no dealings, legal or otherwise, with either couple. "Brownes' lawyer is Dave Henderson. Not sure about Cocineau. You talk to Mr. Henderson, you don't have to tell him I told you."

"No problem there. Do you know about the trouble?"

"Why don't you tell me what you know and I'll answer to that."

When I started to tell him about Laurant Cocineau's desire to buy into Crescent Moon Winery, he stopped me. "Everybody knew about that."

"What about the scandal that Candice and Laurant created."

"Look, Miss Dru, I knew Mrs. Browne and Mr. Cocineau. I knew Mr. Browne and hardly nothing about Mrs. Cocineau. You see what I'm getting at. How I said the names."

I sure did, since I began to think of Candice and Laurant as a couple.

He said, "Always seemed to everybody that's how they should have been. Candice Browne and Laurant Cocineau seemed to belong together."

"How did the previous sheriff get involved in the scandal?"

He shook his blond head enough for hair to fall onto his forehead. "Mr. Browne was known to carry a gun. Mr. Cocineau did not. The gun went off."

"Where was this?"

"At the Cocineau place, by the mill." His coffee cup was empty. The waitress replenished it and passed the pot over my head. My cup was full and cold.

Avlon said, "A bullet hit Cocineau in the leg, so the *story* goes."

"Story?"

"He tried to treat himself but it got infected so he went to a vet. The vet was a friend of the sheriff. By the time it was looked into, the story had various versions."

"So the Cocineaus left town."

"Good idea to let the whole thing die."

"No charges?"

He shook his head like I should know the reason why. "By the time I took office, Cocineau had moved to Atlanta."

"But he and Janet returned."

"Not for long. Then . . ." He spread his hands apart as if to say who knows where they are now.

"Tell me about Domingo."

"Have you met him?"

"Sampled his wine and heard a tale."

"Thought I detected sweet alcohol."

"I'm fine to drive."

"I can tell." He grinned and said that Romeo, referring to the vintner, tackled his civic duties with gusto. He donated his time and his wines to festivals and such, and his body to any pretty girl that wanted it. Other than a few traffic tickets, he'd never been in trouble. When I asked him about Domingo and Candice, he shrugged and said other folks' affairs were not his problem.

I gave it a second's pause to think about Avlon and Candice, but moved on. "Any trouble between Emile and the Bonnets before the scuffle yesterday?"

"None I know of. They didn't cotton to his uncle, Laurant. Lorraine's all right. Baron's a joke. Evangeline's pure evil."

I thought about a smart dog who liked her. "I don't know about that."

"She'd run a pitch fork through Domingo if she could, but the feelings mutual. She's got all kinds of ideas about running the winery."

"Enter Emile Cocineau."

He pushed his empty cup to the middle of the table. "She may be ugly, but she's going to have a pot full of money some day." He raised his hand to flip hair back from his forehead. "Now that's my opinion. And it don't mean snot."

"Do you think Baron and Evangeline are behind the theft of Emile's safe?"

"I can't talk about something I'm investigating."

"What do you know about Emile?"

"Exactly nothing. He's not from around here. Lives in England. Comes here to paint. Pretty much stays to himself."

"No trouble?"

"None."

"Do you believe him about the codicil to Laurant's will?"

He laughed. "Could be, or not." He stood. "Time to go."

I climbed the steps of the two-story clapboard overlooking the Cape Fear River. Dave Henderson's gold sign had been screwed into the lintel of the wide verandah. The cushioned swing at the end beckoned. My swollen ankle hurt like the devil had his thumb pressing on it.

I buzzed as the small white placard requested. The door unlocked, and I stepped inside. A young man sat behind a bank of phones and a large computer monitor. "Mr. Henderson is out of the office," he said when I told him I didn't have an appointment, which he knew because the appointment book was open and the lines from eleven in the morning through two in the afternoon were crossed through. The young man saw that I saw and said, "He'll be back at two."

I said, "Long lunch?"

He laughed. "No, three-hour round of golf, followed by a quick sandwich in the golf shop. I'm not being disloyal," he went on, "he works on the weekends to allow for his weekday golf round."

It was one-thirty. I had my mini-computer in my backpack. I asked him, "Mind if I wait?"

He looked at the appointment book. There were no names below the crossed lines. He said, "I can't guarantee Dave—Mr. Henderson—will be alone when he returns." He gave me a pleasant smile. "He often does business on the course."

"If I can, I'll wait on the verandah." I grinned at him. "We'll see when he gets here."

"Be our guest."

I was caressing my bruised ankle when the young man came out and asked if I'd like a drink.

"Water," I said.

"We got some great teas. Raspberry, green . . ."

"Raspberry would be wonderful."

I called Web first. "Yo," he said. "Billie's mad as hell, and she ain't . . ."

"What's Billie mad about?"

"She's here. She'll tell you."

Billie came on with a grumbled greeting. I asked, "What's going on?"

"That Janeway a-hole."

"What about him."

"He freaked when he saw the cameras."

Most people do. Billie comes loaded with at least three hanging off various parts of her anatomy with lenses fat enough to capture the pin-sized zit on your forehead from a hundred yards. I said, "He agreed to photographing the materials."

"He agreed to let *you*," Billie said. "Not me. It's obvious he's

143

got the hots for your ass."

"You couldn't charm him?"

"He's the kind that likes long—long legs, long hair and big blue eyes."

"And?"

"He carried on. Jeez, he shook my three-hundred like it was a kaleidoscope."

I wasn't in the mood for long drawn-out explanations. "Did he show you the documents?"

"Yeah, when I told him I wasn't leaving until he did."

"You photographed?"

"Sure did. Pics of the campsite, ciggie papers, fire pit."

"The signatures?"

"Yeah, funny. Anna Graham and Gene Poole. Blockish letters like kids' writing. Fake, I can tell you."

"What else?"

"Janeway said the kids were having fun with a drunk and the cops."

"I wonder about that."

"Well, their names, for one thing."

"Yeah, but the drunk is dead."

"Whoa." She paused for two seconds. "Drunks do die. Plus, he wanted to know if I know the kid and the old fart that looks like Rhett Butler. I don't, so I told him, but I thought you might like to know he was interested in them."

"Thank you, Billie, I appreciate your help. Send me your bill."

"No problem. I'm to tell you to remember all this is un-official."

"I hope you told him that it was."

"Sure did. I don't have a pony in this show. He said to tell you he'll call you when he's in Atlanta next. Lucky you."

"Bye, Billie."

"There's something about him, Dru."

How many times had I thought that?

Web came back on. "Yo."

"Now that I got Billie's knickers unwadded, what else you got for me?"

"Since we're on the subject of Bernard Janeway . . ."

Boiled down, Janeway's bio didn't reveal anything darker than two DUIs six years apart and a reprimand for unspecified transgressions against locals. Seems he doesn't like the South or Southerners. Forty-five years old, born Concord, Mass. Graduated U of Conn, business admin. Army Corps twenty years, first Gulf War, back stateside 1994. Stationed to Lake Lanier where he'd been trying to get a post back east.

"Working on Sonny K," Web said.

"I know about his education and work. Anything out of the way?"

"Mother and father killed in motorcycle accidents. Both riding on the winding roads, smashed into by a logging truck."

"Who drove it?"

"Malachi Scoggins."

"Related to Boyd?"

"A cousin. Sonny and Boyd are cousins, too. Boyd's been dead almost a month. Officially ruled misadventure with a firearm."

"Where'd you get that?"

"Medical examiner's report."

"How'd you get it?" Medical examiners' reports are not public info, but so much of what Webdog digs up is not either.

"I enjoy circumventing limitations," he said.

"You've graduated to Botdog."

"No need for such radical approach."

"Lot of misadventure going on in Sawchicsee County."

"No powder burns around the entry on the forehead. No

145

casing, no gun."

"He was facing whoever shot him."

"Twenty-two-caliber size entry."

"Hmmm. A rifle or a hand gun. I'm suspicious when people involved, however peripherally, turn up dead."

"Happens to us often, doesn't it?"

"Too much."

Web said, "Getting back to Sonny Kitchens, Sawchicsee County has a rumor mill you can access by Mr. Google."

"That must have been disappointing. No need of C plus-plus to produce your sneaky codes. No spoofing, no cross-site scripting?"

"Where do you get these terms?"

"Are our Win7 patches current?"

"I don't use Win7."

"Continue, O Open Source guru."

"Nor shell scripts or Perl, either. Now, the rag up there, the *Sawchicsee Bulletin,* is noted for who attends weddings, funerals, bake sales, dinners-on-the-ground, churches. And, pertinently, who's sitting or standing with whom."

"Slither over to the pertinent part."

"Kitchens was photographed, not once, but twice, sitting next to Linette Parker. Big question marks, bold printing and snide innuendoes. Don't you love it? Small towns and their rags?"

"Linette Parker," I said. "The body in the lake. Diane's mother."

"Look down the rabbit hole; it gets curiouser and curiouser."

"I'm looking. Tell me what I'm seeing."

"Sonny Kitchens has a very soft spot for Linette's daughter, Diane."

"You're saying?"

"The three were photographed together. The innuendo-prone

reporter hinted a resemblance."

I conjured up Diane's face and placed it next to my mental image of Sonny. "I don't see it, but I know he sees to her when Linette goes off for long jaunts—went off for long jaunts."

I was so absorbed in my conversation with Webdog that I didn't hear the car door, but when I looked down the steps, I saw a man wearing chinos and a golf shirt bumping a large case up the steps.

"Gotta go, Web. Good work. Here's a name for you: Scully Brunty."

"He's Kitchens' second cousin. The ma's cousin. There's another cousin, Orell."

"Good grief, some of those people must be their own grandpa."

He laughed. "Shopkeepers. No trouble with the law. Nice to have a lawman in the family, I say."

I closed the cell as a string bean of a man with a huge nose reached the last step and placed his oversize briefcase on the wooden floor. Around fifty, he had a high brow and a deep furrow between his eyes. I rose, forgetting about my ankle and winced. He reached out his hands as if to catch me. "You okay?"

"Sure, my ankle." I steadied myself and stuck out my hand. "Moriah Dru."

His eyes sharpened on my face. "Dave Henderson," he answered. "Miss Dru, what can I do for you?"

"I won't keep you. A few questions."

His eyes shifted. "I can't promise answers."

While I fumbled in my backpack to get my business card case, he sat in a wicker chair, hitched up his tan pants, leaned back and folded his hands around a knee. I noticed the big college ring on one hand, a wedding band on the other. He said, "Why do I know you're not a prospective client."

I handed him my business card. "This maybe?"

He scanned it. "Miss Dru, tell me what I can do for Child Trace."

As ugly as he was, the man had charm enough to be effective in a courtroom. Not slick-looking, he was a down-home type, wanting to help the jury understand the gravity of the trouble his client found himself in, and how such an upstanding citizen could not, no-way-in-heck, be guilty.

I said, "I'm working on the Browne-Cocineau case."

He nodded. "I deal with PIs. You don't look like any PI I ever employed. Sounds like you specialize in finding children." He leaned back, relaxed as they come.

"Usually. This time I'm working *for* a kid."

The furrow between his eyes became a deep ridge. "Do I know this kid?"

"Evangeline Broussard."

He emitted an unmelodious hew-haw. "E?"

"E."

I explained the circumstances of meeting Baron and Evangeline and told him a little about the judge who had attracted Evangeline's attention. I omitted her attitude toward the girl, but Henderson could probably have guessed it.

"Waste of time and money," he said and looked over at the porch rails as if Evangeline might spring from the roses rambling over it. "But okay, how can I help you?"

"I've learned that you are the Brownes' attorney."

"That is correct. I can tell you that much. But be careful of the privilege."

"Johnny Browne is dead. Does the privilege extend to the dead?"

"Candice is not known to be dead."

"She could be declared so in a few months."

"True in the state of Georgia. Not necessarily in this state, however."

"Wouldn't reciprocity apply?"

He pinched his lower lip thoughtfully. "I hope you understand that I can't and won't tell tales on my clients, dead or alive."

"I understand that."

He breathed out. "And?"

"Can you tell me who represents the Cocineaus?"

He lopped his head sideways. "Won't hurt to tell you. I did until they moved to Atlanta. I've talked to their attorney there. I could have my clerk dig out his number."

"I'll call you if I need it. Do you represent Emile Cocineau?"

He laced his fingers and cracked his knuckles. Such big knuckles. "The privilege."

I took that as a yes. "His safe was stolen."

"And?"

"I was at Beggar's Grind this morning. I met Emile Cocineau, I saw the hole."

"And?"

"Emile claims his uncle's will gives him the right to half of Crescent Moon Winery if Laurant is declared dead."

"That would have to include Candice in the death roster."

"And, once Evangeline reaches the age of twenty-one, she assumes half-ownership."

"And?"

"Emile and Evangeline become partners."

"And?"

"As Johnny Browne's lawyer, I assume you would know if he executed a codicil to that effect."

"Yes I would."

"And?" *Here, I said it.*

"Since Emile let that cat out of the bag, I can tell you I drew up the papers for both Johnny and Laurant when they were present in my office. The instruments were based on Johnny's wishes."

"Odd."

His smile was tight-lipped. "Maybe, but true. E has no say and no money until she reaches her majority. And when that happens, may God have pity on Emile Cocineau."

"You like him?"

"Nothing I know not to like. It's a plus that E likes him."

"She did until Emile started calling her and Baron thieves."

He rose and I stood. "Now I believe I've told you all I can."

Hefting his oversized case, he looked over his shoulder and said, "I can offer this opinion. Emile was a fool to take those documents out of the bank's safe deposit box."

"Without the originals, are they valid?"

"That, Miss Dru, is a matter for the courts. Under the circumstances, I would say the courts will punt given Candice could still be alive."

"So, for now, the vineyard is in whose control?"

"I am the managing director on the board and Domingo is the operations manager of the winery."

"No other directors? Lorraine Bonnet?"

"Lorraine's name only." He walked to the office door. "I believe we've finished our business."

I went down the steps thinking everybody says they're in charge of Crescent Moon Winery. Too many vintners spoil the year.

CHAPTER FOURTEEN

"Della nee Anderson Browne," Lake said. I listened to his voice streaming through the cell phone while I looked out the window at the Atlantic Ocean, the green-gray seas rollicking toward the shore where children were building sand castles and adults were sunning, walking, or stopping to shell. Lake was saying, "Classic case of road rage. Unnamed subject in red pickup truck tailed Della Browne on Interstate Ninety-Five, traveling south at speeds up to ninety miles an hour. Witnesses say he waved his fist at her, honked and yelled out the window for her to get out of the way. She stayed in the passing lane, and he eventually passed her, cutting her off so suddenly she was forced to swerve into a guard rail and flipped. Chest, head, neck wounds, right arm broken, legs crushed. No suspect arrested, charged, tried or convicted. Never found the driver or the truck. She suffered severe brain damage and died six days later." Lake paused. "Did you know fifteen hundred people are killed each year in road-rage accidents?"

"I don't call them accidents." I grabbed my room key, handbag and a beach towel draped on a chair.

"Incidents, then," Lake said as I left the room and locked the door. He went on, "Shrinks say anyone experiencing that kind of rage is suffering from IED, intermittent explosive disorder. It affects seven percent of the population."

Walking down the hall I said, "So?"

"I thought you'd like to know that."

"You get the name of the witness?" I asked, taking the steps down.

"Two teenagers, a boy and a girl. Apparently the boy was doing the manly thing by going ninety miles an hour to help out a damsel in distress. Their statements describe the man as medium looking, red hat, like a baseball or golf hat, red knit golf shirt. The girl thought he was fair; the boy thought he wore sunglasses. They agree that he was in a rage, windows down, fist pumping, yelling, and tailgating. The girl is quoted as saying, 'It was scary. The guy was out of control.' "

"Names?"

"Roy Ortiz and Beth Donner, both from Raleigh, going to Hilton Head where Johnny Browne told police Della was headed for a girls' trip."

Outside, standing on a dune, scanning the happy families and a hunky lifeguard, I asked, "Did they interview the girls Della Browne was to meet on the trip?" I slipped through the sea oats and snugged my bare feet into the warm sand, so soothing to my sore ankle.

"One, Della's best friend, Addie Sweppington, address twenty-one Katy's Branch, Wilmington. She skipped the trip and went to New York. Reports say she didn't know who else was supposed to meet Della there."

"I ever tell you I love you?"

"The very last time I dug up info for you."

"I'm so sweet."

"Moving on to Sean Tyrone Broussard, first husband of Candice, father of Evangeline. A man walked into Greater Citizens Financial Bank and Trust and asked to see Mr. Broussard, who had just returned from a business lunch. The receptionist said he introduced himself as Willis Ephrom. He wanted to negotiate a large deposit personally with Mr. Broussard. He waited fifteen minutes until Broussard finished a telephone conference and was invited into the office. Not more than five minutes later the man calling himself Ephrom walked out. The guard watched him carefully, or so he says. Ephrom didn't run, sweat, or do any of those things that made anyone suspicious. The receptionist speculated that he might have been a salesman and Mr. Broussard gave him the boot as soon as he found out he wasn't a big depositor. She went in to announce the next client and found Broussard slumped over his desk, a hole in his temple. His wallet was all that was missing."

I now shuffled through the surf, hoping salt water would cure my sore ankle, I asked, "When is a bank robbery not a bank robbery by a man smart enough not to use a fake name like Bob Smith?"

Lake said, "The only deposit he wanted to make was in the banker's head."

"Describe the fake Willis Ephrom," I said.

"The receptionist got the best look at him. Brown hair, clean shaven, wore a gray suit, medium height, slender, like any successful businessman."

"A hit man."

"No one ever came under suspicion—family, friends, disgruntled depositors and so on."

"Nary an enemy?"

"Apparently not, except maybe his wife. Broussard left Candice a dollar in his will. She became a statutory dower and holds an interest in certain properties until her death, at which time Evangeline, as Broussard's only progeny, will inherit, including his banking interests."

"I keep hearing about Princess Pita's coming riches. Maybe I should demand a raise."

"Authorities looked hard at Candice, but nothing suspicious turned up."

"With those pirate ancestors of hers, there's got to be one

who kinked the ancestral DNA chain and deposited the rotten egg."

"A year later she married Johnny Browne. If she knew him before Broussard was killed, there's no evidence of it."

"My sixth sense says she did," I said. "It's Thursday. Come up to Southport tomorrow for the weekend." I kicked at a wave. "The seas are glorious."

"Saturdays and Sundays are murder's busiest days. When are you coming home?"

"If you're not coming here, Saturday morning," I answered. "Who's the president of Greater Citizens Financial Bank and Trust now?"

"Stepley Hurst, protégé of Broussard's."

"Murder for a bank presidency?"

"It's up to you to find out."

"You ask Web. I'm overloading him."

"Will do."

"Where are you having dinner tonight?"

"Redd's," he said. "Braves game tonight."

Cop bar, with wings and girls. "Buxom broads tonight, too?"

"Not for me."

"You could watch the game on television at home."

"Then I couldn't see the buxom broads."

I didn't laugh. Those buxom broads are always pouncing on Lake. I've rolled by Redd's late sometimes. Everyone hushes when I walk in. I wish Lake was as ugly as Dave Henderson.

Lake said, "Dru, chill. I'm kidding."

"It's a cop thing," I said and pressed End. I'd lost my desire to bathe my ankle in the surf and headed back to my room. I thought about my dinner with Emile. I had no dress to wear, and I had time to shop. I'd passed a stand-alone resale shop advertising lightly worn couture clothes. I considered my wrinkled silk pants and shirt, and then the visit I could make if I didn't shop.

I can always blow out the wrinkles with a hair dryer.

I looked up Addie Sweppington, Della's friend. She lived just south of Wilmington. Twenty-one Katy's Branch wasn't hard to find. It was a one-house street on a tidal marsh. The clapboard house had at least seven gables atop two or three stories. Set on a slight promontory, it was a phantasmagorical apparition of porches and railings and bay windows built in the early Victorian architectural style. I'd passed two outbuildings, one a barn and the other looked like a summerhouse.

I slowed to a crawl as three friendly spaniels came running to greet the car. I had to crunch over the gravel and approach at a turtle's pace to avoid hitting dogs that wanted to chew on car tires. At road's end, I stopped and rolled down my window. A red-spotted Springer jumped up, paws on window ledge, and tried to lick my face. Watch dogs, these guys were not.

I heard a call. "Bo, Brick, Jenny. Down." I looked past the ears of the one who had to be Brick and saw a woman hurrying down the hill. Passing through the gate of the split rail fence surrounding the house, she waved, and I got out of the car. I judged her to be a shade under fifty. She looked like she'd given up eating three weeks ago. "Behave," she yelled to the dogs flanking me.

She thrust out her hand. "Welcome." Her brown hair, done in a bun with wiry wisps springing everywhere, was streaked with white.

"Thanks," I said. "I'm Moriah Dru."

"Addie Sweppington."

"Just the person I want to see," I said.

She smiled. Her teeth wore the color of one who drinks wine or smokes. "Down kids," she said to the dogs.

The dogs were pawing me, tails wagging. One, the bitch, licked my hand. "Good girl," I said, patting her head. Addie clapped her hands three times and the dogs sat. Just like that. They sat. "The Dog Whisperer," she said and laughed, her eyes blinking against the western sun. "You're not selling anything, are you?"

"No," I said, "but you look like you'd be an easy sale."

"That's me, one of those suckers born every minute. What can I do for you?"

"I came about Della Browne."

She lost her smile. Her lips pressed together. "Who are you?" I had my card handy and she looked at it. She gave it back. "I don't . . . People ask . . ." She shook her head and waved a hand.

"The *Scuppernong* was raised from Lake Lanier."

"Yes," she said and sighed as if Atlas had lowered the globe on her shoulders. "Yes, oh yes."

The lament in her voice didn't encourage me to say that I was the one who spotted it. "The case is back on the front burner."

"And that's too bad," she said, pushing strands of stray hair behind an ear.

I noticed the dogs had risen and wandered off. "You and Della were friends, I understand."

She leaned against my car. "We were." She crossed her arms and looked over the marsh. "Since childhood."

"The authorities say she was on the way to Hilton Head to meet you and other friends."

She looked at her crossed arms, finally raising her chin to me. "Let's walk."

Oh my aching ankle.

First there was the creeping grass and brackish puddles to transition. Addie plowed through giant cord grass and black needlerush like a farmer going after a straying lamb. The wet sour smell of marsh invaded my nose as I hobbled after her. We came to a rise dotted with spike grass and reeds. Way out in the marsh, a small house looked like it had been built smack in the middle of spikes and panicles. I followed her up wood steps and across a boardwalk to a boathouse and storage shed. Two of the dogs bounded ahead as we moved through the shed to the end of the pier. She sat and dangled her legs over the boards. I did the same. Relief to my throbbing foot. Brick sat next to me and I scratched between his ears. It's funny how some dogs take a liking to you, as Betsy had to Evangeline.

"I've decided," Addie said.

This was a time to keep quiet lest something in my voice allowed her a change of mind.

She burped a grunt. "All these years, I've never told a soul. You come here, accusing me of being a pushover for salespeople, and here I am, ready to gush out what I should have told the authorities when Della died."

"Why didn't you?"

"Wouldn't look good."

Wouldn't look any better now.

She said, "Della wasn't going to Hilton Head to have a weekend with the girls. I was in New York." She squinted at me. "I paint." She looked over the marsh. "Marshes and the sea, as you might expect. I had a showing. Small, but two or three times a year I go to a little gallery on Long Island. I sell out because everyone likes waterscapes with birds, and shells, and sea oats. It's how I make a living."

"Are you married?"

"Never been. Got close a couple of times. I'm a pain to live with."

"So am I." My own flipped-out words took me aback, but it was true.

She tossed her head in the direction of the big house on our right. "I inherited that monstrosity but no money. Takes a heap just to pay the taxes."

Maybe that's why she didn't eat.

She went on, "I was already in New York when Johnny Browne found out I wasn't going to Hilton Head. He called the gallery in a rage. He'd somehow learned none of the girls that usually go were going."

"So Della was going by herself?"

"Ha." Her chest lurched. "Della hated the beach. She was going to meet her lover."

"Who was he?"

"I don't know that I should say."

"And I don't know why not."

She spoke in a chattering whisper as if to get it over with. "Because, in this town, around here, actions tumble like dominoes and affect so many lives. That's why it could never get out."

I doubted that it never got out. "How did you know?"

"She told me, as a friend."

If Della told one friend, she probably told all. "Was he the only lover she had while married to Johnny?"

"Oh my no." Seconds seemed to turn to minutes before she explained. "An outsider would call our old families incestuous—not so much literally, but because we resemble one large infighting group. The lust for prominence and power goes back to colonial days when an invitation to a cotillion meant you'd arrived. Take my family. Toliver Sweppington came to Wilmington when it was called New Liverpool. Toliver established a small community south of today's Wilmington and north of Southport. My rundown house on the hill over there, named Highland, was built on a colonial site established before the Revolutionary War."

"That old?"

She grinned. "The original Federalist house was destroyed by a storm—one assumes a hurricane—in eighteen-forty. By that time, Victorian architecture had reached the New World."

Some would say that was a pity.

She went on, "Toliver was a cabinet maker from Virginia. He moved to Cape Fear to go into shipbuilding using slave labor. By all accounts, not a nice tyrant. Twenty years before the Civil War, his descendants established a rice plantation here at Highland—which the new money in our historical society calls Sweppington House. I haven't had Highland on the tour in several years, but each year they ask me. Maybe one day I'll say yes and they can see what happens when a Daughter of the American Revolution runs out of money."

I said, "It's a beautiful piece of property, must be worth millions."

She shrugged like it didn't matter and said, "At one time there were over a hundred slaves working the land. After the Civil War, my ancestors added peanuts and cotton and used freemen, who were former slaves. My ancestors were senators, congressmen, governors and councilmen—until my father, who woke up one morning and found himself penniless. My grandfather was a kind and gentle man, lacking the personality of a greedy man."

When she paused, I murmured, "Happens."

"There are ten families who have the same pedigree and some are in the same circumstance as me. Political fortunes crested and waned if the tyrannical DNA was diluted by kinder threads."

I said, "What you're saying is the founding families warred, but closed ranks against outsiders."

"You got it."

I was dying to ask who Della's lover was when she said his name.

"Dave Henderson was Della's lover."

"Dave Henderson, the lawyer?"

"Yes," she said. "Della was Henderson's client. He was dipping his privates into an already messy situation. He knew that Della and Johnny were beginning to hate each other."

"Are the Brownes one of those closing ranks families?"

"Not the Brownes. Johnny's family is two, three generations here. Della's pretty close to old family, but Dave Henderson is one of those ten, which is why I didn't tell what I knew."

"Didn't the sheriff ask you questions after Della's accident?"

"It was murder."

I looked at her and knew that she was thinking of the murderer.

"Johnny went after her in a rage," Addie said. "It's my belief he intended her to die."

Which she did. "And neither you nor Dave Henderson said a word?"

"Laurant alibied Johnny."

I love epiphanies. *So Johnny gave half the winery to Laurant in exchange for an alibi, only later to shoot him in the leg for fooling around with Candice.*

Addie said, "And Janet Blair was a friend."

"Janet Blair Cocineau," I said.

"Descendant of one of the ten families."

"Married to Laurant," I said.

"Who alibied Johnny."

My mind was spinning, trying to wrap itself around those four people.

"Snakes in a pit and I'm one of them." She got up suddenly. "Now get me back to my old house before I tell you everything I said was a lie."

160

I limped back to the house on the hill. She walked slowly to accommodate me, but never asked why I limped.

On my way back to the hotel I noticed fog drifting in from the sea. It looked to be the kind that portends gloom. And doom. *I only thought that because it rhymes. Didn't I?*

CHAPTER FIFTEEN

I was getting ready to head out to Beggar's Grind when Portia called. "I got a call from the precocious little horror," she said, not happily.

"Why did she call you?"

"You are not keeping her informed. She said she's been to your hotel three times and you pretend not to be in."

"I don't pretend. I'm not in."

"She heard noises."

"Probably the maids."

"They've finished the autopsy on Linette Parker."

"Cause?"

"Could have been strangled initially; the hyoid bone has an irregular mark. Her clothes kept her torso intact enough to show where the knife nicked a rib on its way to her heart. No weapon left in the body. No precise time of death. A week, about."

Surely the astute medical examiner wouldn't label this as a misadventure, too. "What's happening with Diane?"

"In conjunction with the Superior Court, she's under my jurisdiction. Child Protective Services will investigate."

"Relatives?"

"None located."

When I told her about the Sawchicsee newspaper insinuations, I heard her snort. "Up there, everyone's together in church. I talked to Sonny. We temporarily settled Diane's working schedule and living arrangements. Turns out she's a good student. If her grades slip, she's out of the diner and she understands that. And as far as I can tell Linette wasn't a half bad mother. Just a poor judge of men."

With that she ended the call.

Driving through thickening ground clouds toward Beggar's Grind, I called Web. "Anything interesting on Emile Cocineau? I'm on my way to dine with him."

"*Oo-la-la,*" he said.

"Do I have to watch myself?"

"I think not, although I've just begun to take him apart. He was born in Canada twenty-nine years ago. Emile's father died when Emile was six. Laurant became his guardian. Emile spent most of his childhood in Canadian and English schools. Never married. He lives in Chipping Campden, a popular Cotswold tourist stop. Lots of arts and crafts and games. Emile paints and tends bar. He lives in a flat on High Street. I haven't gotten into his financials yet."

"Dig deeper into Domingo Cardona. I have an odd feeling about things here."

"Your odd feeling is my command."

"Talk later."

"*Bon appétit,*" Web said.

Past the mill at Beggar's Grind, the car rocked deeper into murkiness, passing gardens that threw vaporous patterns over a house hunkered into the shadows. The door flew open and Emile bounced down the terraced steps. I got out of the car. He called, "Stay there."

I stayed, and he hurried forward, hands in the pockets of baggy trousers made from the finest gabardine, the kind you itch to rub between your fingers. His shirt was starched white linen with an oversized collar and cuff links. With the beard, he looked like an elegant gentleman from the past. "Good evening," he said. "We're off to The Grind."

He sprang to the passenger side and flung open the door. Scooting in, he said, "The table's laid. Hope you're hungry."

"We're having dinner in the mill?" Thoughts of being tied to a wheel turning slowly into the water ran through my head.

"Yes, ma'am."

I smiled at his slight British accent.

The car carried us through eddies of vapor and sighing mist. "We're low here," he said. "Always foggier than anywhere else."

When I could see the big mill loom like a ghost house in a gothic novel, Emile reached into his pocket and took out what looked like a cell phone. He held it up, pressed a button and floodlights made haloes in the haze. "We have lights," he said. "Don't want you to worry we'll be partaking in miasma's dim glow."

So dramatic, but he stirred my affections and that made me think I should be on my guard. "Wasn't worried," I said.

"I know you want to pick my brain, and I'll let you so far as I can, but first we dine."

Emile and Domingo had something in common, eating and drinking came before the inquisition. "My pleasure on both counts."

I glanced at him; his teeth flashed and, since his face was in shadow, I felt more than saw his eyelashes bat at me. "Park on the verge there," he said.

He was out of the car and bounding around to open the door before I could turn the ignition key. He reached down for my elbow, saying, "Watch your step."

I caught myself before my ankle cried for mercy.

"What's wrong?" he asked.

"Sore foot."

"Then we'll take it slow." That suited me since he was a bounder by nature—as was I without a sprained ankle. Holding my arm, he led up a slanting walkway, past the wheel rotating at a measured pace. Dripping water cascaded down the paddles into a pond below. The rippling splashes could effortlessly lull me into Morpheus's dreams. This was the stuff of enchantment and that began to worry me. I recalled Web's *Oo, la, la.* But Web had put a notion in my head.

Emile took my hand. "Water comes from a spring over there," he said, pointing.

The warmth of his hand comforted, and I looked at him rather than his pointing finger. Here I stood admiring this enigmatic stranger, bathed in floodlit radiance, who could be a murderer. *No. Don't be so dramatic. He only wants to steal the winery. But it's not stealing if it's rightfully his. Addie's story demonstrates it might be—if Johnny gave half to Laurant in exchange for an alibi. And if Laurant is dead.*

Emile interrupted my thought. "You still with me?"

I half smiled. "Yes, go on."

He said that electricity had been installed in the nineteen-thirties. Laurant put in a septic system and phone lines and that he, Emile, brought in broadband for the computers.

He touched my shoulder. "This is my home when I'm in the United States. The house is a dump."

Inside the double door, he opened an electrical box and flipped a couple of switches. Lights beamed onto gears and chains and wheels and a fat pole—all looking silver-dollar shiny.

Emile said, "This is the sack floor. They used a wooden drum and chain to hoist sacks of grain up here. Downstairs is a pit wheel that is mounted on the same axle as the water wheel." He pointed to the fat pole. "A system of gears turns that driveshaft from the bottom to the top of the building."

"Fascinating," I said.

His palm went to his chest as if saying the Pledge of Allegiance. "Really?"

"Really."

He lit up like a kid. "The sacks are emptied into hoppers. The grain falls through a runner stone to the floor below us. The milled grain from the runner stone—cornmeal—gets fed down a chute to be collected in sacks on the meal floor."

"The grist for this mill was corn?"

"Could also have been any grain."

I followed him across that room and through an open door. The door was one that closed on rails, vanishing into the wall. One of the first lessons a cop learns is to mark the exits.

Soft strains of Cole Porter's "Night and Day" filled the room. I looked at Emile, who was looking at me. It was an interesting choice of music, and I hoped he couldn't read my mind. "Divine," I said.

There was nothing come-on about his stare or his demeanor, and I liked him for it. The thought crossed my mind, though, that highly accomplished seducers know how to play their quarry. Being police, then PI, I am not easily seduced.

The room was a rectangle with no electronics or machines in evidence. A round ebony table sat smack in the center of the room on top of a rug of sumptuous reds and yellows, a sunburst to light a flame in anyone's heart. Cole's lyrics—surround-sounding in the room—had me imagining what an overturned lantern would do to this exquisite room. The walls were covered with walnut wood panels that had been polished to a patina. Eight chrome sconces, casting elongated silhouettes, had been fastened to the panels. The stained glass windows must have cost a prince's ransom. Standing in a corner by a short flight of steps was a sleek floor lamp with chrome curves shaping a woman's body. The glowing upturned porcelain shade served as her head. A mirrored corner cabinet with smooth round edges beckoned, and I walked to it and stroked the sweeping lines of the black lacquered wood. "Heavenly."

He stood by the dining table. "Art Deco," he said.

"I know."

"Originals."

"I never thought they were reproductions."

"I brought it all from England and France."

I surveyed the ceiling where a series of trays and coffers rose at least fourteen feet, each section having its own personality defined by color and geometry. A tiered crystal chandelier, looking like an upside-down pagoda, hung over the dining table, conferring rose light on the silver and glass settings.

"I'm not much of a cook, I'm afraid," he explained. "So I contacted an excellent caterer." He pointed to a basket on a lacquered chest. "Fortunately, it's supposed to be eaten at room temperature." He placed his hands on the back of a padded chair and leaned in. He batted his eyelids. "You know, of course, that Art Deco style implies pleasure, ease, overindulgence and unfettered allure."

I had a flash of paranoia. He was trying to seduce me. I said in a nervous hurry, "I love those old movies. Can we smoke?"

Surprised, he stood erect. "Outside, if you wish."

"Gatsby didn't go outside to smoke."

"Gatsby didn't have a two-hundred-year-old wooden grist mill to protect."

"And I don't smoke."

His lips turned up. "Ah, Americans. Land of the free except for smoking."

"Reformers syndrome," I said.

He flipped a hand and walked toward the woman-shaped lamp. "I smoke. Like the English, I love my ciggies."

I said, "Did Candice Browne . . ."

He raised a finger. "Ah, ah . . ."

I said in a rush, "Did you and Candice share architectural ideas?"

He grinned like a sly black fox. "She never spoke of architecture."

"What was your relationship with her?"

He closed his eyes like he wanted to beg off the question. "Must we . . . now?"

"Simple question."

"No relationship. I couldn't see her appeal, but that's me."

"How about the appeal between your uncle and her?"

"That never concerned me. It doesn't now. Come," he said, moving spritely. "We've more to see before we lose the colors that fog at sunset creates."

"Colors in a sunset fog before dinner?"

He took my elbow. "Unless you're terribly hungry."

"No."

He stopped at the bottom of the steps. Tantalizing aromas of oils, turps, brushes and canvas leaked from above. He said, "My studio, my domain." Climbing, he looked back at me. "We'll have our cocktails here."

"I wondered when strong drink would be served."

"Very soon we shall have our poison." He lifted a foot into the door frame. I was right behind him. He raised his hand, perhaps to flip on a light, when a shot roared through the rooms.

My gut leapt; my breathing stopped. No question it was a gun—heavier than a thirty-eight.

Emile sunk forward.

Unthinking, I grabbed for his belt. Another shot and he reeled backward. I braced my shoulder to halt his rearward fall. Holding him against my shoulder blade, I staggered down the stairs anticipating another shot. I managed the steps with his dead weight, but after the last, I couldn't hold him. He slid down my body and landed next to the floor lamp.

I laid my back against the wall; half hidden by the lamp, but should the shooter come down the steps, I was a dead girl. No way would the lamp shield me or be a weapon against him—or her.

Run, you fool.

The silence ticked and I drew in a lungful of air. Cole Porter played on. I looked at Emile, at the blood spreading on his starched white shirt. One bullet had entered his right shoulder. Suddenly the clamoring of feet resounded upstairs, someone running away. Moving away from the wall, watching Emile bleed in a garish pool of lamp light, I looked up the steps into the studio. Who was fleeing? Who had ambushed him? Evangeline, then Baron, then Domingo flashed through my mind.

The sound of running footsteps ebbed, and the hitch in the footfalls meant he was running down back steps, the way he must have entered the studio.

I bent to Emile and pressed my fingers to his neck. Weakening pulse. I ripped his shirt at the buttons and exposed two bullet holes on his right side. The most serious was the one below his clavicle; the other was just above his waist. The blood seeped rather than gushed from the clavicle hit, and I figured the bullet had hit a vein, one of the ones within the chest wall that carries blood back to the heart. I dashed across the room, looking for a telephone. Emile said the mill had telephones. I ran around the walls, two jacks but no phones. I searched the furniture surfaces, no telephones.

My cell. In my car.

I whirled around and looked at Emile, the strains of "Night and Day" crashing against my ears. *Stop that music.* I knelt; his eyes fluttered. "Stay with me, Emile." He groaned. I had to staunch the bleeding before I went for the cell. The flimsy table napkins were inadequate. No drapes in the place. I dashed up the studio steps and flipped the light switch. Overhead cans lit the room. All the walls were windowed. Spotting a corner closet, I opened it and pulled out rags, sponges, and tape that lay near rolled canvases. Gaffer's tape. Cloth, but durable enough. Back at Emile's side, I plugged a sponge into the bullet hole below his shoulder blade and taped it. The side wound, mostly a skin and muscle wound, leaked blood. A rag and tape would stem the flow. I grabbed plates off the table and stacked them over his chest wound. I said out loud, "Emile, I'll be back." He moaned. He was awake but in shock. "Listen to the music," I said. "Sing the words. I'll be back."

He moaned again.

Dashing through the sack floor, I got to the walkway. At the top of the incline I saw the great wheel rotating, but when I drew near, it stopped. I looked behind me. The shooter was close by. Waiting. I felt his presence mingling with the mist, watching, holding the gun like I would, like a cop would.

Nothing to do but run. Fast. On an injured foot. Reaching the gravel, I sprinted across the lane and dashed around the car, knelt and peered over the hood at the mill. No one. When I reached for the passenger door, I heard something. Movement. I knelt and picked up a rock.

A voice whispered, "Stop." It came from behind me. "Drop it."

I stood and let the rock fall from my hand knowing he had a clear shot at my back, my lungs, my heart. Unless he got off a head shot, I'd be better in profile, my arms shielding my stomach and lungs. I half turned and breathed out, "Why?"

"Don't move."

"I need to get help for Emile."

"No."

It could have been a woman; there was no way to discern the vocals. I judged him—I thought *him*—to be no more than four feet from me, otherwise I wouldn't hear the whisper. I asked,

"Why did you shoot him?"

"Shhhh."

"Emile didn't tell me anything," I said, feeling he wasn't going to murder me or he would have by now. I realized then that he knew Emile hadn't died and wanted to keep me here so that Emile would worsen, then die. I leaned toward the voice. "I don't know who you are and I need to get help." What else could I say? With a quick swizzle of my head, I made out a shape in the fog. Not tall, nor bulky, coat on, hat on. "I'm going home tomorrow," I said. "I don't know anything. Honest." I took two steps and he warned me to stop. I pleaded, "Let me get help." He started forward.

I pivoted on my left foot and back-handed the gun from his hand with my right fist. He lunged. I grabbed an arm and tried to spin him around, get a choke hold, but he was too fast and my ankle screamed. He elbowed my gut. Releasing my hold, I bent over in pain. The gun lay at my feet. Did I have time to reach it? I looked up. He came at me, fists balled and held like a prize fighter. I forgot pain. Crouching gave me an advantage. I rammed my shoulder into his solar plexus. He folded and gagged. I swooped up the gun.

"Bitch," he cried, then twisted and fled up the lane.

I cursed that I couldn't go after him. I'd never shot a man in the back. Although this assailant deserved it, he would not be my first. He wasn't the killer of Emile yet, and wouldn't be if I could help it.

When I pressed 911, I *knew* before I looked at the display. No cell service in these boonies. I shuffled and hopped toward the mill, up the ramp and into the sack room, into the dining room. There must be a phone in here. Desperate and sweating, I ran around the walls searching to another crescendo of "Night and Day." *I'll never have music on a loop again.*

Emile lay as I'd left him, paler, eyes closed. The plates didn't move on his chest and blood had spread and dripped down his side to the floor. I rushed into the studio. No phone. Emile had said . . .

Then I saw it. By the easel. An old-fashioned candlestick phone. I grabbed it. Please, please don't let the lines be cut. I lifted the horn-shaped receiver and got a dial tone.

"What's your emergency?" the 911 operator asked.

Chapter Sixteen

Ear-splitting sirens pierced the music while I lay on the floor at the bottom of the stairs. I could see through the high windows of the studio. The fog had lifted and the beautiful plum and orange streaks backlighting the dying sun were what Emile and I were to enjoy, not bullets and blood while lying together on his Art Deco floor.

Wailing horns joined the sirens. Untold times I've heard the cacophony of rescue, but I still got a chill as I lay across Emile's body. I'd rolled him to better plug the holes in his chest and side. "Hear that, Emile, they're coming," I said. His eyelids fluttered into near unconsciousness. I patted his cheek and told him to breathe steadily. His eyes fixed on me, then blinked rapidly as if he'd pinched himself from some untapped nerve source.

Sheriff Avlon rushed into the room, his gaze shifting from me, the human tourniquet, to the man himself. "He still breathing?"

"Chest rattle," I said. "Big gun. Forty-five. It's on the table."

He motioned two deputies with guns drawn toward the studio. "Check it out. He's got a weapon, shoot."

They scrambled over Emile and me.

"Shooter's gone," I said, rising. "I took his gun."

Avlon looked disbelieving, but he watched paramedics tube Emile for first-line drugs and patch an occlusive dressing on his chest and abdomen wounds.

"Where can I cut that damn music?" Avlon asked.

"Don't know," I said. "In some cabinet . . ."

I stood a little away. Emile's head lolled and his eyes opened. *Oh, Lord, don't let those eyes glass over.* When paramedics rolled him away, I looked down where he'd lain at the blood pool and prayed he'd make it. And realized that my eyes were wet.

Avlon looked down at the blood, then at me. "He's a lucky man, you were here."

I shook my head and pressed my lips together. I picked up the candlestick phone. "I'm calling Atlanta PD," I told Avlon and he nodded to go ahead.

I assured Lake that I was unscathed. Still, he requested and got permission from Commander Haskell to come to Wilmington. I have to admit, it's a fantastic feeling knowing your beloved feels he needs to be by your side after you've tangled with the devil.

I told Lake, "Darling, you really don't need to drive through the night."

"Five hours. I'll be there by one."

"Check the cop shop here first. I doubt I'll be at my hotel."

"I'll stay in touch on the way. How'd you treat Cocineau?"

"My body parts plugged the holes in his."

"I'm not touching that."

"I guarantee Emile and I won't be found in the Kama Sutra Book of Positions. Much too contorted."

The music suddenly cut off and Avlon walked toward me. I said to Lake, "Gotta go give a statement."

"See you in five," he said and clicked off.

Avlon said, "We can sit at that table." He meant the table where Emile and I were to have dined. "Don't suppose the gunman would be sitting down, leaving his prints."

"He never came into this room while I was here," I said.

"We'll wait for the crime scene folks." He pulled out a chair—

polite southern gent that he was—and I sat. He sat opposite where Emile might have sat at dinner. He removed a recorder from his pocket.

"Is this official?" I asked.

His grin was closed-mouthed, sly. "I haven't read you any rights, have I?"

For a reply, I gave him a wry lip twist.

"This is for information," he said.

I went into the minutest of details: our drive through the fog and mist, our conversation about the mill, antiques, the shooting on the steps and my interaction with the shooter. He couldn't believe that I'd disarmed a man holding a gun. He said it in so many ways that I got cranky. "I trained at Quantico so I knew . . ."

His mouth gaped a little. "You did the Yellow Brick Road?"

"Got a brick to prove it."

He looked like he wanted to say something like, *all that training aside, you are still a woman.* "Okay, well, that's enough to get me going. I'd like you to come by the office tomorrow morning. I'll make sure I'm there about nine and we can wrap this thing up."

"What thing?"

He fanned his hands. "You have to stop investigating here."

"Why?"

"Miss Dru. I respect the heck out of your abilities, but with this happening I don't want cross-investigations messing us up."

"I don't want to solve the shooting of Emile Cocineau. I want to find out what happened to three people missing from the *Scuppernong.* Evangeline Broussard hired me to do that, and I'm led here because they were present and past citizens of this state and county." *And yes, I want to find the bastard who shot Emile and escaped my choke hold.*

His blinking eyelids were a meter for a perceived insult. "This shooting might be because you're here, stirring up things."

"You can't seriously believe Emile was shot because I came here to ask a few questions. I didn't know he existed before yesterday. I met him and you at the scene of a burglary, which is more likely the reason he was shot than me asking if he liked Johnny Browne."

"I'm of the opinion that the cases are related with the winery smack at the center."

To refute that would be stupid. "There are a couple of people I need to talk to and then I'm ready to wrap up here."

"Who have you already talked to besides me and Emile tonight?"

"Domingo, Henderson, the lawyer, Addie Sweppington . . ."

"What's Mad Addie got to do with anything?"

"She didn't seem mad to me. Quite lucid on the background of this region's history. I find that it's a good thing to find out about the community where . . ."

"All that old family bull crap isn't this region's history anymore. She lives back then."

I didn't want to tell him that we were delving into Della's accident, so I hoped he didn't ask, and he didn't, yet.

"Who else do you want to talk to before you leave tomorrow?"

"I'd like to talk to the servants at the Browne house."

His eyes narrowed. "Evangeline and Baron okay with that?"

"Why wouldn't they be? They hired me."

"All I'm saying, and I'm saying a lot more than I need to, is that the Cocineaus and the Brownes were tight for years over wine-making. Now with the sailboat surfacing and it likely that the people on it are dead, Emile Cocineau was robbed and shot when he claimed an interest in the winery. There's a solid connection, and I aim to find it." His eyes shifted to where Emile had lain and then back to me. "And in the process I just might discover what happened on that sailboat for you." Their dominant glint irked me even more.

He looked up to see two men in white lab coats standing in the doorway. "Now if you'll excuse me, Crime Scene is here and we got work to do."

So do I.

Once I neared Southport, I had cell service. Lake was not surprised at Avlon's attitude. "He hasn't figured out yet that he's a fool. I'm nearing Columbia, South Carolina."

"You charter a plane?"

"I've been working, too. I've got Web and Interpol onto Emile Cocineau's life and times."

Paul Ardai, an Interpol cyber cop from Lyon, is more than happy to help Web ever since Web helped him track a Frenchman who was stealing the identities of international travelers.

"You got any reason to think Emile's some kind of international criminal?" I asked.

"Dru, he's been burglarized and shot at. Something's up with this guy. And he doesn't reside in this country, but in England, so if he's a criminal that makes him international."

"The sound you hear is me smacking my forehead, saying, 'Of course, why didn't I think of that.' "

"I'm completely overwhelmed by your capitulation."

I'd reached the hotel and said, "I'm home, dear."

"Remember our checklist. You don't know who's hanging around to get back at you for taking away his piece." *To say nothing of keeping alive the man he wanted dead.* "Keep me on the line until you're safe inside."

I sang lyrics from "Night and Day" about him being the one.

"You carry a nice tune so I won't reserve a place for you in treatment."

I found a parking place at the side of the building. "I shall go in like I was an FBI agent raiding a bordello." Locking the car, I searched the street. The mist had turned into a warm rain. I could smell the sea. The waves breaking on the shore sounded like the swish of brushes on a kettle drum.

"I wish you had your Glock," Lake said.

"Me, too. I doubt I can get a special permit from Avlon to carry now that I've been booted."

"We'll get him straightened out in the morning."

"You at the North Carolina border yet?"

"Not quite."

"I'm climbing the steps," I said, turning the corner into a cross hall. "Nothing as I walk down the hall." I came to my door, the metal key in hand. "At my door now."

"Any indications?"

"No, but this is an old place and uses metal keys. The lock looks like it's been picked a hundred times. Now I've turned it and opened the door. Don't talk. I'll find a weapon. Here's a lamp by the door."

"How about a knife from the kitchen."

"If I tried to cut myself with it, it would take all night."

"You're talking."

"This place is small."

I checked the two rooms—under bed and desk—the closets, bathroom and tub shower. I held the cell to my ear. "Clear."

"I'll see you in an hour."

"Bye, love. And thanks, I now know you care."

"This proving can be fatiguing."

Sitting on the bed, the Cole Porter song humming on my brain's main stage, I unbuttoned my bloody blouse and held it to my face. It smelled of old iron and gun. Wearing someone's life blood is unsettling, but this was Emile's. I stroked the streaks and prayed, then went in for a warm bath. When I came out, I spotted the black rose on my pillow. A note underneath it read:

"Emile is not worth your life."

Stupid shit, you forgot to lock the door once you raked the place.

I doubt I'll ever remember the words Lake and I exchanged when he came through the door. His whole body was taut and fierce as his lips pressed mine. My heart trembled in the hollow of my chest while passion bloomed throughout my body like a rosebud to full flower. We moved toward the bed where I'd pulled the duvet down, expecting a storm of unfettered craving and need and desire that would sweep us into each other until I couldn't separate myself, my own sex and personality, from his.

I don't remember falling asleep, but I awoke with the first smear of a foggy dawn and reached for my lover. I heard someone bang on the door, then I heard her voice.

Evangeline.

I sat up. Lake wasn't in the bed, and I intuited he wasn't in the suite. Was last night a dream?

Bang. Bang. "Miss Dru, it's meeeeeee. Eeeeeeee."

I knotted the robe around my waist and opened the door. She rushed in looking as venomous as an asp being prodded by teenage boys. "Ha!" was all she said as if preparing to strike.

"Evangeline. Good morning." I turned to look out the blind's half-closed slats. "Do you know what time it is?"

"Six-thirty by the clock," she said, as if I didn't know what six-thirty she meant.

"You'll have to excuse me," I said, going to the sink to pretend to make coffee. I can't stomach those little cups of coffee from hotels. I turned on the water tap. "You've awakened me."

Thumbs and fingers went around her waist. "I didn't sleep all night." She really was a gnome of a child. "You've been avoiding me." She sure didn't seem like a curious girl of twelve, more like a bitchy hag of thirty-six. What happened to Valley Girl talk? Or Goth?

"No, I haven't, Evangeline," I said, turning to her. "Tell you what. Let me get dressed and we'll have something to eat. I didn't have dinner last night."

"We invited you. But you didn't want to eat with us."

"That's not true, and I suppose you haven't heard the news."

The asp lunged with its fangs set. "What news? What are you keeping from me? I am paying you."

I held up my hand. "Stop, Evangeline, while you still have a private investigator." I went to my suitcase.

She relaxed for a fraction of a second. "Are you going to quit?"

Pulling out underwear and slacks, I said, "I never quit once I start, but if you insist on these tantrums, I'll give you your money back and go it on my own." I went to the closet for a sleeveless blouse. "I found that sailboat and I want to find out what happened to the people on it. With or without you or your money." *What am I saying?*

Her features made a pile in the center of her face. "You're supposed to give me reports."

"I got terribly tied up last night. Now go down to the porch and I'll be there in fifteen minutes." Wait. I didn't want her seeing television or hearing radio before I told her about Emile. I said, "Better yet, just sit down in that chair by the desk, and I'll be dressed in no time."

"You put on a lot of makeup?" she asked, sulking but inquisitive.

"Only when I go to cotillions, but I do need to brush my teeth." I took my clothes and twisted for the bathroom.

"I'm going to watch TV while you're in there," she said.

"I don't know how to work it," I said.

"I do. Channel Eleven has a flick I started watching before Uncle was up. *The Bride of Godzilla.*"

Fits. "Where is Uncle?"

"Downstairs. He's sitting on the porch with that snotty policeman that was at the lake with the dog."

I didn't have to wonder where Lake was any longer. "I'll be right out."

The four of us sat in granny rocking chairs staring at a transoceanic ship passing by.

Evangeline said to Lake, "Show me your gun."

Lake said, "I'm not wearing it now."

"Why not?"

"I need to introduce myself to your sheriff first."

"He's okay. You can wear it."

"E," Baron said. "You don't know the law."

"I'll find out for you."

"Thanks," Lake said. "Now, Miss Dru has some rather bad news to tell you."

"Bad news?" Baron said. "What bad news? I didn't hear anything on the television this morning."

"Emile Cocineau was shot last night," I said. "As of one this morning, he was alive."

Evangeline's eyes popped and her voice frayed into a ragged croak. "Another stunt of his."

I swear I almost burst into cynical laughter, but seeing bloody Emile . . .

I explained that Emile had been shot in the right side and shoulder. Precocious Pita wanted to know how I knew so much and I told her that I was present when it happened. She sulked for half a second then asked for details. I told them most of what happened, leaving out the mill and Art Deco history. And, too, my wrangle with the shooter. Baron, quick on the uptake, observed that the gunman could have shot me, too. Then I said that Sheriff Avlon thinks my asking questions probably got Emile shot.

"Bunk," Baron said. "He's in with a drug bunch."

Who, Avlon or Emile? "Nonetheless, Sheriff Avlon has asked that I stop investigating."

Evangeline bunched her fists. "He can't run you out of town?"

"Nothing so dramatic," I said. "But he doesn't want me to ask questions any longer."

Evangeline turned her head toward Lake. "Is that why you're here? You're going to ask the questions?" Say what you will, Evangeline was a sharp cookie.

Lake rubbed his knees like a toothless hillbilly ready to expound. "No, Miss Evangeline." She smiled and ruffled her shoulders like she was a princess. "I'm going to try and convince the sheriff he needs to keep Miss Dru asking questions. That's the only way he's going to solve who did this to Emile."

"Will Emile live?" Baron asked, the first indication these two cared.

I felt my eyes water. "I hope so."

Evangeline looked at her shoes, which didn't touch the porch floor, and Baron looked embarrassed when he asked, "What are we going to do?"

Lake said, "I can't think on an empty stomach. Where's the nearest breakfast place? I could go for a half dozen donuts."

Baron grinned like Rhett Butler and rose. "Our place. Frankly, the best damned breakfast place out of Charleston."

Boy, did he set us up for that.

CHAPTER SEVENTEEN

Lake followed Baron's car. I asked him, "What time did you get up?"

"About an hour after you fell asleep."

"You anticipated the visit from Evangeline?"

"The sheriff, but he didn't show. That's maybe the way they work here, but there's something off about this. You're a valuable witness, yet he wants to get rid of you. For all he knows, you could have been the target."

Lake had figured that out, too, but then I don't bond with idiots. "I'm supposed to report to Avlon this morning at nine."

"He can't compel you."

"He can show up in a squad car and arrest me."

"For what?"

"Do they have a material witness law here?"

"Probably."

"I told him I wanted to talk to the Brownes' servants. He didn't tell me explicitly that I couldn't, but . . ."

"So we're on our way to talk to the servants. See, I set you up for the chat."

"You set yourself up for a free breakfast. After brekky I'm going to see Emile." I hummed a few notes of "Night and Day" . . .

"You sang that last night. I thought it was for me. Is there something about Emile I should know?"

I reached over and rubbed the top of his shoulder. "Let me

183

tell you about the song. It played over and over while Emile showed me his very pricey digs."

"Money. Drugs."

"I don't think Emile was subliminally telling me about those unless he was going to offer me a post-prandial joint or five-hundred bucks for a romp. Do you remember the movie, 'De-Lovely'?"

"Yes, you liked it and I didn't."

"Because . . . ?"

"I don't like films that romanticize homosexuality."

We'd cruised along a two-lane until it widened into a four-lane flanked with fast food joints and gas stations. "I hate to stereotype," I said, "and I don't have animosity toward gays, but I can't help but think Emile is gay and was telling me so. The mill's beautiful interior—here I go stereotyping—is a tribute to a man with great sensitivities, and he is a painter."

"So he wasn't seducing you?"

I remembered his allure line. "We didn't get far into the evening."

"Regrets?"

"I had a few . . ."

We were at a stop sign. Lake reached over and gave me a side hug. "Maybe he wanted you to seduce him."

"That's most likely it." A dark thought took root, and I reached for my cell phone. "I'm calling Webdog, see if he's gotten anything from Interpol."

"The boy has to sleep sometime."

Webdog answered on the first buzz. "Yo, morning. How's Cocineau?"

"Alive far's I know."

"His set in England would be devastated to hear of his demise."

"Tell me about his set?"

"He's one of a thousand painters in the Cotswolds. He tends bar and lives in a flat on High Street, but in London he hangs with a group of school-tie swells, half are homosexuals and the others are addicts with various tastes. Now this lifestyle takes some serious dough. When Laurant disappeared, there went that money source, but Emile isn't hurting. In fact, he seems to be coining cash."

"His art selling big?" I asked.

"Nope. Paul Ardai says he's sold five thousand Euros' worth in the last year. Hardly enough to buy canvas and paint. He's got over a hundred thousand pounds in five banks on two continents. Paul found it fascinating that I was asking about Emile Cocineau. Seems Emile makes a lot of trips to Nice and Milan and Turin—with his art, of course. Paul and associates believe he has ties to the Albanian mafia, which has taken control from the Italian mafia, in the drug business anyway."

"Hmmm. Are they about to move on him?"

"Not that Paul's saying. These things take months to set up and prove. Deposits and withdrawals from his English community bank are for the usual stuff with an average balance of five thousand pounds. The four other accounts show large transfers in, then smaller ones out, like he'd sold a painting then portioned the proceeds into the other accounts."

"Most interesting, Webby." I watched Baron turn into the Brownes' driveway and said, "We're arrived at the home of Princess Pita."

Web said, "Portia said to call her when you get time."

"Will do," I said, pressing End.

Baron drove through gates that had parted electronically, revealing a lane hidden beneath live oaks. Lake said, "Emile's a money launderer?"

"He could be smuggling powder into the U.S.," I said.

"Not in quantities to keep up his lifestyle without risking his neck."

Once through the live oaks, we emerged into a sylvan meadow where horses grazed inside stone and wood fences.

I said, "Whoever burgled Emile's house wasn't interested in wills and codicils, but bank books and business accounts. Remember Laurant's Talisman Corporation?"

Lake gave a short head-bob. "Could be. Anyhow, the numbers aren't adding up and someone in his crowd doesn't trust him."

"It's someone here, not in England or Europe.".

Baron stopped at the curving drive of a limestone Federalist mansion with four white columns reaching to the roofline.

Evangeline darted from the car and skipped back to wait for Lake and me to get out.

"How do you like it?" she asked.

"Cool," I said, looking over the house and gardens.

She frowned as if she didn't expect cool to come out of my mouth. Maybe the word had gone out of fashion in her world. "It's old," she said. "Pre–Civil War and it takes gobs of money to keep it up."

Baron swanked forward and said, "E, the lieutenant and Miss Dru aren't interested in old houses and their upkeep."

Since we'd been talking about money, I asked, "The Browne pockets are pretty deep, I figure."

"Real deep," Evangeline said.

"Let's go inside," Baron said. "We've yet to have nourishment."

Inside, the foyer floor and walls, at some point in their history, had been lined with travertine. Rather ostentatious, I thought, and definitely not pre–Civil War.

Two large rooms went off the foyer. I'd seen this architectural feature before. They were parlors, or withdrawing rooms, representing separate relaxation areas for men and women.

Pocket doors closed off each room for real exclusion, probably to leave the men to their splendid Victorian isolation. The furniture went to French Provincial with some country French accents. Impressionist paintings hung on the walls.

Evangeline skipped past a staircase. At the back of the house an enormous pantry included a flight of steps leading to servants' quarters upstairs. A Hispanic woman stood at the door. She smiled at Evangeline like she had a knife hidden in her apron.

"That's Soledad," Evangeline said, tossing her hand toward the woman.

"Morning, Soledad," Lake and I said.

Her face broadened into a beautiful grin. "Mornin'."

In the kitchen, we met Benny, the cook. He was a large black man with a face so round and eyes so wide he couldn't scowl if his life depended on it. "I got your message, Miss E. We're all set for a meal fit for a hungry policeman."

Not me? Am I chopped liver?

Evangeline grabbed Benny's hand with both of hers and held it to her cheek, the first endearing gesture I'd seen. "Did you make sugar donuts, Benny?"

He beamed down at her. "I sho did, Miss Evangeline."

She swung hands with him as they walked over to a platter covered with chef's cloth. He picked up the cloth and she started to take a donut.

Soledad spoke from behind us. "Miss E, your guests come first, and you must wash your hands."

Evangeline turned, flames threatening to leap from her black eyes.

Soledad smiled at Lake. "The table is set on the verandah." She looked at Evangeline. "Your hands, Miss."

"My hands are perfectly clean," Evangeline said and stalked to the kitchen door, dashed out, and held the door for us to step onto the covered verandah.

It was a gracious setting, the stairs going down to a lovely garden featuring oleander and crape myrtle. Gardenias, planted around the balustrade, provided the scent. On my left, I spotted a pond with a water fountain. I walked to the rail and smelled the clean air of water and wind. Then I saw a tee box. I laughed. "Evangeline, who plays golf?"

"We all do," she said. "That's my practice tee for getting over the water."

"What's the carry? A hundred yards?"

"One-twenty. My success rate is one in three, but it used to be one in ten."

"Progress," I said.

We settled at the table, and Benny and Soledad brought out silver-plated dishes of egg casserole, bacon and sausage, a heaping plate of fat biscuits, gravy, cheese grits and, of course, the donuts.

"I love donuts," Evangeline declared, picking two off the Spode plate. They were so fresh, her fingers imprinted them.

I love donuts, too, and they love me so much they stick around, lazing on my hips and thighs. I didn't feel like running a marathon today to shed the donuts, but I did take a biscuit and butter. Eggs I can do without, but the cheese grits were too tempting. Okay, a half marathon today. Lake, of course, was filling his plate like a lumberjack who'd gone without food for three days.

An old Springer spaniel wobbled up the steps. "That's Dixie," Evangeline said. "She's named after the song." She rocked her shoulders back and forth and sang, *"Wish I was in Dixie, Away, Away . . ."*

Baron said, "We're at the breakfast table, E."

Lake looked up from his plate. "Dixie. Written by a Yankee. Most folks don't know that."

188

Evangeline bristled. "Daniel Emmett didn't write that song. His minstrel show performed it. The lyrics were written by an African-American woman named Evelyn Snowden to her father because she missed her home in Dixie. Some idiots see it as racist, but it is a part of everyone's Southern heritage." To emphasize, she shoved half a donut in her mouth.

I piped in. "My schoolbooks said the word *Dixie* devolved from the man who drew the north and south borders called the Mason–Dixon Line."

Swallowing, she looked at me like I had the brains of a rabbit. "Then it would be Dixon, or Mason, or Mason–Dixon."

"You make a point," Lake said with his mouth full.

Evangeline said with utmost authority, sugar-coated lips be damned, "The South is called Dixie because of money."

"You don't say?" Lake said and smiled at me. *Money* seemed to be the watchword this morning.

Evangeline informed us that a "dixie" was a ten-dollar note issued by the banks in Louisiana. The word came from *dix,* which means "ten" in French and they called that part of the south Dixieland. When the South seceded from the North, Dixieland came to mean all the southern states, even those that used Confederate money. Aunt Lorraine, with her tax fraud background, told Evangeline that fortunes were made back then trading dixies and Confederate dollars.

Lake looked at me. We nodded in our mind-meld way. If we were right, Emile was a master at currency manipulation, too. Euros to pounds to dollars. In Swiss, Mexican and Caribbean banks. To say nothing of good old American mega banks where they even set up corporations for the purpose of exporting money all over the world, corporations like Talisman.

Baron dabbed at his moustache the way I'd seen Rhett do in *GWTW,* and then said, "Never argue with E about anything she gets interested in."

Evangeline squared smug shoulders, letting us know we'd been *told,* and the meal continued in silence.

After it was over, I said, "Excuse me," and rose.

Evangeline looked up, her fingers coated with sugar. "Where are you going?"

"To talk to Soledad and Benny."

"Why?"

"Doing my job. Don't forget I work for you."

"I won't forget. But . . ."

"My job, Evangeline, is to ask questions of everyone who came in contact with Johnny before he died and Candice before she vanished. I have to be at the sheriff's office at nine o'clock. A little thing about Emile's shooting last night . . ."

"Johnny and Emile don't matter."

"Johnny and Emile do matter," I said and looked her in the eye. *Don't give me any backtalk, Snotface, or I walk.*

She mentally stepped down by shrugging. "Whatever."

In the kitchen, standing at the island, Soledad and Benny were enjoying a cup of coffee. Both looked behind me to see if the menace had come inside, too. I said, "Miss Lopez, Mr. Lott, I'd like a word with you."

Soledad frowned. Benny hadn't the capacity, but his eyes got a little wider. "Sho, Miss Dru."

Soledad said, "I can't talk about people living in this house, Miss. It wouldn't be right."

"I wonder," I began, "has Miss Evangeline said anything to you about hiring me?"

Both bobbed their heads yes. Benny said, "Sho did, Miss. Said you'd be heppin' her find her mama."

I said, "We haven't long to speak so let's get to the basics. What were Candice and Johnny like before he died and she disappeared? Did they get along? Were they planning anything out of the way? I'm looking for things that might have gone wrong, that you observed."

Soledad found something interesting on the fancy range top. Benny rolled his eyes toward the back door. But he shook his head. "Can't say," he said.

Soledad edged toward me. "He was leaving her," she whispered. "Kicking her out again."

"Again?"

"Other men," she mouthed.

"Was Johnny seeing anyone?"

"There was talk," Soledad said, leaning closer. "No one particular, like with Miss Candice."

"And Laurant?"

"Yes, ma'am. And that nephew of his."

"What?"

"I know for a fact."

"She was intimate with them *both*?"

"The uncle more," Soledad said. "She had them here. A scandal, it was. People may not say, but they see."

"How long was this before the Brownes went to visit the Cocineaus in Atlanta and disappeared?"

"Days. Him and his son was here. They locked themselves in the carriage house apartment upstairs. That's Miss Candice's private apartment."

"Did Evangeline know about this?"

Her eyes shifted. "She's not to go up there, but you ask me, Miss E don't miss a trick. She's ears-at-doors. Her mama's screamed at her over and over."

"Did they have a good relationship?"

"Miss Candice said one time she didn't know where that child came from. The devil maybe. Sad thing, I know Miss E heard her."

"That is sad."

Soledad's head bobbed, but her mouth turned up. "She'll be

fine when she grows up. She's at a stage."

I looked at Benny. "Do you agree with Soledad?"

"Mostly," he said. " 'Cept I think what they was up to, they was planning no-good."

"What kind of no-good?"

"Laurant and his boy wanted the winery."

"Johnny Browne had already given Laurant half."

"There was conditions, I heard," he said.

"That's right," Soledad said. "Mr. Johnny said, 'They won't get it all. Over my dead body.' "

And he was dead not long after that. The silence in the room hung with the thought.

Before I left, I took a business card from my pocket and handed it to Soledad, "If you think of anything that might help find out what happened on that sailboat, would you call me?" Soledad and Benny nodded. "Can I call you?"

She leaned closer. "Not on the house phone. You-know-who listens, but I have a cell number." She went to a recess that served as a desk for the kitchen staff and wrote on a pad. Tearing it off, she handed me the paper with her cell phone number.

"Thanks. Sometimes things occur to me that a simple answer will clear up."

Before I left I gave Princess Pita a short summation of my session with Domingo.

"My mother didn't like Domingo," Evangeline said. "She called him a greaser."

On the way to the sheriff's office, I gave Lake the information I'd gotten from Soledad and Benny.

"Somebody's lying," Lake said.

"Everyone probably," I said.

"So we have Johnny involved in two crimes that Laurant covers up—Della's alleged murder and himself being shot in the leg by Johnny. Johnny pays off by giving Laurant half the winery. Along comes Emile, being investigated by the international police. He maintains legal documents giving him rights to the winery have been stolen. Who stole them? Who benefits?"

"Evangeline for one," I said.

"She's as strong as potash, but I don't see her raising a safe."

"Pita had inadvertent help. Someone stole the safe for his own reasons, thus aiding Evangeline's cause."

"A possibility. Who?"

The same s.o.b. that'd left a note on my pillow, but Lake wasn't going to know that. The same s.o.b. who wanted Emile dead, but not me. That would mean Emile's attacker knows me and doesn't want me dead. Why? Because he liked me, or wanted me to finish what I started, that being to find the missing boaters. Who? Domingo? Henderson? Addie?

"I hear the wheels, Vanna," Lake said.

"I'm trying to turn the right letters, Pat."

I looked at the city sign. "Here we are in Pardo Town. How are you going to find out? Avlon isn't going to let you poach."

"I'll talk to the Feds."

"They surely know about Interpol's investigation."

"Don't bet your pension," he said. "Bureaucracies don't like to share, and the foreign police don't like the Feds any better than we do."

I said, "Emile's got a lot of money flowing in; he assumes, or knows, that his uncle is dead. He's done up the old grist mill like a Fred Astaire–Ginger Rogers movie set; he's suspected of being in cahoots with international drug cartels; he lives like a painter in the Cotswolds, but hobnobs with rich swells in London; and, to top it off, he's been robbed and shot."

"To say nothing of inviting you in for a cozy chat about his life and times."

"If he's playing hide-and-seek with international currencies, he has to be washing dollars with something that smells good."

"Eau de Heroin," Lake said.

"I'm going to the hospital."

"Why don't you ask him?"

"Think I will."

CHAPTER EIGHTEEN

Avlon wasn't at the sheriff's office. The clerk in the lobby told me he didn't need to see me and that I should have a safe trip back to Atlanta.

Whenever that is, which I will determine.

On the way to the hospital, Lake bet me I wouldn't be allowed in to see Emile, so naturally I took the bet. "Lay out the twenty," I said.

"Gladly." He slapped one on the dash. "And yours?"

"Mine is safe and snug where it will stay."

"No cash on ya, huh?"

Lake carried rolls of bills and hates plastic. I lose bills, so I need plastic.

At the desk of the South Cape Fear Medical Center a middle-aged woman with a sunny smile told me that Emile Cocineau could not have visitors.

"Is Sheriff Avlon here?" I asked.

"Uh . . ." She shook her head, not sure what to answer, but her hesitation said enough.

I asked, "Would you get a message to him?"

"A message? Sure," she said, her Southern voice full of helpfulness.

"My name is Moriah Dru. Tell him . . ."

"Such a niiiiice name you have."

"I'd like to speak with the sheriff if you could relay that message."

She picked up the telephone receiver. "I'll tryyyyy." Her finger tapped the number three on the key pad, and then slipped to the two. Apparently she spoke to a nurse, who put her on hold. Miss Sunshine lifted her face to me. "I'm holdin'. She's gettin' the sheriff. He's in with the patient."

It was an awkward wait, but finally she said into the mouthpiece, "Yes?" Then, "Oh . . . well, she's right here, if you . . . Oh, surely, I will." She hung up and looked at me. "Uh, he can't be seein' you right this minute, I'm afraid."

"I'll see him later," I said, turning to leave. I paused and looked back at her. "Is there a ladies' room on this floor?"

Happy to be of some help, she said, "Why surely. Down that hall, turn left, past the elevators, on your right."

At the elevators, I pressed the Up button for three.

The door opened on the third floor. I had two choices: left or right. A sign with an arrow pointed me toward ICU. At the end of the corridor I passed through double doors. I immediately encountered a sign that read: "ICU Waiting Room. Visitors time with patients: five minutes."

Several steps later, I was looking into a glass enclosure. A hexagon-shaped desk was planted in the center of the room, obviously the nurses' station where several men and women looked intense. Small rooms went off a hallway that circled the desk. I could see a man's profile inside a cubicle on the left. Sheriff Avlon. I walked back to the waiting room. He would have to pass it before he left.

It wasn't two minutes before he walked in, looking extremely irritated. "I told the girl downstairs . . ."

I held up my hand. "I have every right to visit Emile. Did you forget who called you? Who was with him when he was shot? Who was mugged trying to get help?"

He held up his hand. "All right, he's been asking for you, but you can't be in there for long."

I rose. "Thanks. How is he?"

He shrugged. "The bullet went through muscle and a main artery. They did a clavicle artery resection and put in a stent. He's got a catheter to deal with and aneurysms in other blood vessels."

"Will he live?"

He shrugged again. "Thanks to you he has a chance."

I swished past him, and he called from behind, "I'll be here when you get out."

I fluttered my fingers at Emile. He smiled, showing the tips of his bright teeth. His face lacked color, and he had various IV poles and monitors mounted around him. When he spoke, his pain was obvious. "How are you?"

"Fine," I said. "You're looking better than the last time I saw you."

His voice was weak and whispery. "You saved my life."

"I only have five minutes, so can we talk about what happened and why?"

He breathed in shallow huffs. "Someone shot me."

"Do you know who?"

"Didn't see." He gave me a long doe-eyed stare. "If you weren't there, he'd have finished me."

"Who stole your safe?"

I knew he was going to duck that. He said, "I told the truth about the will and codicil."

"I believe you."

"I want to help Evangeline." He winced in pain, not, I think, at the idea of Evangeline. "She's always gotten a raw deal, being . . ."

"Ugly?" He nodded yes. I said, "Evangeline will do very well for herself."

"I don't want the winery." His brow creased. "England, that's where I . . ." He seemed to deflate, like a balloon losing air.

I leaned closer. "Emile, we know you're a money launderer."
His eyes shut.

"We know you're being investigated by Interpol."
His eyes popped open.

"You have a connection here in the Cape Fear area, don't you?"

He almost grinned. "I could marry you . . ." He blinked. "But I'm not putting myself in jail for you." That much talking deflated him further.

I scowled at him without feeling rancor. "Emile, if they locked you away for money laundering, it wouldn't make one scintilla of difference in the flow of drugs or money, otherwise, I'd bust my butt to put you in jail."

"I guess I owe . . ."

I interrupted, "Who tried to kill you?"

His swallowed with some effort. "I put you in danger."

"Did you know you were in danger when you invited me for dinner?"

His sudden erratic breathing alarmed me. "I would never . . ."

"Is it heroin money?"

He shook his head.

I folded my arms.

He said with much effort. "I shift paper . . . That's all."

"Guns, human slavery?"

He grunted and shook his head.

A nurse ran in and looked at Emile as if he might expire on the spot. A male attendant, or maybe a doctor, stood behind her.

"Fine," Emile said, waving his hand, trying to suppress another cough. "Fine."

The female nurse looked at me, the male hanging back. "Your time's up, Miss," she said. "Past up."

Emile shook his head, his hand moving from his mouth. "I'm not finished talking . . ." He wheezed like he had pneumonia.

"I'll get the doctor," the nurse said, rushing past the attendant who came to the bed and readjusted Emile's tubes and bedding.

"Take it easy, man," said the attendant.

I looked past the nurse and saw Avlon standing at the nurse station. The attendant went out.

"They're going to boot me, Emile. Who shot you?"

He hesitated, then looked past me. I turned.

Avlon stood in the door. His manner was brusque. "Time's up. You got the nurses upset. Emile's their favorite patient."

Emile's eyes rolled to my face. He wheezed, "Come back."

Avlon said, "She's headed for Atlanta."

Emile breathed out, "Ahhh."

I smiled at Emile. "Maybe I'll stick around and we can talk some more about lacquering pine furniture."

Avlon made a boorish noise. I bent and kissed Emile on his cheek.

"My angel," he whispered.

I laid a hand on his cheek. "I'm coming back for that dinner, don't forget."

His eyes closed, but his lips smiled. *"Au revoir."*

I passed Avlon without a word. Two female and two male faces tracked me out the door.

Downstairs, at one end of the lobby, Lake had settled in where dispirited people waited at the clinic to be called for their sniffles or bunions. He was so engrossed in the newspaper, he didn't hear me sneak up on him, holding out my hand. When he finally peered over the top of the broadsheet, I noticed the twenty rolled up and stuck behind an ear. I also noticed a young man with his arm in a sling and a calculating look on his face, no doubt figuring out how to boost a bill off an ear. I snatched the twenty, winking at the boy as if to say, *this is how you do it.*

"Don't be so grabby," Lake said, rising, his gun showing from beneath his arm. The boy's eyes grew wide, his mouth parting, his front teeth protruding. Lake plays games with youths who are sooner or later bound for prison.

Walking across the lobby, Lake asked, "Get much from the transfer agent?"

"I made him feel like he owes me."

"I know that feeling."

We walked out the doors into the sunshine. He asked, "Where to for lunch?"

"It's not near lunch time."

"I'm hungry."

"I'm still bloated from brekky at the snot's house."

"I kind of like her. Knows what she wants, just like you."

"You're cruising for something."

"Not before lunch. Eating a hearty breakfast makes me hungry for a hearty lunch, an early hearty lunch."

We passed through Pardo Town, going south on Highway 17 when a cop car with lights winking from his grill pulled behind us. He yipped the siren in case we didn't think the lights were for us.

The sheriff got out. "Uh oh, what have you done now?" Lake asked.

My skin hummed against my bones. *No.* Tears came into my eyes. I knew when Lake rolled down the window. The sheriff nodded at Lake, who said, "I'm Lieutenant Richard Lake with the Atlanta Police Department."

Avlon introduced himself.

Lake said, "We came by your office earlier. I'd like to carry. My guns are locked in the trunk."

Avlon said, "We can talk about that later." He leaned in, saw my face. "Emile died."

I couldn't find my voice.

He said, "I'm sorry, Miss Dru. They figure an aneurysm. Nothing you did."

"He'd grown so frail before my eyes." I moaned and rocked forward.

I felt Lake's hand on my arm. "Easy."

"He never said another word after you left," Avlon said, his long hands hanging inside the door.

Au Revoir.

"Thanks for letting us know," Lake said.

Avlon shook his head. "It touched me, him saying '*O vaa.*' "

I thought about my efforts to save Emile while he bled on his Art Deco floor to the tune of "Night and Day." I stared at Avlon and felt certainty burgeon inside me, making it almost impossible to breathe.

Avlon stared back, the silence lengthening uncomfortably, until he said, "There's a souvenir tourist trap about five minutes from here. Got a few tables and chairs and sells some fine coffee. Follow me. I'll answer all I can."

I sipped hot coffee, letting it scald my tongue as penance. Emile was dying and I just walked out of the room. Why didn't I sense it? Why didn't I instinctively know? I was born with a caul over my face. Mama said it made me prescient, and there are times I believed I saw events before they took place. This was in retrospect, of course. At my birth, my father photographed the shimmery caul coating my face. He wrote on the back of the photograph what my mother said when she rose up on the delivery table. "She's bound for glory." Given my mother's dramatic tendencies, it didn't impress my father or anyone hearing the tale afterward.

"Miss Dru," I heard Avlon saying. "Lot of problems come

with blood loss like he had. You did all you could, and then some."

I had missed a big part of their conversation because I cried through it. Bawled like a baby. For Emile. For me. Lake handed me a napkin. I rubbed my eyes. "Sorry," I said.

"Emile was a nice man," Avlon said. "Kept to himself. Never a problem with the law until that burglary at his house."

I asked, "What do you know about the Talisman Corporation?"

He tried to hide his surprise and scratched his neck. "Defunct, far's I know."

"Shell corps are a way to funnel money."

"Then it's a job for the Feds, and they don't tell you bull crap about what's going on."

"Anything new on the safe thief, possibly his killer?" Lake asked.

"I guess we're looking for a killer now."

I said, "You guess?"

Lake apparently didn't like my tone. He put his hand on mine and warned, "Dru."

"I'm fine." I looked at Avlon.

He said, "Your sketchy description's out there. The gun might give us a name."

"I doubt it's registered to the killer."

"Prints. He didn't expect you'd get it away from him."

"He wore gloves."

"He loaded it. People load their weapons with bare fingers."

Lake squeezed my hand to keep me from further mouthing off. He said, "It's early yet." He looked at Avlon. "Don't know if you are aware . . ."

I felt myself stiffen. Lake looked at me and said, "Got to."

While Lake unloaded the information Web had gotten from Interpol on Emile, I asked myself why I felt so protective of him, a man I hardly knew. I've felt bereft before, but never for a person I'd known for a day or two. Somebody killed that beautiful stylish man who laundered illegal profits to support his lifestyle. Why didn't I loathe Emile? I think because I believed in his inherent goodness, but what if I was wrong? What if he had me fooled? I was in the room when his breathing labored, yet I didn't suspect those were his final moments. But he did. How horrible for him. For me. He said goodbye—*au revoir*—his last words, and I turned my back and left.

"Dru," Lake said, "let's let the sheriff get back to his investigation."

"You're just saying that because I'm crying," I sobbed.

Avlon rose. "Take a walk on the beach, it'll do you good."

I almost said, *I can't drown; I was born with a caul.*

When he stared down at me, an avalanche of ice tumbled through my body. I stood. *I know who killed Emile and I'm going to prove it.*

He put on his wide-brimmed hat and looked at Lake, who was standing too. "Lieutenant, in this state and county, out-of-state law officers may carry, except in public or private places where it's expressly forbidden. So strap on if you like, but I don't take kindly to folks going around me in an investigation." He looked at me. "Sworn officers of the law or not." With that, he walked out.

"You shouldn't have told him," I said.

"Why not?"

"You were going to the Feds."

"I still am, but I'm obligated to aid his case any way I can."

"Well," I said, walking away. "I'm not."

He caught up and fell in step with me. "Dru, my cooperation forced Avlon to let me carry and you to continue your inquiry."

We walked through assorted geegaws—cups, lighthouses, postcards—advertising the fabulousness of Cape Fear and

North Carolina "Where are you going?" he asked.

I glanced at him. "Take me back to the inn. For a walk on the beach. To think."

CHAPTER NINETEEN

When I walked up the last dune and crossed the highway, I saw Lake sitting in a rocking chair on the porch. I kissed his cheek and sat in a rocker next to him.

He was back from FBI's bureau office. He'd skipped lunch, dropped me off at the inn and, making sure I didn't have a razor at my wrist, went to consult with the Feds.

"You feeling better?" he asked.

"Some. How'd it go with the Fibs?"

"No one home. On a case."

"Emile, perhaps?"

"Don't know. You feel like something to eat?"

"Hadn't thought about it."

"Nourishment. Keeps the body and soul strong."

"I have nourishment in mind, but not with a fork or spoon."

"Ah, you want the strongest tonic known to man, or woman?"

"Something very therapeutic."

This wasn't a race up the stairs, clothes tossed hither and thither for a bone-jumping good time. This was a slow and thoughtful kind of love-making. The kind you savor with every stroke and nuance. We'd opened the windows to hear the surge of the sea. Nothing like moving to the ancient rhythm of our primordial birthplace.

Satisfied, we lay apart, lazing, with sweet sweat cooling our bodies. Lake rolled toward me and stroked my shoulder. "I don't know if that was for me or for Emile."

I knew he was going to say that, and I didn't mind. He knows. "It was for me. And I thank you for your help."

"I got as much out of the therapy as you."

"They say therapists do." I sat upright. "I have to talk to Baron."

"Great minds think alike."

"Trouble is Evangeline."

"Emile gave you some good advice. Put her in her place. She's twelve."

"I must get Baron alone, totally away from her."

"You'll think of a way."

"I already have—on my walk on the beach." I got out of bed, reached for a bathrobe, and said, "Rhett Butler." Lake had a curious expression, and I said, "You, my sweet love, are going to call and remind Baron of his meeting with the Rhett Butler Regulars or whatever their club calls itself. Judging by his bloodshot eyes this morning, Baron enjoys a tipple or two."

"And if Evangeline answers?"

"Here's the deal. I call Soledad on her cell and ask her to have Baron call you. You invite him to meet and drink under some Rhettlarian guise."

Lake laughed. "Frankly, my dear, that's a capital idea."

I went to my backpack and dug out the paper with Soledad's number on it.

Soledad answered in Spanish. *"Hola."*

"It's Moriah Dru."

"Hola, ¿por qué me llamas? ¿Está todo bien? ¿Puedes hablar español?"

"I know a few words. Everything's okay." I wouldn't tell her Emile was dead.

"Me dirijo a ustedes en mi lengua maternal."

I held aside my cell phone. "Lake, she says she will speak in her native language." I spoke again to Soledad, "Is Evangeline near you?"

"*Si, por favor. Yo estoy en el kitchen que en la despensa de cortar las galletas.*"

I said to Lake, "Here's a hot flash for you. Evangeline is baking cookies."

"Are you sure she doesn't understand Spanish?" Lake asked.

I asked Soledad and she said, "*No lo hace. Ella tiene las orejas grandes.*"

Big ears I can believe. "*Bueno.* What I'd like for you to do is have Baron call me at the number on the card I gave you. We need to talk to him without Evangeline around."

"*Yo comprendi.*"

"Does Baron, in his role as Rhett Butler, attend any meetings or anything like that?"

"*Si, mucho. Hay un nuevo libro acerca de Rhett Butler, algo acerca de su pueblo. Se diseccionar que en los bares y las bibliotecas.*"

I told Lake, "She says there's a new book out about Rhett Butler. The league meets to dissect it in libraries and bars, something like that."

I spoke to Soledad. "No libraries, please. Explain that I need to talk to him alone and pretend he's calling one of his buddies to have drinks and discuss something this evening. It's very important, Soledad."

"*Eso es fácil.*"

"*Gracias.*"

"*Gracias. Adios.*"

Half an hour came and went. Lake paced as I followed his every step and turn, my blood racing through my veins. "You're making me more nervous than I'm making me."

Finally, at long last, my cell rang.

Lake dashed to it. "Hello."

"George!" Baron's voice was overly hearty. "I forgot all about the meeting. So much is consuming my time now."

"Not too late," Lake stressed.

"I was just looking at my planner and lo here it is in black and white. You say I'm not too late to join the league tonight?"

"Come right along," Lake said.

"Well, then, I'll be at Pirate Coast Inn at six."

"Good," Lake said. "Thanks for letting me know you'll be joining us."

"Bye, then."

"Bye."

Lake took a deep breath. "It's on. Where's Pirate Coast Inn?"

"We have an hour to find out."

CHAPTER TWENTY

It wasn't hard locating Pirate Coast Inn. North of Long Beach, it had been built off a white gravel road and looked like a coaching inn out of Elizabethan England—half timbering, faux thatched roof, lanterns, wide courtyards in front and back. The entry door sported authentic leaded windows. Inside the small foyer, a door opened to the right and one to the left. True to English form, one was the lounge, easy to identify: sofa, chairs, no bar, and no sign of Baron. In the pub bar, I spotted Baron seated on a barstool, he and his companions having a fine time. He saw us. "Hail!" he called.

"Good evening," I said.

Lake gave him a pat on the shoulder. "Baron, good to see you out this evening."

"Good of you to call me out, I can tell you," he said, flashing his trademark grin. I was reminded that Clark Gable had false teeth. So did Baron.

"Great place," I said.

"One of the gems we hide from tourists," he said.

Lake said, "Can't hide a fine establishment."

"The society built it in the twenties," he said.

"The Rhett Butler Society?" I asked.

He shook his head. "The Stede Bonnet Society. *Gone with the Wind* wasn't released until the nineteen-thirties. How about a pint or a glass of your favorite nip."

"Pint for me," Lake said. "Dru?"

When I hesitated, Baron said, "Order up, it's on my tab, and then we'll adjourn to the Stede Bonnet room."

I ordered gin and tonic and, carrying the cocktail, followed Lake and Baron through the lounge, down a hall into a room that surprised me. I was thinking ship's wheels, compasses, schooners-in-a-bottle, but the Stede Bonnet room looked like a rich man's study. Books, a malachite desk, leather furniture.

Lake and I sat on small sofas facing Baron. He said, "There's a bar behind those doors, so help yourself whenever you need to replenish." He fiddled with his string tie. "Let's get to it, shall we?"

I looked at Lake and gave him the nod. "Emile Cocineau died today," he said.

Baron's eyebrows lifted, but the cagey set of his facial muscles said he'd known Emile was dead. "He was shot. That happens."

Lake said that the sheriff should have been on guard because Emile had been ambushed, and that determined killers get into hospitals by various ruses, even dressing as nurses or doctors.

"Mostly in books," I said, and Lake half-scowled.

"Avlon's no fool," Baron said.

Lake trained stubborn eyes on me. "He was fine when you went to see him, Dru. Then he died, suddenly. Smacks of something sinister to me." He sat back and crossed his arms.

Baron sipped his Scotch and settled the Waterford onto the coaster. "I can't thank you enough for getting me out of that house."

"Evangeline getting to you?" I said.

He took a deep breath. "I get no peace from her."

"Get in the car and drive."

He laughed. "I'd have to pull the spark plugs out of the other cars and take them with me or she'd follow."

"She drives?"

"Been driving golf carts around the winery since she was six or so. Graduated to tractors and trucks. Once, when nobody was home and her cat was bitten by a snake, she drove it to the vet."

"I get it," I said. "She's hard to shake."

"Fortunately, she thinks my meetings are boring."

I suspected E was right, but said, "I hope you removed the spark plugs tonight."

"That would make her suspicious. I told her exactly where I was going. She hates the Rhett Butler League. We can get up a meeting over *Rhett Butler's People* at a moment's notice."

"Rhett Butler's People?"

"It's a book by Donald McCaig. It's fiction, of course, but cleverly gives us insights into Butler's forbearers. Some characterizations don't jibe with Mitchell's, but it's become part of the canon and hotly debated among the acolytes."

Lake had gotten fidgety. "Okay, so we've got Evangeline safely at home, no suspicions about your impromptu meeting."

"Fire away," Baron said, rising. "But first let's refill. I've got a feeling this is thirsty business."

After the refills, Lake said, "You said you and Lorraine share responsibility for the winery's operations."

"That is true."

Lake explained that I'd interviewed Browne's lawyer, David Henderson, and that Henderson claimed to be the board's managing director and that Domingo was the operations manager. Furthermore, that Lorraine Bonnet was a board member in name only. To really rile him, Lake said that Henderson had never mentioned Baron's name.

Baron puffed up like a red-faced cobra. "Preposterous. Lorraine is an officer of the board. Finances, that sort of thing. When she's away I see to things."

"Does she do the billing and write the checks?"

"No, we have a service that does that. He's a contract

computer software guy. Of all the damned nonsense. Henderson wanted Emile in there so he would have control. Emile
wasn't going to come over here to run a vineyard. Domingo is
tight with Henderson, too. You can bet they're licking their
damn chops waiting for Candice to be declared dead. They'll
throw Lorraine out in the street, too."

Lake said, "They're dangerous people. She might want to
watch her back."

His head jerked. "What? Why, I never thought about it." He
shuddered, rather dramatically. "Preposterous."

He was all about preposterous.

Lake pressed on, "Lorraine had problems with the Internal
Revenue Service. What was that all about?"

If he weren't half soused he might have realized what was
happening. He said, "Lorraine doesn't talk about it. Goes back
to when Candice was married to Sean Broussard. Lorraine did
a favor for Candice."

"By cooking books?"

"It was over a corporation that went bust. Don't ask me more.
Lorraine's debt is paid."

I asked, "Why did Broussard leave Candice a dollar in his
will?"

He still hadn't caught on that he was being cop-teamed.
"They would have been divorced if he hadn't . . ." He sputtered
out, "Sean Broussard was a prig. Candice wasn't."

"I see you use the past tense. You think she's dead?"

"Nothing else to think."

"It's interesting about Broussard's murder," I said.

Cutting off my interest in Broussard's murder, Baron rose to
fetch another Scotch. I shook my head. Lake went for a beer.
Back in his seat, Baron said, "The slickest of the bunch is Laurant." He certainly wanted to segue from Sean Broussard's
demise.

"He was one of Candice's lovers, wasn't he?"

"Common knowledge, but she wouldn't run off with him."

"What about Domingo?"

"Johnny knew. Lorraine knew. Hell, everybody knew."

"Did Candice have an affair with Johnny while she was married to Sean?"

"What difference could it make now?"

"Broussard was shot in a funky bank robbery."

"You're off the mark if you think Candice had anything to do with Sean's death. She was inconsolable when he was killed." He tried to rise, but the Scotch had a grip on him.

"Sorry," Lake said, his face a study in regret. "Questions from cops can get ugly. We came here to find out what was behind the scuttling of a sailboat, and one dead man and three people missing. Now we have another man killed that might relate to the sailboat case. Candice is at the heart of it all."

Baron had his handkerchief out, wiping his forehead. "She's my sister," he breathed out. "She had her ways . . ."

"Like running off with Laurant?"

He snapped out the words. "Candice has the blue blood of Stede Bonnet running in her veins. She wouldn't run off with anyone."

The same Stede Bonnet who was hanged.

I asked, "While we're on the subject of blue bloods, what do you know about Addie Sweppington?"

He shook his head. "We Bonnets are transplants from Charleston. I can tell you with all sincerity that I wish I was back in our town."

Lake said, "Would it surprise you to know that Della Browne was likely murdered?"

Baron waved his glass. "There's always talk. I don't get involved." He swigged half the liquid and wiped his mouth.

"You know what I think," Lake said. Baron drew in his

shoulders for the onslaught. "I wouldn't be surprised if Johnny killed Sean *and* Della."

Frog-eyed now, Baron grunted. I could tell this wasn't a new concept. "Well, *he's* dead, we know that for a fact."

"And," Lake said, "Candice knew it."

"Preposterous. I dare you to prove it."

Lazily rubbing his cheek, Lake said, "What if . . . ? Let's say Laurant gave Johnny an alibi for the time Della was chased by a road-rage killer."

Baron sat up and struck his knee with a fist. "By golly, Laurant did. He said he was with Johnny at the vineyard when it happened. Candice was nowhere around at that time."

"But that would give Johnny a reason to give Laurant a piece of his vineyard."

"He wouldn't," Baron declared in drunken assurance.

I asked, "Who was Della Browne's lover?"

He raised his chin, his puffed face looked like a full moon. "She had two."

"One was Henderson. Who was the other?"

"Avlon. Jealous man. Very jealous . . ."

"You're kidding."

Baron hiccupped, then spread his lips in a knowing grin. "Some have it that Avlon was the man in the red truck."

"Then who was Avlon's alibi?" I asked, knowing damned well who.

"Addie Sweppington," Baron answered. "Before becoming sheriff . . . was a lawyer."

"Why didn't they marry?"

"He's . . . not old money, hic."

Aside from reiterations, we learned no more and so wrapped it up with a few questions about Rhett Butler to get Baron back in character.

Lake went into the bar and got Baron hooked up with a

member of his league who promised to see him home safely. His name was George.

We had dinner at a little place on the beach. I've never eaten better grilled swordfish and rice with rosemary and red curry. Lake, the complete beef man, gave in and ate grouper and fries. We walked back to the inn carrying a bottle of Blue Sapphire, weaving between late-night families on vacation and lovers leaning against each other. "I'm living with dead people," I said. "I'm a coffin case."

Lake looked at the waxing gibbous moon shining nearly as bright as a full. "Don't go preternatural on me, darling."

"I'm going to bite someone pretty soon."

"You can start with me, but leave my arteries alone."

In the kitchenette, Lake poured two gins and dropped a lime curl into mine, two olives into his. We toasted, drank off half the glass and walked to the French doors. A widow's walk went around the inn. I followed him outside where he anchored himself against a post, and I leaned into him and unbuttoned his shirt. The hair on Lake's chest is dark and sparse, enough to be sexy but not animal. I nuzzled my mouth into his neck.

"Ummm," he said, reaching his hand behind my head, pushing it more firmly into his neck. His soft full lips moved across my temple in little kisses until they reached my ear. It was my turn to say "Ummm."

"Better go inside," he whispered.

"Ummm."

We didn't take our time as we did when I went into therapy. Tonight was one that when need rises, need takes hold and says, *foreplay be damned. I come first.*

Feeling like I'd run the hundred-yard dash in record time, I lay with my leg across his body and marveled at the uncountable times we've made love and how deliciously unique each was. It should be ever thus. "You've raised me from the dead," I said.

"It's the least I could do," he said, his voice dog-tired.

"Want to do it again?" I asking, swirling a finger in his hair.

"Give it a try," he moaned.

"You owe me."

"I always will."

Closing his eyes and wriggling into slumber position, he was soon breathing deep and steady. I slid from beneath the sheet and walked to the window. The moon hung overhead, its light shimmering on the black sea. *No,* I told myself, *you cannot dig into the graves this night. You will not think about this day because this night is for recuperation, to rest and ready yourself for battle tomorrow.*

I returned to Lake's side and was asleep as soon as my head landed on the pillow—only to be immediately awakened. Lake leaned and whispered into my ear, "Wake up sleepy head, we've got to go."

Dawn was just thinking about rising so I could barely see his face. "What? Where?"

"Atlanta."

"Later," I said, moving to turn over. "You go on."

"Portia called."

My head came around. My body rose but I had no recollection of making it do so. "What's wrong?"

"Diane Parker is missing."

CHAPTER TWENTY-ONE

It was three o'clock in the afternoon on another scorcher of a Georgia summer day when Lake pulled the squad car onto the gravel lot of Trader Joe's. The car next to ours belonged to Portia. She got out. The sheriff's car wasn't here. Sonny Kitchens had invited Lake into the investigation in the expressed hope that the Atlanta Police Department's presence would keep the GBI presence less invasive. *How naive.*

Portia came hurrying up. " 'Bout time," she said, folding her arms over her chest. "Moriah, would you please call that pushy horrid child and give her your cell number?"

"What does she want now?"

"Where are you with *her* case?"

"I'll call."

Lake spoke up. "Any news on Diane?"

"None. Brunty's inside. He was the last to see Diane . . ."

I thought Portia was going to say *alive.* Instead, she compressed her lips so as not to go ballistic, I think.

Scully Brunty sat in a booth, chin nearly touching his chest. He didn't look up when Lake opened the door. There was no one else in the diner and Portia said that the entire county was combing the highways, hills and rills for the girl. They had dogs, she said, but not Betsy.

"Betsy's a cadaver dog," I said. "God forbid that we need her."

Sonny Kitchens walked in the door. "Hey folks, sorry to keep you."

Brunty lifted his head. "Sonny, this ain't necessary."

"Diane missing makes it necessary, Scull."

I believe they were talking about us being here. We pulled up cane-backed chairs to surround the booth and sat. Lake said, "Let's start at the beginning. Yesterday when she got here. When and how?"

Scully pointed at Sonny. "Him. He dropped her off, like usual."

"What time?" Lake asked.

"Noon." Scully looked at Portia. The oblique light on his glasses made it hard to read his eyes, but his body language said irritated. "Can't work but from noon to five. I got to get help in the mornings and evenings."

Portia said, "You're lucky I let her work that much."

"She's not overworked here."

"I'm looking out for her welfare, Mr. Brunty. Someone has to."

"We do fine here." He didn't seem to care he was on thin ice.

Sonny intervened. "Scull has kept to the rules, Judge. To the letter."

Lake projected a disapproving throat noise. "Except he let her walk out yesterday on her own."

Scully said, "It was her time to leave. She wanted to walk and catch up to Sonny."

Sonny's hardened shoulders pulled at his shirt. "I told Scully sometimes I can't be here on time, and he said he'd let her stay without working her."

Portia said, "Accusations over."

Lake asked Scully, "Did you see which way she walked?"

Scully stared directly at Lake, and I caught the light blue of his magnified irises. He said that Diane headed toward town and that it was also the route to her home. "I'm not her keeper. Someone else is, from Atlanta, taking her away from the place where she earns her keep given her mama was trash."

"No need to name-call," Sonny said.

I asked Scully, "How did Diane seem?"

He stared at me as if he didn't like me much; understandable since I'd sicced Portia onto him.

Portia said, "In case you don't remember, Miss Dru works for the state courts."

Scully studied me several seconds longer, giving me a chill. "Seems ever' one's an investigator. Special ones for special people."

I said, "Children *are* special people."

Scully said, "The girl could marry so she's no child."

"What exactly are you saying?" Portia's nose twitched like she smelled something foul.

"She's got her woman's days."

I could see thunderheads gathering. "How do you know that?"

"I got eyes. I had girl kin."

"You'd better be careful . . ."

Lake interrupted before the storm. "Did she have these *woman's days* yesterday?"

"Not that I know of," Scully said, looking down at his twiddling thumbs.

"What was her mood?" I asked.

He stopped rolling his thumbs. "Twitchy-like."

I remembered Diane. Twitchy-like described her the day Lake and I ate here.

Lake asked, "Who were your customers yesterday afternoon while she was here?"

Scully rubbed the light stubble on his chin and explained that he didn't have many customers at lunch. Sonny was there, he said, since he took such an interest in Diane, which made

Sonny look like he wanted to curse Scully to hell and back. A man and woman came in—strangers that Scully didn't know. Also there were two biker regulars from Gainesville; Orell, his cousin, got a sandwich; and another regular he called Bernie.

"Bernie who?" I asked.

"Janeway, the park ranger."

"Did the men flirt with Diane?" I asked.

Sonny slammed his hand on the back of the booth. "Miss Dru, I don't appreciate . . ."

Portia interrupted, "Shut up."

Sonny fired back, "I filed to be her guardian, for the love of Christ!"

Silence invaded the place like an army of denunciation.

Portia said, "Miss Dru did not besmirch you. Go on, Mr. Scully."

Scully shook his head. "Boys always cut a light tone with a girl."

"Janeway, too?"

"He was serious-like." Scully's mouth twitched. "When he left, Diane rushed off to the girls' room."

Sonny glared at Scully. "Why am I just hearing this?"

"Didn't know it meant anything."

"You saying she was upset?" Lake asked.

"Didn't ask her."

"What about Janeway?"

"Always the same. Uppity."

I turned to Sonny. "Where's Janeway now?"

"With the searchers."

That was it. Scully swore he knew nothing else and lowered his chin to watch his nervous thumbs roll over one another.

Lake, Portia and I were off to Landing Creek Park, but first we stopped next door. Orell was closing Trader Joe's to drive a busload of searchers somewhere. He said he hadn't seen "hide-nor-hair" of Diane after he left the diner at lunchtime yesterday. We got on our way, and I considered that searching this county would be a daunting undertaking. Three-quarters of it was national forest—dense old Southern forest with steep rises and deep ravines. A favorite place, I learned when I was with APD, for suicides to find a shallow cave in the limestone outcroppings or low-branching trees to shoot or gas themselves, not to be found for months or years until some hapless hunter wandered upon the scene.

Lake drove slowly along capricious Route 128. I couldn't see the searchers, but we spied three television trucks from Atlanta at a wide spot where, years ago, a wooden orchard pavilion had been left to rot. It served today as the search leaders' bivouac.

Lake and Sonny spoke on the radio. Sonny said he'd contacted the Hall County sheriff to find the bikers who were Diane's last customers.

When Lake finished his call and disconnected, I said, "It was Janeway that upset her."

"Sonny overreacted to the suggestion of unnatural interest in Diane," Lake said.

"Every man does these days," Portia said.

At the park Lake flashed the pass Janeway had given him, although the lights flashing from the grill would have done the trick. We passed parties of searchers and Lake spoke an old refrain: "We need to locate Diane's father, or relations."

Portia said, "No father listed on the birth certificate. Linette was a runaway from Tennessee. She arrived here when she was seventeen and has kept quiet about her hometown and any relatives."

"There's DNA," I said, unwisely, because . . .

Portia said, "You going to test every man in Sawchicsee and surrounding counties, as well as every Tom, Dick and truck driver passing through?"

"How about possibles, starting with the sheriff."

"I asked him outright if he was her father, given his interest in becoming her guardian. He volunteered to take a blood test. We've been busy up here since you and Lake went cavorting in wine country." She managed a dark grin.

"And witnessing an especially delicious murder," I said, eyeing her.

"You'll mend," Portia said. "You have God on your side." That impressed me all to hell. Porsh and I attended parochial school together, but neither of us came out particularly religious.

Diane, Portia explained, had moved in with Connie Scoggins, who was being vetted by CPS. I suggested that Connie could be a suspect if her husband was murdered and flinched at the expected rebuke.

Portia didn't like her judgment questioned and was always abrupt in saying so. But in this case, I heard caution in her tone, too. I said, "Someone up here knows what happened to the sailboat people."

"Connie?"

"Also Scully, Orell, or, yeah, even Sonny and Janeway. It's a small county."

"You'll never get people to talk up here, that's for damn sure."

We'd circled the park back to the gates. No Sheriff Kitchens or Ranger Janeway in sight, but a church bus was emptying its load of citizen searchers. Two deputies were shepherding folks past the gates. One deputy shouted specific instructions through a bullhorn.

I didn't think Diane was dead, maybe because I'd had my quota of death for the month, but if she was, whoever disposed of Linette in the lake might do the same with her daughter in some act of convoluted malice or contrition.

Portia said, "Diane wasn't reported missing until early this morning. Everyone thought she was off on her own. Even Sonny, who should know better. He mentioned Diane had a special place she liked to go to sort things out."

"He tell you where?" Lake asked.

"North of town, near the cabin where she lived with her mama. The cabin was a rental. The rental folks get it back next week."

"Let's get there," Lake said.

He picked up his radio and called Sonny. The sheriff told Lake he was on his way to the park with Janeway. Lake said, "Give me directions to the Parker place."

There was a moment of silence from the radio. "We searched it thoroughly, Lieutenant."

"I'd like to go there, but it's your call, your jurisdiction."

"I've no problem, but you'll have company. The GBI is on the way."

Lake cursed. "In that case, we'll wait for you here."

My cell phone played the concerto. "Yeah, Web?"

Lake and Portia were all ears. "Evangeline's jerking me," Web said. "Mind if I get the office number changed?"

"Then I'd have to give her my cell number and that ain't happening. Who's in your cross-hairs?"

"The affairs of the late Sean Broussard first. The FBI's got a list of corporate bank accounts that appear bogus. What they're looking for is terrorists' secret funds, but they're also rounding up shell corps that might be laundries. One is the Talisman Corporation. The agent being Emile Cocineau. Also Stepley Hurst, Broussard's successor, bought some of Emile's art. Seems there's a connect between the missing Laurant, his late nephew Emile, Dave Henderson, Adele Sweppington, and Stepley Hurst."

"I can't worry about the mess in North Carolina," I said.

"Now about your campers, I found Anna Graham and Gene

Poole. Facebook names and YouTube slapstick, but it was videoed five years ago. Nothing since."

"No clue about their real names?"

"In the skit, she called him Henry; he called her Boleyn."

"Henry the Eighth and Anne Boleyn."

Web went on, "Anne of the Goiter and Henry the Fat, but Anna Graham/Boleyn said off-hand to Gene Poole/Henry, *That's pretty dirty, Tommy.*' The skit wasn't high-minded. Rather crude, actually. Check it out on YouTube. They looked to be college age, southern accents, but not mountain types."

"So his name may be Thomas or Thompson," I said, watching the sheriff arrive with Janeway. "Keep Webbing."

I fell in step with Portia and Lake. "Web found the campers, but nothing since five years ago."

"They're key," Portia said. "If they're still living."

Inside the ranger's cabin, we stood in a ragged circle, Portia next to Janeway. She came to his shoulders, and I think he liked looking down on her. He'd learn soon enough.

Janeway stared at me then batted his eyelids. "Sorry you couldn't make it the other day. That spunky gal you sent hit me with an attitude."

"I wonder who hit first," I said.

"They were for your eyes. I put myself on the line with those documents."

Lake said, "We're over the documents. We're here to find a missing girl."

Janeway breathed in and pressed his lips, apparently seeing the wisdom of cooperation. "My people are all on it."

Portia said, "We know that you spoke with her at the diner yesterday and she seemed upset. What was that about?"

He zeroed in on the top of her head. "I gave Diane my condolences. It was the first time I'd seen her since Linette died."

"That all?"

Janeway frowned. "I don't know what you're getting at."

"Did Diane cry?"

"There were tears; to be expected." Janeway stepped back two paces as if to distance himself from her. "I always felt sorry for her—her mother and all."

"What about her mother?"

"I'm sure you've heard about her ways."

"You ever practice some of those ways with her?"

Janeway grinned. "If I were to practice those ways, Judge Devon, it would be in Gainesville or Atlanta. This is a small place, in case you haven't noticed."

"I noticed, and I haven't forgotten that this park . . ." She stabbed her finger at the floor. "That this park, which comes under your supervision, is where some kids saw a boat brought out of the water the night three people disappeared. It is from the boat ramp in this park where, most likely, Linette Parker's body went into the lake."

Janeway lifted his chin. "I can't answer for the vagaries of kids on dope, and yes, somebody can put a boat in and out of the water at night. If you can find some money for me, I'll hire a night security guard."

Portia closed her eyes for five seconds. "Once you said *your condolences* to Diane Parker, thus upsetting her, did you ask her to meet you somewhere?"

Janeway exploded, "No, I did not ask her to meet me. The implication is horrendous, damn near slanderous."

Portia waved her hand back. "That's all."

Janeway marched out and Sonny said, "Never want to be in the box in your courtroom, Judge."

"Don't want you there," she said, and stalked out, maybe to catch up to and harass Janeway further.

CHAPTER TWENTY-TWO

Lake drove Portia back to the diner and her car. She was bound for Atlanta as the guest of honor at a media event where she would be roasted. I was to attend, but the investigation trumped a night of humor.

"She's a kicker," Sonny Kitchens said as we got in his cruiser and headed for the boat ramp.

"She'll bust into hell to find Diane," I said. "So will I."

His eyes blurred with care and he nodded. "That little girl thinks she can solve her own problems now her mama's gone." He looked out the windshield and let his eyes roam the sludgy lake. "She never had a real childhood. Her mama started leaving her by herself when she was six, seven years old. You grow up fast in the country, but not that fast."

I got out of the cruiser and walked onto a long, narrow dock beside the boat ramp. The stagnant shallow water smelled of dead fish and old motor oil. "How long is the shoreline in this county?" I asked.

"About half mile west of here," he said. "Couple hundred yards west of here, Sawchicsee County ends. Sawchicsee is the state's newest county. It was created when the Corps made the lake. They blasted rock here to make a ramp. Where we're standing is the only access to the lake from the park." He turned to face west. "There's a marina off the main channel 'bout where the county starts."

I looked east, to where a mass of stones created a ridge.

"Someone could throw a body off that ridge."

"Wouldn't carry out into the lake. Be stuck in trees and ravines."

"I would say that's a good place to dump a body then."

"Used to be a lot of feuds over moonshine, marijuana, and plain ol' meanness . . ."

I picked out random details of the land. "You saying plain ol' meanness isn't happening now?"

"More than ever, but things change. Several years ago, climbers found the remains of five people, all in different stages of decay. Rappelling the other side of the cliff has become popular, so bodies aren't turning up any longer. They still find guns though."

Lake's squad car pulled up and I watched as he walked the boards, his brow pulling together like his mind was churning on something. My best guess, he'd gotten a call from the brass.

I asked Sonny, "Where's a good place to stay overnight?"

"Sawchicsee Inn, a mile from the diner, near town." I'd seen it. A white concrete block motel that had maybe six doors. "Nothing fancy, but clean," he said.

Lake came up. I said, "Lieutenant. You look hassled."

"Got to get back. Suspect arrested. You going or staying?"

I didn't have to think twice. "Staying. There's an inn."

"Thought so." His lip twisted; he didn't like it, but said, "You need a car."

I looked at Sonny. "Any rental agencies around?"

"Cumming. I can get you there."

I turned to Lake. "So I'm set."

"Cumming's not too much out of my way," Lake said.

I turned to Sonny. "So I'm set."

"I guess you are," he said. "I'll see to your room at the inn."

"Take care of her," Lake said.

"Sure will, but I got a hunch she's good at taking care of herself."

"Bet on it." Lake backed away, taking my arm. We walked to Lake's car. "I don't like leaving you here."

"I'll be fine. You heard the sheriff."

"What do you plan to do?"

"Go to the Parkers' cabin. The GBI won't mess with me. I believe Diane's hiding herself."

Lake folded his arms across his chest. "Because she doesn't like what's happening to her?"

"Either that or she's afraid. I'll need to get my gun. Snakes in the woods."

"Yeah, and not only reptiles."

My gun was in the glove compartment of his car. I'd have to talk to Sonny about carrying it. Lake unlocked the glove box and got out my ankle holster that carried the Glock 33, with nine .357 SIG rounds in the magazine.

There was a tap on Lake's window. Sonny. Lake slid the glass down, and I watched Sonny's eyes widen. I held the gun up. "Permission? I'm licensed."

He studied the gun and silently assented. "You're all set at the motel," he said, backed away and waved.

I strapped the holster to my ankle.

"Don't get into a situation where you have to use it," Lake said.

"Have I ever?"

"Too many times."

On the way to Cumming, Lake said that his FBI friend in Atlanta told him that Stepley Hurst had been canned by the bank's board of directors. He was undergoing interrogation with his attorneys present and had been relieved of his passport. But did Stepley have Sean Broussard murdered, arrange the theft of Emile's safe and, in the end, arrange Emile's murder?

He wasn't the son-of-a-bitch I had in mind.

At Thrifty Rentals I got a mid-size Ford. Lake complained of hunger and spotted a hometown take-out place that fried the best chicken I've put in my mouth. I hadn't eaten three squares in a row in some time and didn't realize how starved I was.

Meal over, it was time to let go of Lake. For no particular reason, I hated to, but on the other hand, I had a few places I wanted to go, and it's hard to wrestle the lead away from a bona fide police lieutenant, even if he pretended to let me.

The western sun had begun its descent into the forest. It looked like a basketball with the tree branches holding back its fall through the hoop of leaves.

I'd cell-phoned the sheriff on the way back to his town. Search parties had boarded buses back to base. No sign of Diane. I drove into the town proper. No one on the streets. The fading day and the reality of an unknown tomorrow seeded the furrows of my brain with blind belief. Blind because I had no guide through the darkness except belief that I would find Diane, and when I did I would find the missing boaters. My eyes roamed the town square with skittish anticipation and settled on the ice cream store that was still open. Not surprising since there were no liquor stores or bars in Sawchicsee County. What else to comfort the savage gut? Two-bit wine? I'd traveled a long way from Cape Fear's grape country, so very far away from the late Emile's and Domingo's sophisticated lives.

Pulling the rental into a slanted slot, I got out and walked in. A meaty-looking woman worked behind the counter, making what looked like waffles. She said, "Jist a minute."

"No hurry," I said, sitting on a stool and watching her. She put the lid on a round waffle maker and wiped her hands on her chef's apron. It looked clean, except for a few swipes of batter.

She had a jolly face, all cheeks and chin. She looked familiar. She said, "What can I get you? Supposed to be closed up now, but I had some folks a little while ago wanting ice cream. They'd been going all day looking for a girl what wandered off."

"I know Diane," I said. "From Scully's diner."

"Ahhh, t'was bad. Shouldn't of happened, but some folks don't live according to the Lord."

"How well did you know Diane and her mother?"

She looked back at her waffle maker from which steam poured. "Say," she said, walking to it, "those cones are 'bout to come out. Would you like a fresh one?"

"Please."

She opened the appliance, picked up a long fork and urged the flat waffle from the bottom of the maker. She laid it on wax paper to cool. "Won't be but a minute, I can roll it. What you like in it?"

"Chocolate."

She grinned, showing crooked teeth. "Chip, almond, Swiss, plain?"

"Plain."

She flipped the flat waffle cone over, then picked it up and twisted it into a cone—just like that, and said, "Let 'er cool some more, or you'll have chocolate soup."

"Let me introduce myself," I said. "I'm Moriah Dru."

"I know you, Miss."

"My goodness, if I've forgotten your name—I'm . . ."

"We never met. I'm Gussie, Orell Brunty's wife."

"Nice to meet you. I bought wine from Orell."

She shook her head. "Orell pushes that wine off on city folks who don't like it like we do."

"I wanted to try it."

"Well, what did you think?"

"I haven't yet. I've been busy trying to find out what happened to three people who disappeared on that sailboat they found. And now Diane."

"You're a detective, too?"

"Private detective."

She squinted her eyes like I was an exotic bug, and then scooped two giant balls of chocolate into the waffle cone and handed it to me. "On me."

"You work too hard to give your ice cream away."

"I make it back, don't you worry."

"Can I ask you about Diane?"

"You can, don't know if I can tell you what you want to know."

She confirmed that Diane wandered all over the county by herself when she wasn't in school or filling in at the diner for her mama and that Diane now lived with Connie and everyone was keeping an eye on her, but then she just ups and runs off. And, yes, she said it was too bad about Mr. Scoggins being killed like that.

I licked the soft chocolate fast so it wouldn't run down my arm, then said, "Connie thinks he was shot on purpose."

"Everybody's got somebody who'd like to kill them; don't suppose Boyd was any different."

I sucked at the ice cream to stem the flow of chocolate. She went to fetch extra napkins. I said, "He saw those young people camping in the park the night the sailboat sank."

She capped the container of batter and turned off the waffle maker. "You treat everbody with respect like the Lord wants, and you don't have a call to kill or be killed. Mind your own business, that's the best way."

"Was Diane unhappy with Connie Scoggins?"

"The court said, and she went. Poor thing. Hope she didn't run off to Hollywood."

Did girls do that anymore?

I wadded the napkin and soggy cone together, and she took

the ball and tossed it in the trash can. "Tch," she mouthed. "What'd I say about minding your own business?" Gussie untied her apron and came around the counter. "Scully treated that girl right, and what did he get for it? Reported to the authorities."

"I talked to Scully today. He seems an honest, thoughtful man."

"Scully is a quiet man, lives by hisself now his mama died. Five years now she's gone. Seems like yesterday. Always thought ol' Scully would marry after his mama died, but he never did. Ain't good for a man not to."

I got off the stool. "If you think of any place Diane could be, will you let me know? I'm staying at the Sawchicsee Inn."

"That roach trap?"

"Oh my." I have a real aversion to roaches—and spiders. Where's there one, there's a million.

"You want to stay someplace nice?"

Who doesn't? "That would be good, yes."

She headed for the telephone mounted on the wall. Don't see many of those anymore, and I thought of Emile and my dash around his lovely grain mill looking for a telephone. Gussie was saying, ". . . Rent these places. Not many renters in this kind of weather. You take the snow in the winter, you got lovers wanting cabins, going naked in the snow, you wouldn't believe."

"Who rents cabins?" I asked, remembering that Orell said something . . .

"Scully," she said. "The cleanest cabins in north Georgia, and quite nicely decorated, too, if I do say so myself." Ten guesses who did the decorating.

Anyway, a phone call to Scully and I was booked into a roach-less, spider-less cabin. I felt a serendipitous thrill and, at the same time, a peculiar tug of doubt. She drew me a map and told me turn by turn how to get to Scully's Cabins. I started to leave, but asked, "Who rented the Parkers their place?"

"Why, Scully—if you call it rent. He never took a nickel from Linette."

I wondered why.

CHAPTER TWENTY-THREE

The primitive woods hovered alongside the gravel road with the bright moon high and grinning. *Hey diddle, diddle, The cat and the fiddle, The cow jumped over the moon. The little dog laughed to see such sport, And the dish ran away with the spoon.* I recalled the bawdy origins of that rhyme. Diddle is a dance. The cow represents humping or being deliriously happy; which could mean both. The little dog was the Dog Star and the dish was a maid that ran away with a mad man. Candice the dish, Laurant the mad man. Were they off humping and spooning under the Dog Star? My gut said no.

The night was also bursting with stars, but I felt dark and disturbed like I could panic in a blink of an eye. I pulled up to a wood cabin with red shutters and got out of the car. Two rocking chairs sat on the little porch. I lowered my tired body into one. The resinous scent of pine sunk into my skin while I waited for Scully.

He was almost pleasant when he unlocked the cabin door. The cold air smacked me in the face. The air conditioner was grinding like a log truck up a steep grade. Scully apparently had hoofed it up, or down, here to turn it on after the call because, surely, he wouldn't waste money on A/C when no one was here.

Otherwise, the little place featuring an oval braided rug and an Early American pull-out couch eased my tension. Scully set my overnighter down, and I went to inspect the kitchen—one larger than I expected—and a bedroom with enough space for two queen beds and some chests. The cottage could accommodate three hunters, or three fishermen, or an amorous couple looking to romp in the snow. Or me, edgy and dead tired and ready to snuggle into one of the queens.

Back in the living room, Scully stood where he'd entered and appeared to expect a compliment, and I gave him one. "Nice place. I like it."

He shrugged. "Don't provide a phone no more. People bring their own."

"Like me," I said.

He turned for the door. "I put some bottled water in the refrigerator and two Cokes, some juice. Better than drinking from the tap. Bread and butter in the freezer, toaster in the cabinet. I treat my guests good."

"Thanks," I said to his back. "I'm happy to pay you for your hospitality."

"No," is all he said.

"Mr. Brunty?"

He glanced over his shoulder.

"I'd like to ask about the four people who were on the sailboat?"

He bobbed his head. "Okay."

"Is it possible they came into your restaurant at any time in the days or weeks before one was killed and the other three disappeared?"

He had a way of getting light to reflect off the lens of his glasses. "The proper authorities asked me and I told them the truth. It's possible, I reckon, but I don't remember everybody that eats at my place. Four year later, I still don't."

The proper authorities. That's not me, in his opinion. "Do you grow and sell grapes?"

"Me and Orell both grow, but don't sell much except wine."

"Then you wouldn't have done business with Johnny Browne?"

"Don't know him, never seen him except when the proper authorities showed pictures of them four."

"Some years before Johnny Browne was killed, a man named Laurant Cocineau came to this region to scout out vineyards. Since your store is on the main highway, I thought it possible he may have stopped in asking about grapes."

"Don't recall ever seeing a man of his looks." He pushed his glasses against his forehead. "There's more than one eating place in this county. There's places over in Dawsonville and Cumming. People pass by me on the way to them places in guide books, thinking the food's better in a guide book. At gas stations, you'll find where the good places are." Loquacious for Scully.

I grinned. "You serve the best breakfast in the mountains."

"You didn't eat much," he reminded me.

"I'm not much of an eater when I'm on a case."

He grabbed the door knob, twisted, pulled and was out before I could think of anything else to say, like where's the office and when do I pay?

Nothing for it but to call Evangeline. I could always put a block on her calls or change cell numbers later. But I got lucky. No cell service. I went outside and sat in a rocking chair and tried again—nary a dash on the service line. Maybe I'd tell Scully he wasn't doing his guests any favors not having a landline. What if the cabin caught fire?

Inside, I jacked down the A/C, pulled the shades and drew the drapes, then stripped to my bra and panties. Arms to the ceiling, hands clasping, back arched, I stretched, and then collapsed forward to touch my toes. Thus began my fitness routine for my butt, arms, legs, abs. Lastly, I straddled an imaginary two-foot box on the floor and stepped into the box with my right foot followed by my left, then out with my right and then with my left. This I did until my heart started to race. My cardio.

In the bathroom, not a lot of pressure came from the tap, but finally the tub was half full. I stepped into the tepid water. Suddenly, I heard a cacophony of hounds followed by a booming explosion—shotgun. Close. I jumped up and out of the water and reached for a thin towel to cover myself. The dogs sounded like they were about to come through the door. I can dress fast, and did. Barefoot, I hurried to the door. Ear against the wood, I listened and waited. The hounds were outside, whining and moving restlessly as if waiting for the master. Soon the low grunts of a man's voice carried beneath the threshold and hinge cracks. The grunting commands receded along with the shuffle and whines of the hounds. At the window, I drew a drape aside and saw shapes in the shadows, the hounds, a man, the broad shoulders hunched, the hips narrow, wearing a cap. Soon his retreating form was hidden by the thick oaks and scrub pine.

I blew out my breath, realizing I'd been holding it while my heart beat out a rhythm close to a rumba. *What the hell was that all about?* With the cabin lights on, anyone in the woods could see far enough away to circumvent it. Yet, he had intruded. And I thought intentionally. Was it Scully? Was he trying to intimidate me? Why? I reviewed our conversation of an hour ago and the conversation today at the diner. Clearly, he didn't like what Lake, Portia and I represented. Clearly, he didn't like us messing in his life and territory. So why did he let me stay in one of his cabins, suggesting I was a welcome guest, not a prying one? Was he setting me up for some evil deed?

Forget the silk nightie. I put the gun on the scarred maple end table next to my head and lay down fully clothed. I couldn't possibly go to sleep, I thought, right before I spiraled downward into exhausted slumber.

I awoke to the sound of shoes squishing through pine straw and leaves. I reached for the Glock thinking I'd been better off with the roaches and the spiders.

Dry-mouthed, I peered between the crack in the drapes. A man walked forward like a specter from the woods. He was smoking a cigarette. Should I rip open the door and demand an answer for his intrusiveness? At that moment he looked at the window where I stood, the light from the moon reflecting in his glasses. Scully. Damn the man. I almost gave in to compulsion, but he turned and hurried up the path where the hounds and the other figure had disappeared.

I slept on and off while sitting on the pull-out sofa in the living room, gun on my knee, pointed toward the door. My watch said six-thirty when a pinkish glow came through the pines.

Time for a talk with the concierge.

I packed, closed up the place and walked outside. In closing the door, I saw a decorative sign nailed to it that told me I had spent the night in Wolf Cabin. Beneath that sign was a plaque that said if I needed anything or had an emergency that I should go to Fox Cabin. I looked around. There was no other cabin in sight. What good was knowing I should go to Fox Cabin when I didn't know where Fox Cabin was?

I started the Ford. There was nothing to do but travel back the way I'd come, to the highway, to the diner. Going down the decline, I saw an intersecting trail. On a curiosity rush, I turned right and followed the narrow unpaved road. A rustic cabin with green shutters appeared on the right. I got out and knocked on the door of Deer Cabin. I wondered what the occupants thought about being near Wolf Cabin. There were no occupants to consider it apparently and I drove up the lane and came to another cabin. Larger than the other two, it had blue shutters and was Hunters Cabin. Deer Cabin didn't have a chance. A window was open so I didn't knock. At lane's end, I found Fox

Cabin. It had yellow shutters. If this was Scully's shutter scheme, there was some color in the man. A sign on a post told me this was where I could report outages and emergencies and inquire about reservations.

Gussie Brunty came out the front door carrying a laundry basket with lamps in it. She watched my car approach and when I parked, she smiled her little teeth smile.

"You got lost?" she asked.

"Sort of," I said, looking at the small plastic Tiffany-style lamps. "I stayed at Wolf Cabin. I'm checking out and want to pay. Any word on Diane?"

"Not one, and you won't be paying, neither." She carried her load toward a pickup truck.

"Where's Scully live? Around here?"

She shook her head. "You go on to the diner, you want to talk with Scully."

"How does he make money?" I asked, looking back at Fox Cabin. I'm not sure about yellow shutters on a wood cabin.

"He makes do," she said. She had noticed my interest in the cabin. "This here's where Linette and Diane lived, if you want to know."

I wanted to know. "You said he never charged Linette rent."

"Had a soft spot for her since she came here a runaway. Thought they might wed one day, but she took off with some boy, no account from over Dawsonville way. Wanted to drive race cars."

"Diane's father?"

"Nobody knows but the poor girl that's in her grave."

"Is she there already?"

"Way of speaking," Gussie said. "They got a service for her ashes coming up."

"Where's the service?" I asked, wondering if Diane might come out of hiding for it.

"Little Church in the Wildwood. Sonny said she told him once that's where her service should be and she should be burned and scattered in those woods around it." She cocked her head, assessing me. She was shrewd enough to know I'd be going there. "We use the old logging road but best if you go up the hard road. You'll see a little wood sign. Turn right, you'll go into the forest. Pretty little church, don't hold many folks. 'Course the way she died and all, lot of people will come to the service."

She plunked the basket holding the two faux Tiffanys on the truck bed.

When she saw me study them, she said, "Don't belong to Linette. Orell lent them. He told me to get them back for to sell in the store. Soon as the state police leave us be, we can clean out the cabin of Diane and Linette's things." She meant the GBI, but *state police* sounded vile and were outsiders to a lot of country communities. Lake would agree.

I said, "A pack of hounds came by Wolf Cabin last night. Someone fired a shotgun. Like to scare me to death." I can't say she was flabbergasted, although she tried to hide her alarm by looking at her muddy shoes. *Muddy? When did it rain here?* "I'll have to thank Scully for coming by in the middle of the night to see if everything was all right, but I don't think he should be smoking in the woods with it so dry."

"Scully don't smoke."

"But there was a man . . ."

"Weren't Scully."

"Does Scully have security? A night watchman?"

"We ain't Atlanta," she said and went to the truck's driver's side. "Got to get me going. Open the store at nine, I do. Come on by after you eat at Scully's place. Nothing like a sweet to cut through the bacon fat."

CHAPTER TWENTY-FOUR

The Little Church in the Wildwood. The title sure fit. It was little and it was in the wildwood—a simple wooden structure built on a stone foundation with a steeply pitched roof and a steeple projecting from the highest point. A wooden cross painted gold hung above the door. Three stone steps led into the building.

I pushed the door in and paused to listen. A preternatural hum came from the church's very existence. Lake, of the excellent hearing, once said that living objects like a deer standing still or a snake frozen in the grass make their own noise, if nothing more than that which emanates from pulsating innards. Inanimate things like rocks and metal create sound by simply affecting the flow of air around them. Though I don't have excellent hearing, I can attest that buildings are noisy. I've been in some that creak and groan like old arthritic gnomes. Not this place. It had the nuance of a lonely structure, a vague creak, a soft sigh, a *sssssss*.

I crept into the gloom. The walls had once been a soft white. Now stripes of water ran down where the vaulted ceiling leaked at the corners and rain had pushed past the casement window frames. The stained glass was a work of art with its lovely centered rose and delicate white lilies. Christ wore a gold halo and looked upon his three shepherds, thus bestowing glory and kindliness to this small sanctuary.

Five rows of worn pews lined the right side of the little

church. Maybe five people could fit on a wooden bench. On the left side, in front of three rows of pews, a long wooden box with a single wide stair had been constructed. It was a fundamentalist baptismal fount enclosed by a surround. I stepped up to look into the white tub. It appeared someone had walked in it. I hurriedly stepped down. When I was about ten, I went to the church of a neighbor whose daughter was baptized. They dunked her backward into the tub. Scared me to death.

Ah ha! At the head of the tub, where plumbing was housed inside the surround, I saw a cabinet door opening to a cut-out for needed plumbing exigencies. Besides pipes, the small space was empty, but not dusty. Skinny Diane could wrap herself around the pipes.

On the other side of the room, a narrow door led out of the sanctuary, probably to the church office. Approaching the altar, I noted that the cloth was freshly ironed, the wild flowers recently picked—as if for a service, perhaps a funeral service.

A sound reached my ears, a sough vibrating on the air and emanating from the office door. "Anybody here?"

At the door, I knocked. "Preacher?"

The sough subsided. Either it was my imagination or, as Lake would have it, the little building had decided to take a deep breath when somebody was paying attention.

The air was still now, but watchful. So was I.

I opened the door and gazed around the small room. A faint smell came to my nostrils and lingered, and it wasn't ecclesiastical. Not long ago someone with body odor had come looking for Diane, or perhaps it had been Diane herself. A desk chair was overturned, revealing the desk's knee hole. Church garments had been pulled from a small closet. A door led out the back. I opened it and walked into filtered sunlight and onto the brown gravel parking lot. At the back of the lot, a decrepit cemetery was fenced off. On brief inspection, no gravestone was later than the fifties. I found myself on a path into eerie dense shade. I listened for sounds that would tell me something— something positive here. The pine siskins busily pecked at the bark covering the heart of pine. A woodpecker rat-tatted. A squirrel tossed acorn hulls. Normal forest sounds.

Ahead I noticed a glistening outcrop and walked to it. I thought about inanimate objects and the noises they made. This boulder, this piece of granite that had been here since time began, was whispering something—a kind of ghost writing on the blackboard of my mind.

Slip-sliding on pine straw, I circumnavigated the boulder and saw that it butted against a wall of rock covered in lichen and blackberry vines. I walked along it and discovered that it was a man-made stone fence like you'd see in England and Wales. But here? In this forest? Fencing what in? It encompassed roughly a square of maybe two hundred yards. The woodland gently sloped up and down, and I thought it odd that someone had built a stone fence around a small patch of forest that was guarded by a boulder. Was this a place of sinister worship?

My stomach had been threatening to growl since I parked in front of the church and now was emitting enough noise to frighten the birds.

Back in the Ford, I drove to the main road, my mind flickering on the little church. Then I called Web. He told me that Orell Brunty was a deacon of a church, that he was married to Gussie who gave birth to one child that died in childbirth; and that Orell drove a school bus before buying Trader Joe's and a shop in town. Interesting that he progressed from school bus driver to retail entrepreneur.

Trader Joe's parking lot was filled with people and cars and media trucks and I wondered if there was news—if news had happened while I roamed the hills of Sawchicsee County trying to figure out what happened up here.

In the diner, men milled around, talking, drinking coffee, and holding napkins while stuffing pastries in their mouths. I saw Scully in the window behind the counter, busy, the lenses in his glasses reflecting the sun rays tilting into the diner's windows. He looked up suddenly. I waved and he nodded.

Outside again, I went into Orell's store. He stood at the register. "Hello, Miss Dru," he said, holding up a finger. "Be with you in a minute."

"No hurry."

"I'm driving the bus."

"I heard you were a bus driver in a different life."

He looked confused, maybe it was the idea of a different life. He said, "Oh, the school bus, yes, part time. Still do when something goes wrong with the regulars." He shook his head. "They don't know how to handle the kids just right. Be too soft, they run over you. Too hard, they tell their mamas. Kids words' taken over grown-ups." He shook his head again. The way of the world.

I put a finger to my lips. "I need to ask you something confidential."

"So no one knows?" He was sharp.

"Right, just something nagging my head."

"You go right on and ask."

"You heard about those campers and what Boyd Scoggins said they saw?"

"Nobody minds what Boyd says when he's bad with drink."

"The male camper was named Tommy. We believe he could be from around here and that night was using a made-up name to camp with his girlfriend. Did someone named Tommy come into your store that day?"

He frowned and tugged the skin under his chin. "Can't recollect."

I said, "Tommy was kind of punk, college boy, likes acting, cutting up."

He shook his head. I noticed the muscles around his deep brown eyes were pulled together by curiosity. "We get kids passing through wanting a Confederate flag if he's going to a Southern school, but I can't recall that boy."

I brightened and grinned. "Or maybe he came for your wine."

"Sure, kids come for the wine. They like sweet when they smoke that dope."

"And it's cheap."

He started to take offense when the door opened and Gussie bustled in. Damn, I wasn't finished with him. She said, "I got here quick as I could, Orell." She hurried behind the counter and shooed him away. "Go on now; get that bus out to the searching."

He didn't have to be told twice and scooted for the door just as I heard the yip of a siren. Just a short blast. I thought of Lake because he does that sometimes to say hello when I'm jogging the sidewalks of Atlanta and he's driving like a man in a hurry. Such was my thought when I turned to leave and nearly ran into Evangeline. She'd darted past the departing Orell and almost ran into me.

"What the— ?" I'd halted in time. I don't cuss out little girls, even pitas.

This little pita's britches were filled with bees. "I knew you'd be up here."

"Good morning, Evangeline," I said, then looked at Baron who had followed her into the store. "And to you, too."

His smile blossomed. "Top of the morning."

"Or the bottom. You two come to join the search?" I stepped around them, going for the door.

"We came to find you," Evangeline said.

"You found me," I said, leaving the store, them trailing.

"I want my money back," Evangeline said.

"I think I gave it back already."

"We made up."

"We did?" I said, and, looking past her head, saw Lake. That answered the yip of warning from his cruiser. "Excuse me." I charged away, heading for Lake.

Evangeline was on my heels. "You said you would call me yesterday."

I said over my shoulder, "No cell service."

"I found out, but you could have gone to a town and called me."

"I could have, but I didn't."

Baron said, "Come Evangeline, these people have a girl to find."

"And—and—and I have a *mother* to find." She'd started out petulant and wound up crying.

Even little horrors touch my heart when they cry. I saw Lake fold his arms as if to wonder what I was going to do about it. I said, "Evangeline, stop right this minute or I'll never find your mother."

She brightened like she was three, and I'd given her a lollypop after I put a funny-face bandage over the boo-boo on her elbow. She asked, "You're looking for her?"

"I am, yes. I *am* looking for her."

"Up here, with these . . ."

"Don't you dare say anything pejorative about these people."

She giggled. Her nose wrinkled and her eyes squeezed together, not a pretty sight, but engaging enough. "I know pejorative," she said. "I'll like the people here because Mama liked them." She folded her arms in a challenging way. "She was happy in the photograph. She's laughing. Mama doesn't laugh if she's in a place she doesn't . . ."

"What photograph? What place?" I said, sharper than I should have.

"Of her and Laurant and Janet in front of this store." She pointed at Trader Joe's sign and the Indian. "Johnny took it."

Lake and I looked at one another like we couldn't believe we were such asses not to have asked Evangeline and Baron about photographs other than those in the media.

Evangeline said, "I didn't know where it was taken until I just got here. This is it, isn't it, Uncle Baron?"

"If I remember correctly," he agreed.

Lake contained his excitement very well. "Do you have that photograph?"

Baron answered, "Should still be in the picture drawer in the wine cellar. I've never had call to look again. There's dozens just like it."

Evangeline piped in, "Johnny was always saying he was going to make a book out of their wine trips. He never did. We *knew* he never would. When Mama comes back, we'll do it together. She'll know when it was taken."

Lake asked, "Do you have a fax machine?"

"Is it important?" Baron asked, looking around. "I mean . . ."

Lake grew cautious. "It may mean nothing. We have to see it first."

The Brownes and the Cocineaus were here at some time posing for photographs before whatever happened to them happened; and Princess Pita and Faux Rhett didn't need to know and spread that about—until the time came to spring.

I looked at Gussie looking out the window at us. The photograph didn't prove they'd been inside Trader Joe's or the diner, or had anything to do with anyone in town, but it was a stretch to think four people stopped here just so Johnny could photograph his wife and best friends in front of a general store that looked like every other mountain general store.

"Rendezvous," I mouthed to Lake and said to Baron and Evangeline, "You must be thirsty. Go into the store and get a drink."

"You want to get rid of us," Evangeline said.

Perceptiveness can be a pain in the tush. "We can't stand around speculating about an old photo while people are missing."

We walked to Lake's car, and he said, "If the photograph is date-stamped, that could prove they were here around the time they disappeared."

"Any time within a year would be good."

Mentally crossing my fingers that the photograph hadn't mysteriously disappeared, I thought that this was wonderful evidence of their presence here, but didn't answer the question, why were they so far away from their marina, so late at night, after Johnny fell or was shoved overboard? And that begged another question, at that time, were they still in charge of the sailboat?

Lake said, "I'll inform the sheriff. I'm to meet Sonny at the funeral home. Linette's body has been released." The implication was Lake was going to examine it. I wrinkled my nose.

"Who's Linette?" Evangeline asked. She and Baron had quietly eased to where we stood.

Lake and I exchanged glances.

Baron said, "Linette is the lady in the lake. Her daughter's the one that's missing."

"I have to go," I said.

"I can help," Evangeline said. "I want to find her." Her dark serious eyes pleaded with me. "I can, I know I can. Me and Uncle Baron, we can."

I smiled at her. "I appreciate your faith. I have an idea. A bus just left for Landing Creek Park. Why don't you two follow it and join the searchers?"

Lake looked intrigued at the prospect, either of getting rid of the two of them or the idea that Evangeline might actually be helpful.

"Landing Creek Park," Evangeline said, excited. "There's another picture. It's of Laurant and Johnny standing by a sign in a park. That's the name of the park."

"Evangeline, I need your help with the photographs." To say she was thrilled would be the same as calling her meek. She called Soledad, giving the woman permission, instructions and the numbers to fax copies to Webdog and the Sawchicsee sheriff's office.

That arranged, I called Web and told him to be on the lookout and investigate what he got from the photographic evidence. Also, I asked, "What's Scully Brunty's home address?"

I heard his keyboard click. "It's a post office box number. His land is in the hills off State Road 128. It touches the federal forest. That's the best I can do for now."

"Thanks."

"Before you go, this will hearten you. The Atlanta newspaper reporter is in Wilmington now. Be glad Bonnet and Evangeline are in Georgia. He's looking for them."

"What did you tell him?"

"That I didn't know where they were, which was true at the time. He's onto the bank stuff, fishing around. He wanted me to confirm and enlighten, which I didn't."

"You're a treasure."

He rang off.

Lake swore Evangeline and Baron to secrecy regarding the photographs and sent them on their way. Finally, we were alone. "Come with me?" he asked. I looked at him, something about the way he'd asked.

"The Crime Lab finished with her body."

He shrugged. "I think about her kid. Somebody killing a hapless woman and tossing her away. Somebody needs to pay attention to her."

Lake has a reverence for the dead not found in most homicide detectives. It appeared that we'd separately come to the conclusion that, even though she neglected Diane, Linette wasn't a bad person and didn't deserve her fate. Crazy as it sounds, there comes a time when I know—by instinct—that I'm being led by some force seeking justice. I'm a believer that the unjustly dead want us to know what happened to them.

I said, "Linette's service is at the Little Church in the Wildwood. I've been in it; it's a baptismal place. The murderer will be there."

"So will everyone in the town and county."

"You go on and see Linette. Tell her we'll get justice for her."

"I like vengeance better."

Lake gave me his slyest grin. "Did you exist in a bad cell last night or was that for Evangeline's benefit?"

"Bad cell."

"I tried to call. Thought you'd taken up with a fly-by-night in that motel."

"Ah, but I didn't stay in the motel."

I told Lake about the mysterious happenings at Wolf Cabin.

Hey, diddle diddle. The dish ran away with the spoon. He happily concurred.

CHAPTER TWENTY-FIVE

Scully was sitting at the counter, his hands wrapped around a cup of coffee. I sat on the short stool next to him and asked if he used security at the cabins. He looked perplexed and said he did not.

I said, "Someone was hunting near Wolf Cabin last night."

"Shouldn't be."

"That's not the point. He was. I caught a glimpse of him . . ." I let the trailing word have meaning, one he understood.

"It wasn't me."

"He discharged a shotgun. I'd say less than thirty feet from the cabin. The hounds were with him."

His complexion paled. "Coon hunters."

"You got someone in mind?"

"Not particularly."

"Where's your house?"

"Over the state road."

"I ask because shotguns are noisy and maybe you heard."

"There's hollows and blowing wind."

I griped about not having a telephone in case of emergency since I couldn't use my cell phone. And I got him to admit that Linette and Diane had served as managers of the other cabins.

"This state has innkeeper laws," I said.

"You surely know your laws."

"Where is Diane?"

He shook his head. "If I knew, I'd tell you."

251

I believed him; she was probably as far away from him as she could get. I got up. He kept his gaze steady on his cold coffee. "I'd like to pay you for last night."

He shook his head slowly. "Wouldn't be right."

"I don't like to be beholden."

He looked up, angling his glasses so I couldn't see his eyes. "You're still not paying."

I headed for next door. Scully had to know I would. Gussie didn't smile when she looked up and saw me. I asked her if Fox Cabin was opened and she said it was not, that the state police didn't want people in and out. When I said I'd like to inspect it, well, look up intractable in the dictionary. There's Gussie with her mouth zipped tight and her brow pulled together. "The state police investigated the cabin. I did, too."

"I need to see for myself."

"Why?"

"To get a clue where Diane might have gone. I don't see why you would object."

"No objecting, just protecting Scully's property." *Like I was going to burn it down.*

"You know you can trust me, Gussie." Her mouth parted enough that her teeth showed. "Did you stay in Fox Cabin last night?"

"That cabin's been part of state police business since they found Linette."

"Since investigators are finished with it, maybe Diane stayed the night in her old home?"

"Tell the truth, she might have. Connie Scoggins ain't all she's cracked up to be. Sonny don't know everything; neither does that interferin' judge. All's I know is it wasn't me staying there. I got me a nice house in a meadow with barns and cattle. Don't take to woods much."

"Can I ask you something?"

"That's better than accusin'."

"I wasn't accusing you. Please."

"If you say. What do you want to know?"

"I'm looking for a young man named Tommy."

She tossed her hands back. "What in the world?"

I'd dumbfounded her, but an unnerving bombshell it was not. I told her we believed the male camper was named Tommy and that he might have come into the shop for a drink or snack. She gave it two seconds' thought and said it was all in Boyd Scoggins's mixed-up head. "Twaddle, that's all that was."

"Can I have the key to Fox Cabin?"

"Scully say you can?"

"He didn't say I couldn't."

She dug into her polyester pants and brought out a ring with five keys on it. "They're marked. Take 'em, bring 'em back."

"Thanks," I said, skipping out before she changed her mind.

On the way to Fox Cabin, I spied Lake's unmarked following the sheriff. Fifteen seconds later, my cell played Mozart. "Where you going?" Lake asked.

"Fox Cabin," I answered. "Find any clues on the body?"

"There was a needle prick in her left arm at the bend in her elbow. The Crime Lab noted it in their report, but not that she was left-handed. Sonny told me that."

"That'd be a good trick to shoot up in the left arm using your left hand."

"Someone didn't know that," he said. "Scully would, since she worked for him and he's observant."

Lake also said that Evangeline's photographs arrived at the sheriff's office, which was where he was headed. With a rush of exuberance, I said, "We're getting close."

"Yes," he said.

"The boaters are dead."

"Yes."

"The YouTube video may not be our campers; they may be dead, too."

"Yes."

"Diane's afraid of someone."

"Yes."

"Four years ago, when she was eight years old, she saw the boat people or something connected with them, which she didn't comprehend. Recently something prodded her memory."

"Yes."

"Does Sonny see it like we do?"

"Mostly."

"Are you sure he's told you all he knows?"

"Reasonably."

"Diane won't be in the park."

"No."

"Okay, Lieutenant Garrulous, I'm off to find her."

"Good."

Fox Cabin looked like a quiet, pleasant place to grow up in if you like growing up in woodland cabins. I hadn't noticed what a dollhouse it was when I'd met Gussie Brunty here, or that the clearing allowed enough light to grow tomatoes and cucumbers and peppers. They thrived in a garden alongside the cabin, the neat rows picked clean of weeds, gum balls and pine cones.

Stepping onto the porch, I smiled at the stenciled bird and butterfly appliqués on the window frames and thought of the thin girl who had waited on us that first morning. I was certain we'd find her, most probably when she wanted to be found.

Opening the door, I expected to feel a forlorn stitch in my chest. Oddly, despite a touch of mildew in the air, the place gave off a blush of invitation. The air-conditioning, on low, still hummed in the window. The room was sparse on furniture, and I assumed Gussie took more than two lamps. Only a sleeper sofa and coffee table sat on the ubiquitous rag rug. The fireplace hadn't seen a fire in months. I looked up into the chimney. Nothing but sooty kiln walls.

In the back room, a bed had been removed, but left its mark on the rug. There was a tall boy and a vanity dresser—the kind a skilled man would build and for which an adept seamstress would sew a skirt. Drugstore makeup was arranged neatly on the glass top. An oval antique mirror hung on the wall above the vanity and an ice cream stool served as the vanity seat. If I let myself, I could shed tears for that orphan girl, and even a few for her misguided mother.

Sucking up the melancholy, I pulled aside the skirt and rummaged through odds-and-ends boxes, through hair paraphernalia, ribbons, ointments, coins, wallets, but nothing that would give away Diane's whereabouts. The tall chest yielded zero. Of course, the GBI would have taken anything pertinent. Contrary to what Lake thought of them, they were thorough at searches and wouldn't overlook the obvious. What I was looking for was the unobvious, and I had no idea what that could be.

I tackled the shallow closet and its contents. Nothing in pockets, nothing hiding in shoes, the rug was secure on the floor, no attic access in the closet ceiling, but I wondered about the high pitch of the roof and went in search of a stair or small opening somewhere in the cabin.

The surprisingly large kitchen had a pantry, but no attic opening. A can of beans and a tin of sardines sat lonely on the shelves. The cabinets contained cheap crockery and glasses; the drawers even cheaper utensils. In the fridge, a box of baking soda had been left to keep the interior fresh. A toaster and a tiny microwave sat on a Formica countertop.

On the screened back porch, I found the pull-down ladder. A

pull on the leather strap and the steps unfolded at my feet. The ladder wasn't wider than my two feet together. I climbed up and poked my head into the attic's hot black air. There was a small dormer on my left, and soon my eyes accustomed to a lighter, charcoal interior. I listened for the sound of human presence hiding behind objects, the feel of eyes watching, perhaps waiting to pounce, the scurry of mice feet. But nothing. Life did not exist here at the moment.

The floor's bearer beams had been covered with plywood and that was heartening. I wouldn't be falling through the ceiling to the floors below. Standing was problematic and I hunched toward the naked light bulb and pulled the chain. The 60 watt lit the small space. There was surprisingly little dust, and I smiled seeing the old camel-back trunks like those in my family's attic. I spied a springy rocking horse and a scooter, beloved toys from childhood, too precious to toss or give away. A dollhouse sat in a corner. These things, even though old and used, looked cared for. Compared to my attic—I shuddered to contemplate.

Okay, someone came up here often. All these cabins were alike, so no one would overlook this attic as Diane's hideout, but if my hunch was correct, she'd found a way to make it safe. How? Where?

I walked around the plywood walls and knocked for hollow sounds. I was looking for attic bypasses. The GBI's forensic team would have too, if they were thorough. Attic bypasses weren't necessarily built as hidey holes, but some could be used as such if they were large enough. These bypasses could be the flue housing, or for pipes, even wiring cages beneath the floor or in the walls. Sometimes builders got sloppy and left holes where insulation should have been installed.

I came upon a possibility in one wall where the dull thuds halted and the chock of hollowness echoed beneath my fist.

When I pushed away the wooden dollhouse, I discovered that it hid a vertical half-panel. Three feet off the floor, the panel had a horizontal seam. It looked like a carpenter had nailed a three-foot section to make it fit to the floor. But a close inspection showed the nails didn't fasten the pieces together and the bottom piece was loose. I was testing it for hinge access when I heard a sound.

Outside, a car crunched gravel, and then braked. The dormer window didn't overlook the driveway so I couldn't know who was out there. I turned back to the rigged panel that most certainly hid a hollow in the cabin's frame. All I had to do was find the way through the three-foot section, because this was the place Diane could hide if someone came looking.

As I pried at the wood with my fingers, I heard two distinct voices. Female. "Yoo-hoo, Miss Dru?" That was Gussie. I made a snap decision to try out Diane's hiding place. My fingers hit on the knot that occurs naturally in plywood. The knot fell into my hand, leaving a hole in the wood and cool air fanning my hand. It came from the cabin's living quarters. The faux nailed section didn't lift up as I'd thought. By using the hole for leverage, the panel slid between its fellow panel and the frame post. Thank God I'm slim, but my height wasn't easy to stuff through the opening. Before I slid the section back into place I replaced the knot and pulled the dollhouse toward me. It wouldn't be flush, but it would withstand casual inspection.

There I was, behind the panel, hidden from Gussie. If she found me, so what, I can think fast. In a corner lay a cartoon thermos bottle and a lunch box. I sat on a blanket that was cleaner than expected. The space was wide enough for me to sit, but would be uncomfortable before long.

I listened for foot falls and wondered who the second woman was. They were in the kitchen below. In seconds, it seemed, they spotted the ladder, and in a few more seconds one woman climbed it. "You up here, Miss Dru?"

The heavy tread crossed the plywood floor. "Ain't here," she said.

"That ain't the car she had before," the second woman said. Connie, it had to be.

"She got herself a rental." I could tell Gussie was near the dollhouse. Would she move it? Gussie said, "Probably walking the woods. Silly girl."

"She better watch for drop-offs," Connie said and hacked out a gruff cough.

"Serve her right, coming up here, nosing around. Ain't right for a woman."

My friend Gussie.

There was a stir and Gussie said, "What the matter with you, Connie?"

"My ol' back." I heard her shuffling and coughing. Climbing the ladder and smoking probably did her in.

Gussie said, "I'll do the flowers and get the church ready for tomorrow. Orell will set up the chairs."

"I take that kindly. My old back ain't up to hauling chairs." After a short pause, Connie said, "I hope Diane don't want this old junk. I ain't got room for it."

"Don't have to worry about it for now. State police don't want us to touch anything or move anything. Bastards take their time with other folks's lives." She'd moved away from the panel. She said, "Be glad when that service is over; puts an end to things."

"No bringing Linette back, poor thing." Connie's croaky voice receded and the ladder creaked with her weight. "Now we'll never know who's Diane's daddy."

"I already know," Gussie said.

"Who?" Connie barked.

"Just never you mind. Let's go, I ain't got time to wait for

Miss Up-Your-Ass to show herself." Gussie was on the ladder. She spoke but all I heard was, ". . . At the church . . ."

I heard the rackety sound of the ladder being pushed up into its hutch. The front door slammed, and a car started up. I squeezed out of my hole in the wall and looked out the dormer and saw the truck wobble up the woods' trail, disappearing into the pines. So Gussie had come to check up on me and didn't seem perturbed not to find me. What to make of that?

I loved the irony. Diane hid out, right under their noses, safe and insulated, so to speak. But where was she now?

CHAPTER TWENTY-SIX

The ladder pushed down easily and I left the cabin—eager to get away before the truck retraced its way back down the trail—and saw the sheriff's car bobbling and plunging up the road with Lake following.

I stood on the porch. Lake got out of the car, grinning.

"What's so funny?" I asked.

"What are you trying to do to your hair?"

I reached up and pulled pink insulation from the tangles. "Playing hide and seek."

Sonny laughed. "Black and pink go good."

"Come inside," I said, "I got something to show you. And tell you."

"Make it happy," Lake said. "I could use some."

"I had visitors here. Connie and Gussie." Lake opened his mouth, but I cut him off. "But I was well hidden."

"Here?" Sonny said.

I followed the men up the ladder and three of us filled the small space. Lake said, "That rabbit of a girl that served us breakfast didn't look like she had the smarts to do that."

"She's got country smarts," Sonny said. "School smarts, too."

Lake and Sonny inspected the hideout and when we'd climbed down the ladder I asked him where the road alongside the cabin went, the one carrying Connie and Gussie. I'm sure they hadn't come from that way. I would have heard the truck coming down the hill.

"That's the main branch of an old logging trail. It parallels the hard road for a couple of miles. Other trails branch off it and go into the hills. Quarter of a mile up, you take a left for the hard road."

"Diane has to be hiding in those woods up there," I said.

"Lots of caves thereabouts," Sonny said. "Good thing Diane knows every cranny in this county. Some of those caves are gained by holes in the ground. They're like honeycombs made by underground streams and tree roots. Hunters stumble into them and have a devil of a time crawling out." He shook his head. "We won't find her if she doesn't want to be found."

I had to agree. "Portia told me about an underground waterfall near her cabin."

"That's south of here, called Weeping Rock Falls." He motioned his head toward the woods' trail. "Up north of here, 'bout a quarter of a mile through the woods you come to a cliff. In the rainy season you see nature at her best. Water tumbles out of the face of the rock cliff, kind of spinning to the base, then disappears into an underground stream that ends at Sawchicsee Pool, although there's other names for it. Cavers went down there one time. Liked to scare them to death. Said they were lucky to get out alive."

I asked, "Where would they go down if water is coming out of the wall?"

"Cavers are a crazy bunch. If you don't mind getting wet, you can squeeze through openings at the bottom of the cliff. You couldn't pay me."

"Me, either," Lake said.

"How did they get out?" I asked.

"Same way they crawled in. Rope and tackle back up through the cracks."

"This isn't finding Diane," Lake said.

"No," I said. Instead of talking about underground pools, I

should be exercising my gray matter, which was stretched to a flat field where ghosts cavorted and adolescent girls played hide and seek. Thinking of adolescent girls, I wondered how our Evangeline was coping with the local adults, or how they were coping with her.

I said to Sonny, "Tell me about the photographs."

"A courier's bringing the originals to the Crime Lab in Atlanta. Meantime, what we can see on the copies is Laurant standing in the middle with Janet on one side and Candice on the other. All arm in arm, smiling happily for the camera. But what's interesting is someone's looking out the store window at them. Couldn't tell who, but the lab can fiddle with the originals." He moved away from us. "Now I got to get back."

Walking to the cars, I asked him if he'd shown the photographs to the Bruntys or Janeway and he said he hadn't caught up with Orell or Scully yet, but Janeway denied ever seeing the couples in the park. I asked Sonny to give me directions to Scully Brunty's home.

He scratched his head. "I wouldn't go there by myself if I was you. Scull and Orell share ancestral land and they don't invite company, if you get my meaning."

I thought of Connie with her shotgun, but at least she had a reason, being a woman and living alone on a mountainside. "They're awfully secretive for tradesmen."

"Probably because they're trade, they want to keep part of their lives private. You think Diane's there?"

I shrugged.

When I didn't go on, he cocked his head. "I've not been in Scull's house since his mama died." He smiled as if a funny crossed his mind. "Maybe he doesn't want a private detective getting a notion to check his pillows to see that he didn't rip the tags off them."

I really did appreciate his humor. "He's certainly not happy with me acquainting him with certain laws."

A lull developed in the conversation and I believed Sonny was still contemplating my interest in the Bruntys' homes. In the end he capitulated with directions but warned me not to go sneaking around if I didn't want a hind-end full of buckshot.

"When is Linette's service?" I asked.

"Tomorrow morning, ten thirty. They've probably started burning her already."

I shuddered. This was my chosen end, but I wasn't up to the reality of the flames just yet. I told Sonny that I was headed to the Wildwood church and that Gussie told Connie she would get the sanctuary ready for the service.

"Connie hasn't told me that yet," he said. "I pick her up and take her when she does the little church. She's fussy about it."

"Let me know what the Bruntys say about the photograph," I said.

"Sure, but it's hard telling if they'll own up to anything, especially with the mystery surrounding those missing folks. As I've told you, folks here pretty much keep out of other people's business."

"It could be Gussie in the window."

Sonny thought about that. "You take the two of them, Orell and Gussie. Gussie'll arm wrestle you till your wrist breaks."

"Could either of them kill a person?"

Sonny took his time. "They're mountain folks. They protect their own, so I guess they would if something threatened their own."

"Why would the Cocineaus and Brownes threaten them?"

"That's *if* they did, and I see no reason for them to. No one up here knew them."

"Or admitted knowing them. I have a theory."

Sonny smiled; all women have theories, like intuition.

"Now that we know the two couples were here, at least one

time, my thoughts have gelled into a supposition. What if Johnny Browne did business with Orell or Scully?" Sonny cocked his head, curiosity lines etched on his forehead. "Grapes. Johnny was looking to expand his winery and he liked to use local grapes; Domingo said he had suppliers in the North Carolina mountains, in Virginia and some in other states. What if Johnny contacted Scully or Orell and that led to a sale?"

Sonny nodded. "Orell mostly makes wine with his, but Scull has been known to sell his grapes. Scull even developed one for export—starts with an M—in the last ten years. What are you getting at?"

"Johnny strikes a deal to buy his crop . . ."

"That could be, I suppose."

"And what if the bargain wasn't kept?"

"You mean Scull didn't deliver? I wouldn't put much into that. Those boys might not be important in the sophisticated big city, but they are men of their word."

"It's the other way around. Maybe Browne didn't keep his end of the bargain. He didn't pay."

"That would explain the photograph, them being here about the grapes." In no hurry now to leave, he leaned against his squad car.

"The Cocineaus and Brownes had no other connection to this area. They didn't own land, have a boat dock, a cabin, or kin. No reason to come here except to purchase grapes—or extend their credit."

Sonny shook his head. "There would be no extending credit with either Orell or Scull. They believe in hard cash, on time, or they'll sock you with interest no bank would dream of charging."

"Does Scully own a boat?" I asked.

Sonny looked at me like he was ready to reevaluate my intelligence. "Both do. Big cabin cruisers. Everybody owns a boat here. Orell and Gussie liked to sail."

I hurried to assuage my stupidity. "Can the cabin cruisers be trailered?"

"Good size trailer, sure."

"Let's speculate that Johnny told Scully where the *Scuppernong* would be docked and that he was going to visit the next day to work things out, but that he sure as hell wasn't paying full price. So the Brunty boys motored the cruiser to the sailboat that night. Now the couples had been drinking all day. Orell and Scully board the sailboat. Cocky Johnny, who we know gets killed, puts up a fight and they knock him in the head and he goes overboard. That means they had to kill the others who were too drunk to defend themselves. Orell sailed the boat out of its slip and Scully drove the cruiser. Since they hadn't planned on murder, they didn't have containers for the bodies so they brought the bodies ashore to bury in these mountains, having first scuttled the sailboat in deep Waterfall Cove."

"Burying in the holes up here has been done in the past, with revenuers that we know of," Sonny said.

"Which," I said, "is what the campers saw. Scully and Orell taking the cruiser out of the water."

"Orell and Scull have slips at the big marina. Why not go back to it?"

Lake said, "They wouldn't want to carry bodies off a boat at a busy marina."

Sonny seemed skeptical. "Same thing at the park. They would have witnesses. If that's what happened, they did." He hadn't protested on the Bruntys behalf, and he seemed to give the theory serious thought.

Lake said, "The campers never came forward. Scoggins and Linette are dead. That tells me something."

Sonny blinked several times. "You think Orell and Scull added the campers' bodies to the other three, disassembled

265

their camp and stole their vehicle?"

"And killed Scoggins for obvious reasons, and Linette for something she saw or knew. Maybe about the grape business since she worked for Scully."

Sonny got this wide-eyed look. "My God." He wiped his forehead where beads of sweat simmered. "The grape thief."

"The grape thief." The phrase caught in my throat. I reiterated, *"The grape thief.* Domingo said one of Johnny's suppliers called him the grape thief because Johnny refused to pay. The supplier threatened to collect the debt his own way."

Sonny appeared to be hyperventilating. "Funny how the mind works. Scull said one time in passing that they sold their crop to a grape thief who refused to pay. Lord, I never associated it with those missing people. He never said the grape thief's name."

"It wasn't your case," Lake said.

I said, "According to Domingo, Johnny refused to pay the supplier because the grapes were inferior."

"Scull's grapes have never been inferior," Sonny said. "Treats them like pampered poodles. Orell's can sour on the vine if they go too long." He opened his car door. "I have to look into this."

"Be careful how you ask things," Lake cautioned.

"Don't you worry," Sonny said.

"I'll go with Dru to the church," Lake said. "We'll catch up later."

"Sure," Sonny said, getting into his multi-antennaed squad car.

When he was on his way, I said to Lake, "You don't have to babysit me."

Lake slipped into the seat and closed the door. He turned and touched my nose. "You're going to need me some day."

"I need you here and now."

"Ticks and chiggers," he said. "And I don't carry an air mattress for just such occasions."

The deep-rutted logging trail jostled the car side-to-side as Lake downshifted. He said, "I suppose the mind could forget something like ol' Scull calling someone the grape thief."

"If you believe he meant Johnny, and if you believe Sonny forgot."

"It tripped from his tongue easily enough," Lake said.

"But that doesn't mean Sonny knew the grape thief's name was Johnny Browne."

"Hard to believe he wouldn't have asked. They're all cousins."

"Hmmm. So how's Sonny involved in the murders?"

"Not so fast, Speedy Moriah. We still don't have bodies. You weave a nice tale, but we need remains and facts."

"Mere obstacles to my brilliant theory. Notice Sonny didn't stick up for his kin, Scully and Orell."

"Sonny serves and protects until he detects a higher power closing in."

"Sinister, Lieutenant, very sinister."

"Why are we going to the Little Church in the Wildwood?"

I told him that I believed Diane went back and forth between the church and the cabin, and that when she heard cars or voices, she hid.

"If you say so," Lake said.

The seductive power of the car's engine and the rocking motion lulled me as trees and rocks slid by like hallucinations. I was sleepy. Lake's voice came as if in a dream. "Hey, dopey, I see a clearing ahead. There's a side shoot right here where I can pull off."

I shook myself. "Good idea."

Outside the car, the hot air, heavy with humidity and buzzing insects, didn't do much to energize me. I don't know why, but I felt beat to hell. Walking the hundred or so yards, I said, "I'll go in. You stay outside in case she runs."

Inside the church, the atmosphere was fraught with cold fear.

She was here. My eyes were drawn to the baptismal tub.

"Diane?" I said.

Time ticked, eager to explode.

"Diane, it's me. Moriah Dru. I'm here to help you."

She became a human flash sprinting for the door into the church office.

"Diane, wait!"

Running, I got to the office threshold and saw her flee through the exterior door, flinging it backhand.

I knew what I'd see when I opened it. Diane struggling in Lake's arms.

"Diane," he said several times, holding her wrists up while her feet scampered in place, her butt swaying back from him, her shoulders pulling away, her face distorted. "Please, please."

I came to her and smelled the acrid odor of terror and filth in the sweat from her pores. She hadn't bathed and her adrenaline never abated while she was on the run. "It's over, Diane. You're safe."

She stopped struggling and hissed at me. "It'll never be over 'til I'm dead."

"It will," I said, extending a hand to this underfed child who had masqueraded as a woman since she was six. She froze, her eyes fixed as if afraid to blink or shift. Her hair was stiff with grime and flecks of pink insulation.

Lake said, "Let's go sit in the police car where we can talk. You'll feel safe in it."

His words didn't do much to quiet her anxieties. "I'm in trouble."

He said, "You're not in trouble."

"I—I need to stay here. My mama . . ."

"We'll be back tomorrow for the service," Lake said.

Her wistful submission, as if her emotions had been thoroughly milked, ragged the edges of my heart. I could so easily cry for her.

As we walked down the trail in silence, a noisy flock of masked birds with yellow tail tips showed off their aerodynamics. Diane looked up; her voice quivered when she said, "Cedar waxwings."

In late summer, they'd show up in my yard to pick the bushes clean of berries. I said, "You know every bird in the forest, don't you?"

Sniffling, she said, "Just about."

She sat in the front passenger seat. I sat in the back. Eyeing the shotgun, she said, "You ever shoot that?"

"I have," Lake said. "Do you hunt?"

She played with the hem of her t-shirt. "I don't kill things. Would you kill a bad person?"

"Depends on if he's trying to kill me, or someone I love, or someone I'm sworn to defend."

"I wish I could," she said and shook her head like she was waking from a bad dream.

"Does someone want to kill you?"

She developed a sudden interest in the woodpecker rat-tatting on pine bark. "Red-bellied," she said.

"Diane, this is important," Lake said. "We know a lot about what went on up here."

Her head whipped around. "You couldn't."

"We do. We know someone in Sawchicsee County killed those four people in that sailboat and maybe the two campers from the park."

Her brow pinched together. "I don't know about . . ."

"Who don't you know about?"

She started to shake. "No one."

"Someone is frightening you. Who is it?"

She pushed back strings of hair from her forehead. "I

can't—no one."

"Why did you hide?"

"Mama died." She spoke it loud as if being assertive allayed the grim finality.

"Who killed her?" Her head moved like it floated from the bottom of a nightmare. "It is someone you know, isn't it?"

I could see the outline of Diane's white skull. The weight of the question seemed too much to bear. She bowed her head and let the tears race down her thin cheeks.

"I'm sorry," Lake said, starting the car.

I asked, "Is it Scully who frightens you?"

Her shoulders went rigid, her fingers stopped moving, her whole body looked like if I flicked her shoulder bone with a fingernail it would break and cascade like precious crystal to her lap.

"We'll be getting back to town soon," Lake said. "I'd like for you to tell me why Scully Brunty frightens you."

"I can't." Her gaze darted to him. "I won't."

"All right, it's up to you, but you know you can talk to us, or to the judge."

"The judge . . ." Diane said, as if it hadn't occurred to her to go to the judge, or that the judge could help her.

Before we left the forest, Diane and I exchanged places in the car, and Lake told her to relax in the back seat. She curled into herself like a baby in the womb and occasionally let out a whimper.

Having alerted Sonny we were bringing Diane in, that she was frightened, and that it was best to keep her secluded, we arrived at the sheriff's back door. I've never seen a man more overjoyed to see a ragged, dirty girl in his life. He'd told us that he'd confided to his deputy, who hailed from Utah with no ties to the community, that Diane had been found. Then he sighed. "I'd better call off the search. When folks learn, they won't like searching for someone's not missing anymore."

Outside, Lake said, "Where to now?"

"Connie Scoggins's place. She knows . . ." A car came around the side of the building. "Oh crap," I said. It pulled into a parking place, and Evangeline and Baron got out.

Evangeline skipped up. "She's not there." She almost outranks Portia in greeting cordiality. "We looked everywhere."

Baron scoffed. "Not everywhere, E."

"I can tell. I knew when we got there she wasn't in the park. Nobody thought so."

"What do you mean?" I asked.

"Nobody was looking for her."

Baron gave a half laugh. "Some brought picnic baskets."

Evangeline threw him a look. "A man said it was a waste of time searching the park. He said she was hiding in the woods back of the Devil's Arse."

"What?" I said.

Baron laughed. "The Devil's Arse. Fella said it's a falls."

I looked at Lake, then held up a finger. "I'll be right back." I turned toward the sheriff's building.

Lake didn't seem happy to be left standing with Evangeline and Baron.

I went inside and found the sheriff in his office speaking into a cell phone and Diane making herself as small as possible in a leather wing chair, half hidden by the door, out of sight of any personnel who might walk by.

When he saw me, he waved me in and spoke into the phone, "Just tell Orell to bring 'em on back." He put the cell down and walked around the desk. "Diane doesn't want to go to the hospital. My deputy went to fetch her clean clothes from Connie's." His eyes narrowed and stuck on my face for a tic. "You look excited."

"Where's the Devil's Arse?" Diane peered around the wing of

the chair, her mouth open, the blue of her eyes frozen on Sonny. "Someone said Diane was hiding up by the Devil's Arse."

"You thought so, too," he said. "It's back of the Wildwood church."

I shook my head. "I didn't see a falls back there."

"Like I was saying about the cliff and the water running over it in the spring; it plunges deep into the ground, meets up with a natural spring that eroded the limestone to create a waterfall. It ends at the back of the church. There's a sinkhole that's the bottom of the fall. It's got a big boulder covering the hole else some hunter comes along, falls in it and never gets out."

Diane shivered and leaned her head against the wing.

"Never?"

"Not if nobody knows he fell in," Sonny said.

"Is that the reason for the stone fence?"

"The ground's never been stable. It's scattered with surface caves. You could slip and fall into a hole that's just been created and break a leg. Geologists are studying the area. One day they'll probably dynamite the whole thing once it clears the Forestry Commission. Meantime, don't go walking back there." He looked past my shoulder.

I said, "I'd advise a few signs."

He took a step forward. "Hey there . . ."

I turned. Evangeline stood on the threshold.

I moved to block Diane from Evangeline's sight line and said angrily, "Evangeline, what in hell are you doing in here? Go out. Now."

She came in anyway. "You're trying to keep something from me. I'm the one who found out about the Devil's Arse."

I didn't do a good job of hiding Diane. Evangeline raised an arm and pointed. "That's her."

I closed the gap between us and stood over Evangeline. "I've about had it with your intrusions."

She dashed around me and went straight to Diane. Diane looked at Evangeline like she hadn't seen anything so odd in her life.

Evangeline knelt. Diane allowed Evangeline to take her hands. "It's been terrible for you, hasn't it?" Evangeline's voice was quiet, caring.

"Yes," Diane whimpered, looking at their entwined hands.

Evangeline said, "Let's be friends."

Diane bobbed her head. "Okay," she whispered, tears falling.

I looked at Sonny, who had a silly grin on his face. This was a scene from a sappy television show.

Evangeline stood and held out a hand. Diane took it and allowed herself to be pulled to her feet. "Let's go to the girls' room," Evangeline said.

"I look awful," Diane said.

Sonny and I stood guard in the hall and the girls hurried into the restroom. Lake and Baron bore down on us from the back door.

Lake said, "Did I see what I just saw?"

"Instant girlfriends," I said.

"Maybe your client can get something out of Diane," Sonny said. "I sure can't."

Baron said, "If E can't, there's nobody can."

"What and where's the Devil's Arse?" Lake asked.

When I explained, he said, "You thinking what I'm thinking?"

"Pretty obvious."

"What?" Sonny asked.

"Our missing sail-boaters were tossed into the Devil's Arse."

"There's a boulder over it."

"You got a county full of tractors."

"Orell and Scully have a yard full of them," he said, shaking his head. "Lord, don't let it be so."

Lake patted his shoulder.

Sonny breathed in deeply. "I always looked up to my second cousins. Scull was never one to get into a fight even. Orell was a little more hot-headed, good to take offense, but those boys—Old Mrs. Brunty, Scull's mama, who raised both boys, wouldn't stand for them hurting anyone that didn't deserve it."

That didn't deserve it. Who was to judge?

Lake said, "Let's ride to Trader Joe's. Orell will be driving back by now."

Sonny said, "They'll keep. My first priority is Diane."

Baron said, "I'd let E stay with her. She can talk a clam into giving up its pearl."

Sonny thought a moment. "I don't know. This is official business."

Lake said, "Let it play out. If Evangeline crosses the line, shut her up."

Lake was at my side as we hurried down the hall, out the back door and into his car. He turned the key, saying, "This town might never be the same."

CHAPTER TWENTY-SEVEN

Lake drove like the storied race car drivers outrunning the revenuers and braked on the shoulder near Trader Joe's General Store and Diner. We trooped over to a group of folks looking joyous. Word had spread like wildfire in a pine forest that Diane was found safe.

The diner had a CLOSED sign in the door. Trader Joe's was likewise closed.

"What's going on?" Lake asked bystanders. "Where are the Bruntys?"

A man answered, "Scully left fifteen minutes ago, Orell just locked up and took off."

"Did they say where they were going?" I asked the man.

"Neither of them boys is good at telling folks what they're up to."

"Thanks," Lake said and I walked back to the car with him.

"Connie," I said. "The town crier. She tipped that we found Diane."

"Goddamn Sonny's ass," Lake said. "He should know better. Connie's a blood relative to him, but she's also related by marriage to the Bruntys."

We raced over the hills and down the valleys. "Incest of the mind," I said. "Love and hate combined."

"Standing against all outsiders," he said, and turned onto the gravel road leading to the Scoggins's place.

The hounds came running and Connie came out with her

shotgun. I got out of the police car. She recognized me and grinned. Lake got out and she scowled. "Who're you?"

"Lieutenant Richard Lake," Lake said, opening his coat, showing the badge attached to his belt.

"The fancy city policeman I been hearing about."

"Nothing fancy about the city," Lake said with a grin designed to make every woman he meets sigh for him.

Connie was no exception. I thought the shotgun was going to fall from her hands. She said, "Well, city boy, I already sent Diane's cleaned and ironed clothes with the sheriff's deputy. That new boy don't know his arse from a hole in the ground about folks around here."

Apropos, I thought.

"Didn't he tell you not to say anything about Diane's being found?"

"Sure as hell did. Who'd he think he was?"

"Didn't Sonny tell you that also?"

She hunched her shoulders into a deep shrug. "Sonny's a good man. Blinded by that girl, but she needs the steady hand of Scully and Orell."

"And so you called them."

"Felt it was my duty. We're all family here. I couldn't hold back on them."

Lake was moving back to the driver's door.

"Where you going?" she asked.

He stopped and said, "Did Diane hang out in your woods back there?" His arm was raised, his finger pointing over her shoulder.

"She hung out everywhere. You go back there, you'll see some stick furniture she fashioned." She shook her head. "She didn't see who did it. She was working that day. Ask Scully."

"We have to go, Mrs. Scoggins. Thanks for your help."

"How'd I help?"

"You told us the truth."

"You ask anybody around here, they'll tell you Connie Scoggins tells the truth, the whole truth, too, like it or not."

We got turned around and headed back down the rocky road, making it to the hard road without running over a single dog.

"I'm glad you didn't ask where Scully lives," Lake said. "Seems it's bugging you."

"It is, my darling detective, sweetheart of my dreams, but I do know a snitch when I see one."

"She's on the phone to Scully now."

My cell buzzed on my hip. Portia. I answered, "We found Diane."

"Where?"

"In the Little Church in the Wildwood in front of the Devil's Arse."

"Are we in a Damon Runyon play?"

"Oh that we were."

"I'm on my way there. I have two young people with me. Your campers. Meet me at my cabin."

"Not the sheriff's office?" Lake asked.

"Nowhere near it."

I was beyond ecstatic. "Who are they?"

"Tomas Adagio and Jean Little."

I looked at Lake. "They're alive. Anna Graham and Gene Poole."

We sat on the porch. The overhead fan hummed as they began their story. Four years ago they'd been students at the University of Tennessee in Knoxville; both were born and raised in Clarksville and had been "hooked up" since high school.

Tommy and Jean shared the porch swing. They looked nervous, their hands clutched together as though waiting for the ax to fall or the sheriff's siren to shriek.

"Relax," Portia said, coming out of the cabin door with a tray of drinks and snacks bigger than she was. Lake got up to take the tray but she shouldered him away and placed the tray on the picnic table. She'd carried a brown envelope in her armpit and laid it on the table. Pictures, I assumed.

They shook their heads at the invitation to eat and drink. Tommy didn't look much like Henry the Fat of their YouTube skit. Padding gone, heavy red beard, too, leaving a skinny young man with thin blond hair and scruffy whiskers. "These four years have been hellacious," he said. "I'm ready for this to be over."

Nor did Jean look like Anne Boleyn of the Goiter. Henry the Eighth's second wife, Anne, for whom he'd divorced Catherine of Aragon, was said to have an unsightly goiter on her neck. Anyway, Jean wasn't wearing anything like a goiter. Her lank black hair limped down her back, her arms were bare, her neckline dipped down into a suggestion of cleavage.

She looked at Tommy. "I don't think I'll ever feel safe."

Portia sat on the picnic bench and propped her cheek on a fist, a pose she strikes in the courtroom when she's after the tiniest detail, or is bored. "Take your time. Begin at the beginning."

Jean and Tommy had arrived at the campsite in an old Range Rover with a dealer's license plate. It had belonged to a school friend.

Jean was antsy. "He warned us not to talk," she said.

"Who's he?" Lake asked.

Tommy's eyes switched from Lake to Portia and back to Lake. "The sheriff."

"Sheriff Sonny Kitchens?"

"His name was Sonny. He didn't say a last name."

"Did he say he was the Sawchicsee County sheriff?"

"Not that I remember."

Portia sat straight, a little impatient now. "Tell them what you saw on the lake."

"Well," Tommy began, and glanced at Jean, "nothing like what was in the news reports. The guy in the truck called Scoggins said we were smoking dope and drinking with him. We never smoked dope or drank *with* him."

"But you did smoke dope?" Portia said.

"Yes, ma'am."

"Go on."

"It was going on for dark when he brought his fishing boat out of the water."

Jean said, "He was so drunk, the boat almost fell off the trailer."

Tommy snickered. "We thought about having some fun with him, but, man, he was wasted, so we helped him get his boat squared on the trailer."

Jean broke in, "He offered us a drink from his whiskey bottle and said we should get some beer out of his cooler for our help."

"Which we did," Tommy said. "We had our own, but," he shrugged and grinned, "you can always use more beer. We didn't know how long we were going to be there."

Jean said, "He wanted us to take his supper bag. I don't like country ham but Tommy does."

Tommy said, "I was getting hungry."

"You didn't know how long you were going to be there, yet you didn't take food or enough to drink?" Lake said.

Jean answered, "We weren't . . ." She looked at Portia. "You said we wouldn't get in trouble for telling on ourselves."

"You didn't buy the stuff and you didn't grow it," Portia said. "Go on."

"A bunch of us wanted to experiment with hemp and we found this guy on the Internet that would sell us seeds to make a guerilla garden," Tommy said. "And some leaves, too."

"So you connected that night. What time?"

"Supposed to be some time after dark. Turned out to be one in the morning that he came."

"Did he say anything about Scoggins?"

Jean said, "He said don't worry about him. He's into strong drink and can't see straight when he's sober."

"Did you make the buy?" Lake asked.

"Never got around to it. About that time we heard a boat."

"What kind of boat?" Lake asked.

"A small yacht. Sonny went down the trail a little ways then came running back. He said he got a call, an emergency in the county, and had to leave. He said to keep quiet about the meeting and that he'd e-mail us again for another meeting. He ran up the hill to the road above our camp."

"Did you witness him getting a call?" I asked. *Can't be good-looking Sonny* . . .

They both shook their heads. Jean said, "I didn't see him get a call."

"So he left as this boat's coming in?" I said. "Did it tie up?"

"Not right away. The engine cut out, and it stayed in the same place for a while."

"Then," Jean said, "another larger boat came from behind."

"Was it a sailboat?" Lake asked.

"I didn't see sails. It was real dark and cloudy. It rained earlier, but both boats were white so we could see the hulls. When I heard the news about the sailboat being missing, I searched my mind. It could have been a sailboat. It was farther out on the lake than the yacht."

"How much larger was the second boat than the first?"

"Much longer," Tommy said.

"What happened then?"

Tommy spoke like a man who didn't have to give it a

moment's thought. "The larger boat disappeared through the trees. The yacht stayed in the water for a while, and then I heard the motor crank. It followed the big boat. A long time later it came to the dock. A man got off and tied it up."

Jean said, "He lit a match to smoke."

"Can you describe him?"

"No," Jean said. "He wore a baseball cap. It was dark and chilly. He had on dark clothes."

"Was he short, tall, fat, what?"

"Maybe big. Too far away, looking down on him."

Tommy picked up the tale. "In maybe fifteen minutes a double-cab pickup, with a trailer, a pretty big rig, not like a John boat trailer, pulled up and backed toward the ramp. Another guy got off the yacht and the three of them got the boat onto the trailer and they all took off."

"No big sailboats pulled out of the water by a tractor trailer?" I asked facetiously.

Jean shook her head. "We got a kick out of that in the papers. That was the drunk in the little truck saying that. I saw him sit up when the yacht was dragged out of the water."

"Did the drunk talk to you the next morning?"

"We didn't wait until dawn, but we went down and told him we were leaving. He cussed the boat and passed out again."

"The whole thing was creepy," Tommy said. "Something about those people with the boat we didn't like, and the sheriff running off like that. We talked about it later. When we heard about people going missing, we thought about going to the sheriff, but then he e-mailed us not to say a word, that we would go to jail."

"What is his e-mail address?"

She recited it and Tommy said the hemp sheriff drove a Jeep. He wore a commando-style, tight-fitting sweater, field pants and heavy boots. He had a gun and a badge on his belt. Tommy swore that they didn't leave marijuana papers at the scene. "No bottles, no trash, no nothing."

"Did you save the e-mails he sent?"

"Every one."

"Good," Portia said, lifting her head off her fist.

Jean burst out, "Once the news got out—oh God, he e-mailed every day and warned us not to change our e-mail addy. Then when the case didn't get a lot of media coverage anymore, he'd remind us every once in a while that he knew where we went to school, our hometowns, our real names, that we videoed skits for YouTube. He described our place, like he'd been there and stalked us. We deleted all our information and stopped going online. Everything."

Tommy said, "We only used the computer for our school stuff, but he always knew everything we did. Man, he had to be there watching in person."

"Scary," Jean said. She took a deep breath. "When the sailboat was found in the lake, and with e-mail warnings coming every day, we decided we had to do something."

Tommy said, "That's when we heard about this judge who found it." He grinned at Portia. "In Atlanta."

"Coming to see me was the wisest thing you did," Portia said, implying everything else had been brainless.

I thought about the other person who came to see Portia after she'd mouthed off to a reporter. I grinned at Porsh. She batted her eyes and opened the envelope. Handing two photographs to Jean and Tommy, she asked, "Is this Sonny, the sheriff?"

Jean frowned and shook her head. "It was dark. He seemed heavier, but . . ."

"Don't know, man," Tommy said. "He wore a hat to his eyes. You know, he stayed in the shadow of our campfire. If I could hear his voice maybe . . ."

I had one more question. "Did you hear anything unusual on the lake, sounds, echoes?"

"Yeah," Jean said. "High-pitched sounds like . . ."

Like drills and saws.

"Why a guerilla garden?" I asked. That was a garden planted away from an illegal grower's home. "I thought they made growing hemp legal."

We followed Portia's car over the rough road leading away from her cabin. She was taking the campers back to Atlanta. No one would get to them except over her dead body, and she said as much.

"It's not legal under federal law," Lake said. "Its narcotic qualities are pretty poor, but being related to marijuana, it's considered a controlled substance. Georgia law enforcement doesn't pay a lot of attention except in small towns where they can use the penalty money."

"Do you believe that man was Sonny?"

"I can believe anything."

"I hate to be wrong about people," I said, knowing I sounded mulish, "but something was said that reminded me . . ."

We came to the hard road and I unfolded the paper with directions to the Bruntys. Were they ever off the beaten path! "If Sonny Kitchens isn't the hemp sheriff, he's going to be pissed, and I don't blame him."

Lake had gotten used to the twisting turning roads, and I held on tight. I like to be in control when it comes to driving fast. When we were nearing the gravel road leading to the Bruntys' houses, Sonny called. Hopefully, not hemp Sonny. Lake slowed and put the cell on speaker.

"Diane said her mama knew something that Scully didn't want her to know. Diane says she doesn't know what it is. She said Scully took care of them to keep her mama quiet."

"Why did she run?" I asked.

Sonny's voice came loud over the speaker. "Gussie came into the diner and told her to hide herself until the police left and things could get back to normal." He laughed a little. "That Evangeline can charm the spots off a dog."

Tell it to Portia. "Gussie was protecting Diane. Where's Diane now?"

"She's at the office, being looked after by my deputy. Connie's coming to bring her something to eat. She wants to go home with Connie."

"Keep her in your office."

"I got a fold-out she can rest on. Where are you?"

"We're on the way to Scully's house."

"I'm close by. Meet up with you in the valley."

We arrived at the gravel road at the same time the sheriff did. Lake pulled behind Sonny and we got out. Walking to meet the sheriff, Lake said to me in a quiet aside, "You better hope your hunch is right about the sheriff and the hemp."

"More than hope," I said, having figured out why my reasoning was unquestionable. I'd given Lake a few hints, but he hadn't been listening as closely as I was.

When we met up, Sonny said to Lake, "Didn't ask for a warrant. Not enough to get one."

"No," Lake agreed, but Lake was being political. No need to argue with a man who's letting you into his territory.

"How you want to play this?" Sonny asked, his fists resting on his hips, a stance favored by sheriffs and cops all over the country.

"We go to talk," Lake said.

Sonny studied me, and I knew what he was going to say. "This is law enforcement."

"Easy, Sheriff. Dru's there to pay a debt. You and I are there to talk about Diane and Linette."

Shaking his head, Sonny said, "Puts a civilian in danger."

Lake said, "But she carries, don't forget. And she trained at Quantico."

I'd transferred my gun from an ankle holster to a paddle holster at the back of my waist and patted it to show Sonny where it was.

He seemed mollified enough and said, "Scully won't invite us in, but he'll come outside."

We boarded our cars and Lake followed Sonny for a half a mile before coming to a valley.

"This isn't going to go well," I said.

"Some things are destined not to," Lake said.

We pulled behind Sonny's car. He'd stopped at a low stone fence, much like the stone fence behind the Wildwood church. Inside the fence the grass was lush, evidence of a sprinkler system or someone handy with a hose.

Scully's two-story house was an architect's nightmare. It looked like the Brunty family had added onto it for generations, yet it had a curious symmetry in the cedar wood and stone facade. A bare-wood porch wrapped around the front and sides with four stone treads leading up to the floorboards.

"I don't see any vehicles," I said.

"Scully has a barn around back for his vehicles," Sonny said.

I followed the two men up the steps. Sonny knocked. "Scull, you in there?" No answer. There was a push button, and when he touched it melodious chords came from within, odd tones for taciturn Scully. I had the feeling someone watched from a window on my left. He pressed twice more, holding his finger on it too long for etiquette. No answer.

We descended the steps. Lake and Sonny insisted I precede them, thinking, I suppose, that Scully might tear open the door and start spraying bullets. Sonny took out his cell and punched in numbers. "Scully has a cell," he said. He listened for a time then pressed the end key. "Let's pay a visit to Orell."

Lake drove behind Sonny, up a lane perpendicular to the gravel drive. The weeds and grass became brown and unkempt.

Orell's house was an old-fashioned two-story farmhouse with a pitch roof and no porch in front. Sonny walked up three shallow concrete steps. No melodious bell. And no response to his door pounding.

"Is the ice cream store open?" Lake asked.

"Wasn't when I went by," Sonny said, giving the door a last hammering. "Gussie never did keep regular hours, especially late in the day with no tourists. But I'd best check again."

I looked at the sky. The sun, the color of a cooked egg yolk, had begun its late-day tumble through the pines. "Let's go to the Wildwood church," I said. "She and Orell are setting things up for tomorrow."

CHAPTER TWENTY-EIGHT

"So you think something's up tonight?"

Finding Diane had given me the itch that presages conflict. "Yep."

"I'm with you," Lake said, a bit skeptical, mostly because I think he hates stakeouts.

The churchyard was deserted. A yellow bug light lit the front porch. Lake drove into a stand of pines where his car wouldn't be caught in headlights approaching from either direction.

"Give me another hint why you trust Sonny."

"You'll never figure it out. You were too busy running your own mouth."

"Sonny should have gotten a search warrant."

"Maybe he didn't want to alert the county gossip machine. The Bruntys and Scoggins are probably cousins to the judges, too."

We hid in the scrub pine near the church for an hour as the glaring sun made its way down the mountain, creating a blotchy pattern on Lake's face. Lake suddenly straightened; his ears seemed to wriggle. "Vehicle," he said. Seconds later I heard the low moan bouncing along the hills and hollows, and then clearly the sound of grinding gears.

Lake drew his gun and I drew mine.

Last-gasp sun rays caught the vehicle's glass as it came from the direction of Scully's cabins. Passing us, a Jeep vaulted through dips and over rocks at an insane speed. We hoofed it through scrub pines and lost the taillights. Suddenly, darkness burst upon us like a blown fuse. I could hardly make out Lake's face. We assumed the Jeep had turned left at the church; therefore we kept to the woods and reached the church trail. We circled the church and saw the Jeep parked with its headlights on the stone fence, up the hill from the cemetery.

Lake whispered, "Someone's in the church. I heard noise."

"Voices?"

"Thumping."

Before we could investigate, the headlamps of another vehicle swept along the road and turned at the church. We took to the shadows. When it passed, I could see that it was a double-cab black truck with a winch and cables mounted on the side of the bed. It also had a cherry picker in the back and block and tackle on the front.

"Overkill," I whispered. "A winch and chain is enough."

The truck continued past the cemetery up the rise.

The church had no windows in back. Lake crept, gun ready, to the back door. I literally had his back, gun in position.

The door was locked. I moved behind him as we slipped to the side of the church. He peered into the stained glass. "Someone's inside."

I didn't hear anything but our breathing. Lake, however, can hear a tick suck blood. He asked, "You hear that?"

Thud. "Just did."

"Something knocked over," Lake said. "We're going in."

The next sound, a click, set fire to my nerves, but it wasn't the cocking of a gun. Someone unlocked the back door to the church. It didn't slam shut. A male voice said, "Should have done this . . ." I couldn't hear the rest.

But Lake did. He whispered, "Going in." He hurried ahead of me, toward the front of the church.

During our cop beat days of busting into drug houses and

other illegal human habitations, we developed a routine. I'd stand to the right and beat on the door while he covered me from the left. Then when no one answered, he'd kick in the door and I'd cover him. Usually it ended as intended. Usually.

From beyond the cemetery I heard a truck start up and cables begin to grind against the winch. I beat the wooden door with my fist. "Police! Open! Open now!"

I glanced to see Lake still in position.

Boom. A shotgun blew the door off its hinges. Splinters hit my arm. I slammed back against the shingles and watched the door ricochet off the steps. A lengthening silhouette came from the doorway, a knife in one tentacle, the twelve-gauge in the other.

"Brunty," Lake cried. "Drop it."

Orell stood on the threshold. "Get out of here, city bastards," he yelled, swinging his shotgun toward Lake and the knife toward me. I got his full face in the yellow bug light, the look of a maniac snarling. I don't like knives, but Lake was the one in immediate danger. Orell had the shotgun aimed at his gut. With his finger in the shotgun's trigger housing, and at ten feet, I couldn't shoot him; that would kill Lake, too. Lake had to talk him down or shoot him first.

"Drop the weapons," Lake said, his arms out. "I will shoot you." Fragments of panic gripped me, but Lake was deadly calm.

Orell shifted forward. Two shots ripped the air at the same time. Both from handguns. Lake shot Orell in his shotgun arm. The other bullet whistled past my cheek. *From behind me.* I whirled and had the Glock ready to shoot at . . . *no target*. The darkness . . . it had to be the other Brunty. I was boxed. Terror dropped through my body like a jagged rock.

Orell stood in the door, blocking my escape into the church. Scully wouldn't miss me a second time, me in the bug light, him lurking in the dark.

Orell stepped across the fallen door, knife gripped to thrust at Lake's throat. Lake would shoot him with the first move. "Drop it," Lake warned, the gun never wavering in his hand. Pressed into the wooden siding, I was caught between Orell and Scully. It was one of those limbo moments. Empty my gun into the darkness? Run like mad straight ahead? Shoot Orell—who was taking precious time menacing Lake—and escape into the church. A pistol shot sang past me. Orell's head wrenched back. The slug sheared the top of his head. Bone and brains misted down, glimmering red in the yellow of the church's forty watts of bug bulb.

His body sagged with a groan and a symphony of farts while I jumped his body into the church. Lake was beside me. "You okay?"

"Yes," I said, heart hammering. "He's out there."

"Let's do something about him." He raised his gun and stuck his head outside the door frame. "Police! Show yourself!"

I heard the yell. "It's me! Sonny!"

"Show yourself. Hands in the air."

Into the light walked Sonny. He held up a shotgun and his forty-five by their butts. He said, "State's coming. No time to let you know I was here. I shot and ducked." He stepped forward, looking at me. "You looked deadly with that gun." He stepped over Orell's body into the church.

"That was pretty good shooting," Lake said.

"Been toting all my life. Dang it, I missed Orell with the first shot."

Right then, I wanted to know one thing. "Where's Scully?"

He shook his head. "When Orell left the store, I followed him here. Scully was not with him."

The screech of the winch intensified. "Scully's opening the hole," I said.

Lake moved toward me, and, like a lover's graceful shift, he touched my shoulder and then extended his arms around my back. Tugging gently, he urged me to move ahead, further inside the church. Golden light through the blown front door illuminated a bizarre scene. Lake moved up the aisle, me at his shoulder, guns in position. A man was tied to a wooden arm chair that lay on its side. The man was gagged.

Sonny flicked on his flashlight.

"Scully," I said.

At his feet lay a rolled-up rug.

"Cover me, Dru, Sonny," Lake said.

I aimed at the office door. Sonny had my back while covering the front door. Lake untied the gag.

Scully's naked eyes were popping out of his red face. "Get her—in there. Hurry!" he said, signaling with his head toward the rug.

"Hang on, man," Lake said.

"She's suffocating," Scully said, his voice like a frog's. "Don't bother with me."

"Dru, I got the doors covered," Sonny said, shotgun in one hand, the forty-five in the other. "Help the lieutenant."

Lake took one end of the large carpet and I the other, and we rolled it over and over until the body of a woman fell free. Lake turned her face up. She looked absolutely and positively dead. Skin dead white, hair matted with blood, her blue eyes half closed. By the bruises on her neck, she'd been strangled. Still, I recognized her. Blood powered through my vessels.

Candice Browne—Evangeline's missing mother.

Evangeline . . . I loved her at that moment for never giving up.

Lake checked Candice's vitals. "Alive. Get an ambulance."

"I'll make sure, but everything we got is on the way." Sonny was keying his radio when a truck engine fired up from in back of the church. "Who the hell is that?" Sonny said.

"Gussie," Scully said.

"Gussie?"

"The worst of us."

"Anyone else out there?"

"Just her."

I said to Lake, "Back door."

Lake sprinted past the altar into the office. Scully tried to raise his body and the chair at the same time. Sonny finished the call and, picking up the shotgun, went after Lake. I raised my automatic ready for anyone that came in either door. I said to Scully, "Sorry I can't untie you right now."

"How's my wife?" Scully asked in a froggy whisper. "She going to be all right?"

I bent to flick Candice on the cheek. Her eyes began to flutter and she gasped air. I looked at Scully. *My wife.* "I think she'll be fine."

"Thank God, thank God," he said, laying his cheek on the floor.

I contemplated Scully tied to the overturned chair. I longed to untie him but I wasn't laying my gun down. This wasn't over yet. I said to him, "I know what they had in mind for Candice, but what about you?"

"I told them to put me in that hole with Candy," he said, his anguished eyes biting into mine. "They tied me up to keep me from getting away with her."

"They wouldn't put you in the hole, and you wouldn't tell on them for throwing Candice in, am I right?"

He didn't answer.

Shots boomed from outside, a firefight so fierce I couldn't pinpoint the direction for the echoes.

Fearful but bold, I leaped to the front of the church and rammed my back against the wall. Anyone coming in would get a bullet in the temple. I kept my sight on the office door, too.

The shooting stopped and a heavy truck engine revved. Six seconds later it slammed into something, metal on metal. Lake's automatic fired several more shots. An immense quiet packed the atmosphere. Then Lake called from the back door, "All clear. I'm coming in."

He looked at me as he came through the door. "Gussie's dead." He went to Scully and untied him.

I stood next to Lake and we both watched Scully lift Candice's torso and caress her. She buried her head in his neck and whimpered.

"Boy I never would have guessed that," I whispered.

Lake looked at me and winked. "Evangeline told you her mother was alive."

Oh, please.

"I told you my mother was alive," Evangeline crowed, sitting next to her mother's hospital bed.

"And I told you I would find her if she was, or if she wasn't," I replied.

"It's better that she was," Evangeline said, rubbing Candice's arm.

I thought Candice feigned sleep, which I would have, too, had I the decisions she now had to make.

Earlier this morning she was well enough to relate the terrible events.

We'd surmised right that Johnny owed both Bruntys several thousand dollars for grapes. It was Orell's grapes that he considered inferior. The idea, thought up by Gussie, was to take the cabin cruiser to where Johnny and his friends were on a sailboat. They would put the fear of God into Johnny. Waving shotguns, Gussie and Orell demanded payment. Johnny told Orell and Gussie they were stupid redneck fools and he'd pay them when he pleased, or never. Gussie knocked him down with the butt of the shotgun. He landed on a cleat and sliced his skull. Gussie hit him again and Orell chucked him overboard. Janet started screaming. Orell took hold of Janet and they marched her down into the salon where Laurant and Candice sat smoking and drinking, unaware of what had happened on deck. With Gussie holding the shotgun, Orell tied the three up.

Orell sailed the *Scuppernong* and Gussie piloted the cruiser to the deepest part of the lake, where they sank the sailboat. They took their three captives ashore in the cabin cruiser because they didn't want accidental witnesses at the marina or bodies washing up. They knew a place where hidden bodies would never be found, and besides, their boat needed cleaning.

Enter Scully, who got a call from Orell to drive the double-cab pickup to Landing Creek Park and help trailer the cruiser. According to Candice, he was appalled to find three tied-up people in the boat. They drove to Orell's place, unloaded the three doomed people from the boat into a pickup truck outfit-ted with boulder-moving tackle and took them to the Devil's Arse.

Candice had been certain she was going to die. She said, "It's a numb feeling, a feeling of inevitability and acceptance that life is over. Gussie promised us we wouldn't suffer." She swallowed a few times, shuddered and went on, "Gussie said since we knew what happened to the grape thief, despite our promises not to tell, she couldn't take the chance." Candice stared into my eyes. "Would you take the chance we wouldn't tell?"

"No," I said. "But sane people don't let bill collection get that out of control."

She cried when she told the last of it. "She dumped Laurant in first, into that awful hole. She just pushed him in. He was alive and he screamed until we couldn't hear him anymore. She shot Janet, she said, for the hell of it, and kicked her in."

I handed her a hospital towel.

"But you were saved," Lake said."

Wiping her face and cheeks, she said, "By Scully. He told Orell and Gussie, 'I won't have this one going down that hole.' Gussie laughed like the devil herself and said, 'My my.' "

The devil laughed to see such sport and the spoon ran away with the dish.

Candice whimpered while I held her hand. "I'll never forget that—*My, my*. She taunted him. 'Scully has fallen for a pretty face, but you can't keep her, cousin.' Scully said, 'I am keeping her. You want to go in that hole, try to drop her in it.' "

"Did he make you marry him?" I asked.

"Oh no," Candice said. A sad, sweet smile formed on her lips. "I fell in love with him."

"What?" Lake blurted, startled as I.

Lake had been thinking the same thing as me—that she'd had to marry him to stay alive.

Candice paused to stare across space and time and memory and then looked at us. "Scully was a gentleman, the best man I'd ever met. He never so much as touched me until we were falling in love. We talked many times of leaving Yarrow. Things were getting dicey, especially with Gussie. I knew she wanted me dead. I was never far from a shotgun when Scully wasn't around." She took a deep breath. "Then *Scuppernong* was found. We knew . . . I knew it was going to be over."

"Who killed Linette?"

"Orell, and rowed her out onto the lake."

"Why didn't he push her into the Devil's Arse?"

"They wanted her body to wash up for a burial, for Diane's sake. She's his kid. Decent of them, huh?"

"Four years is a long time without someone besides Orell and Gussie knowing about you," Lake said.

"I never left the house, except to go in disguise to Ringgold to marry Scully. We couldn't even use our own names. That was the deal. Gussie promised if she ever saw me outside the house she would kill me. I lived with the idea of her laying in wait."

I recalled how Scully hovered over Diane that first morning we came to his diner. I said, "But there was someone else who found out about you. Diane."

Candice nodded. "She and her dog wandered all over the county. No one thought much of it. One day her dog crawled under our house to escape some animal. She came for it and saw me through a window. It was my fault for watching outside." Candice had tears in her eyes. "She was just a kid and I put her in danger."

"She told her mother. Did Linette get in touch with you?"

"No, but she was brazen, always dropping hints about the woman in Scully's life."

Lake said, "Thus dooming Linette once the *Scuppernong* started to surface. Diane knew who you were when she saw pictures in the newspaper."

I was still trying to sort through all that I had thought and felt. "Scully protected two maniacs."

Lake said, "Kin."

"Where is he?" I asked.

Candice said, "I imagine he's waiting for you to take him away." The tears ran down her cheeks. "He always said our time together would be short."

"Who killed Scoggins?"

"Orell. Because of the drought. Orell kept a close eye on the place where they'd sunk the sailboat. He knew if it didn't rain soon, the boat would be exposed. They even talked about dynamiting it."

Better sense, it appeared, had prevailed.

Lake reasoned, "And if the sailboat surfaced, Scoggins's account would be given more scrutiny since it was found not far from the park."

"That's it," Candice said.

"Are you going back to North Carolina when you're out of here?"

"You bet," she said, squeezing Evangeline's hand. "I've missed my darling E so very much."

"I'll see you there," I said. "I have unfinished work."

"E told me about Emile. Pity. If I can help find his killer, I will."

"Me, too," Evangeline said. "I show up and their goose is cooked."

Brother.

We left Candice in the arms of Morpheus with Evangeline fluttering over her like a wizened Florence Nightingale.

Waiting at the elevator, Lake asked, "You mean it? You're going after Emile's killer?"

"The shooter's probably on another continent. I'm going to prove that the sheriff and the banker were behind it. Avlon certainly stole his safe and injected the drug that killed him, just minutes before I visited. I take it personally."

"Why would they want him dead?"

"Emile was about to go down. I don't think he would have gone quietly. Once Interpol gets onto you, your goose is cooked."

Lake shrugged. "So I've heard."

I walked out of the hospital alongside Lake, feeling my composure starting to splinter.

Lake said, "You always feel let down after a case."

"This one was uglier than most."

"Ah, Dru, they're all ugly."

My cell played the concerto. It was Portia. "Yeah, Porsh."

"The hemp man was Janeway. The kids saw a video with him speaking. He'll be in prison for a long time for that and his part in withholding evidence in the murders."

Suddenly my chest filled like a helium balloon and I felt if I spoke I'd sound as giddy as a cartoon chipmunk. Fortunately, Portia didn't give me a chance to respond before she was gone.

I fixed my clever eyes upon Lake. "There was just something about Janeway." I flipped my hand back. "I knew he was the hemp sheriff."

"You did not."

"Did too."

"Did not."

"Too."

"Not."

"I'm hungry. Let go eat."

"Trader Joe's is closed."

ABOUT THE AUTHOR

A retired journalist for the *Atlanta-Journal Constitution,* **Gerrie Ferris Finger** won the 2009 St. Martin's Press/Malice Domestic Best First Traditional Mystery Novel for *The End Game. The Last Temptation* is the first in the Moriah Dru/Richard Lake series published by Five Star Publishing. *The Devil Laughed* is the second. She lives on the coast of Georgia with her husband, Alan, and standard poodle, Bogey.

www.gerrieferrisfinger.com
www.gerrieferrisfinger.blogspot.com